T0282246

PROXIMITY

A LEXI MILLS THRILLER

BRIAN SHEA

STACY LYNN MILLER

SEVERN RIVER
PUBLISHING

PROXIMITY

Copyright © 2022 by Brian Shea and Stacy Lynn Miller.

All rights reserved.

No part of this book may be reproduced in any form or by any electronic or mechanical means, including information storage and retrieval systems, without written permission from the author, except for the use of brief quotations in a book review.

Severn River Publishing
www.SevernRiverBooks.com

This is a work of fiction. Names, characters, businesses, places, events and incidents are either the products of the author's imagination or used in a fictitious manner. Any resemblance to actual persons, living or dead, or actual events is purely coincidental.

ISBN: 978-1-64875-388-6 (Paperback)

ALSO BY THE AUTHORS

LEXI MILLS THRILLERS
Fuze
Proximity
Impact
Pressure
Remote
Flashpoint

BY BRIAN SHEA
Boston Crime Thrillers
The Nick Lawrence Series
Sterling Gray FBI Profiler Series

Never miss a new release!
To find out more about the authors and their books, visit

severnriverbooks.com/series/lexi-mills

1

Five minutes before sunset, he coasted his stripped-down white side-panel van to a crawl at the bus stop on Watt Avenue at the Interstate 80 overpass, stopping precisely thirty feet past the last passenger shelter. He'd done his homework four months ago on his scouting trip and had discovered the blind spot in the Sacramento County camera surveillance web.

Having committed to memory a photograph earlier today, he spotted the person he'd come for. His partner for this op stepped to the curb, opened the passenger door, and slid into the front seat. He accelerated and took the eastbound ramp one hundred feet ahead without exchanging a word with his new partner. His phone barked directions to the city of Gladding, predicting a twenty-six-minute trip.

They settled into silence, the way he preferred to work. His job as a scout and an on-the-ground observer had him working alone for the past three years. He'd had no one to depend on, but even more satisfying, he relied on no one. Then, following the events in Spicewood four months ago, his role changed. Belcher wanted him to get his hands dirty.

It wasn't as if he hadn't done things like this before, but he'd thought he'd put this type of work behind him in the sandbox. He would have walked if Belcher hadn't offered double his regular fee. Now he had to rely on the assistance of a partner he'd only talked with over the phone once to iron out the op details. With any luck, the newbie with the fresh face sitting next to him knew enough to stick to the script and not freewheel.

Google Maps was accurate. They arrived at their staging point eight minutes before go time and well after the last glimmer of light had left the summer sky—more than enough time to prepare their gear and load the prepositioned second vehicle. He manually popped the old beater's trunk parked under the oak tree on the outskirts of their target's property before tossing the car keys to his partner.

They worked together, transferring six of the two dozen metallic boxes, each the size of a toaster oven, from deep inside the van to the trunk. After locking up the sedan, they donned equipment vests and loaded up with zip ties, duct tape, one-foot-square cloth sacks, and ketamine-filled syringes. Finally, they ops-checked their sidearms and extra ammo. But if this part of the operation went smoothly, the guns would be only for show. That was the optimist in him speaking. The pessimist had him thinking two magazines each wouldn't be enough.

Returning to the van silently, his partner hopped in to drive while he took the passenger seat. They both put on ski masks. His partner then drove down the hundred-yard-long, sweeping dark access road of the target's semi-rural property. This place was ideal for what they were about to do. The front of the house was shielded from the road by trees and shrubs, and the nearest neighbor was an eighth of a mile away. The chance of encountering a stray witness was virtually nonexistent.

At this time in the evening, the husband wouldn't be home for an hour. The maid should have left for the day a half-hour ago. The wife should be in the hot tub on the back deck and at least two cocktails into her nightly routine. The two teenagers should be in their rooms under the pretense of doing their homework. However, *he'd* done his homework. The boy was likely cruising porn sites, and the girl should be on her phone scrolling through her Instagram and TikTok feeds.

Once his partner pulled around the circular driveway, he activated the signal jammer in the glove compartment to disrupt cell service within five hundred feet. The range was far enough to cover the property but not so far to impact the nearest neighbor. He then walked thirty feet to the buried utility box at the edge of the concrete driveway, lifted the lid, and cut the fiber optic service line. The security system sensors would work without the internet, but the camera feeds were inaccessible to anyone inside.

All communication to and from the house was now disabled.

Both approached the front porch. He left an Amazon package near a patio cover post and rang the doorbell before joining his partner to the right of the door out of view of the peephole. A minute later, the door swung open, and someone stepped out. That was their cue. They rushed the person, a quick glance confirming it was the teenage girl. He placed a hand over the girl's mouth, injected her arm with ketamine as she struggled, and began a countdown in his head. They'd have to hit her over the head if she wasn't out by thirty. Arms flailing, she put up a strong fight, but as he passed twenty in his head, her motions slowed and came to a body-limp stop.

He dragged her inside, leaving her on the floor in the entry room with a zip tie around her hands. No one else was in view as he closed the door. Soft music came from the direction of the living room screen door, suggesting the wife had stuck to her routine and was in the hot tub. That meant their next target was to secure the boy. By now, he was pissed off that his porn sites were inaccessible so he could be on the move.

Drawing their weapons, they glided past the formal dining and living rooms and turned down the unlit hallway to the bedrooms, stopping at the second door on the left—the boy's room. The door was halfway closed with light spilling out into the corridor, so he eased it open until he determined the space was unoccupied. Then he heard a toilet flushing from inside. That meant the boy was using the Jack and Jill bathroom he shared with his sister.

He gestured for his partner to take position near the bookcase to the right of the bathroom door. He settled into the corner to the left. Moments later, the boy walked out and spotted him. "What the hell?" The boy pivoted to retreat into the bathroom, but his partner enveloped him with muscular arms, placing a hand over his mouth. Another dose of ketamine and the boy was out in twenty-five seconds.

Tying the boy's hands, his partner dragged him down the terracotta-tiled hallway and left him on the floor next to his sister. That left only the mother, but she would be trickier to capture. They needed her conscious to make a phone call if the husband didn't come home on schedule.

They pushed through the formal part of the house toward the great room and back deck. A loud crashing sound of a metal pan hitting the tile floor shrilled when they entered the kitchen. He looked left. "Damn it," he whispered. The maid hadn't gone for the day. She screamed and mumbled something in Spanish as she grabbed a butcher knife from the kitchen island. Then two loud pops sounded. Her yelling stopped, but her body jerked as two expanding red spots appeared on her shirt near her breasts. Her eyes turned glassy with disbelief before she fell to the floor.

He glanced at his partner, still pointing a semiautomatic sidearm in her direction. "I told you no shooting unless necessary."

His partner glared. "It seemed pretty necessary to me." Newbie had a point. At least his partner was a good shot and double-tapped her center mass.

He heard rustling noises through the deck screen door and trained his weapon in that direction. He pushed toward it and slid the door open against the rails, discovering the wife, dressed in a bikini, toweling off. "Freeze," he ordered.

The wife gasped and threw her hands up, letting the towel drop to the wood deck. She still had quite the physique for a mother of two in her fifties. But based on the amount of money this family had, she likely had a frequent flyer card with her plastic surgeon.

"Where is your cell phone?" He glanced at the table attached to the side of the hot tub. There were three glasses, all empty.

She trembled as much as her voice. "By the hot tub."

He gestured for his partner to retrieve the phone and hand it to him. Stuffing it into his vest pocket, he asked, "Where are your clothes?"

"In my bedroom."

"Go." He wagged the muzzle, encouraging her to lead the way.

Her gait was unsteady, likely the result of the high temperature in the hot tub magnifying the effects of her three-cocktail night. Stepping into the kitchen, the wife turned her head in the direction of the maid, who was now lying in a puddle of blood. She then screamed, clutching her chest. "My God, Amelia."

"Unless you want to end up like her, keep walking." He pushed her along.

"Where are my kids?" Her voice turned from rattled to determined.

"They are unhurt." His impatience was growing. They had a timetable to keep, and coping with a half-drunk, distraught mother wasn't in it. "Now go."

She wobbled through the great room. She glanced toward the front door when crossing the entry area and gasped. "My babies."

"They're just drugged to make them sleep. If you don't do as we tell you, we'll put a bullet in their skulls."

The wife nodded to a weak whimper before continuing down the hallway. Once in the primary bedroom, she gathered the clothes strewn about the bed and put them on, including a pair of tennies.

He cuffed her hands behind her back with a zip tie and considered the next step. The original plan was to wait for the husband to come home in the next thirty minutes and make their demands. However, the gunshots with the back door open had thrown a monkey wrench into the mix. Considering the lack of traffic in this semi-rural area, the closest neighbors might have heard the loud gunshots and reported them to the police. That necessitated a change of venue.

He turned to his partner. "Your little party poppers earlier threw us a curveball. We need to go now."

His partner let out a weighty sigh, appropriately reading blame into his order. Then, without delay, they ushered the woman into the hallway, past her sleeping children, and to the front porch.

He ordered, "Sit on your ass. If you try anything, your kids die. Do you understand?"

She silently nodded, freeing up the two kidnappers, now killers, to retrieve the unconscious boy and girl and toss them into the back of the waiting van. After searching the kids for their cell phones and throwing them into the bushes, he returned to the porch. The wife was sitting with her hands behind her back, looking utterly frazzled as if her world was coming to an end. She wasn't that far off if her husband didn't cooperate.

He pulled her up by the arm, guiding her to the van. "Where are we going?" she asked.

"For a ride." He pushed her through the open sliding door and ordered her to sit. "Extend your legs." He couldn't chance her getting up and overpowering the driver while in transit, so he zip-tied her feet together at the ankles and slammed the door shut.

They hopped into the van with his partner behind the wheel. While they coasted to the main road, where they'd left the second vehicle, he pulled out the wife's cell phone. He held it to her face until the facial recognition feature unlocked the device. He then located the phone app and scrolled through the call log until he found her husband's number. He dialed. The call picked up on the third ring.

"I'm coming home right now, Kathy. I didn't forget your bottle of vodka."

"That's very kind of you, but your wife won't be drinking any more tonight." He used a nonthreatening voice to keep the woman calm. The last thing he wanted was a blubbering mess on his hands.

"Who is this?"

"That isn't important, but the fact that we have your wife and kids is. If you don't do exactly as we say, they will die."

"What the hell are you talking about? Is this some joke?" the husband asked.

"This is no joke." He put the phone on speaker and held it close to the wife's face. "Tell him."

"Pookie, this is real. They've taken the kids and me, and they killed Amelia in the kitchen. For God's sake, Pookie, do whatever they say." The wife ended on a shrill note. She seemed like the type of woman a man would put up with for only two reasons—great blow jobs or a fat bank account. Maybe he'd be doing the husband a favor by capping her when all of this was over.

"Do you believe me now?" If the husband didn't provide the correct answer, his wife would die, and he'd have to answer to Belcher.

"I do. What do you want?"

"We have a job for you, but first, you need to meet us at the old POW site outside of town. We'll give you everything you need. If you do exactly as we say, your family will live. That starts with no police, or we will shoot them and leave their bodies for the coyotes. Say it. No police."

"No police."

"Very good." He kept his voice calm and steady, lacing it with military precision. He needed to set the tone that this man was dealing with a soulless professional, not someone he could negotiate with. "If you're not at the site in fifteen minutes, your family dies. Say it. They will die."

"They will die." The husband's voice cracked this time, suggesting he'd made his point.

He ended the call when the van stopped next to their second vehicle on the main road. He then opened the door and tossed the phone into the heavy brush. Hopping into the sedan, he took the lead toward the abandoned POW camp. Glancing in his rearview mirror, he realized they were leaving a mess inside the house, but it didn't matter. By this time tomorrow, they would have gotten what they needed, or they would all be dead.

2

Lexi pulled open the door leading to the Parkland West Physical Therapy Office. Dozens of memories swirled in her head the moment she walked through. This was the place where she learned to walk again. Today, though, she wasn't here for herself. She was here for the woman she planned to propose to in two nights. Striding down the hallway, Lexi had an extra pep in her step. Today was special, and she wouldn't let anything keep her from being here for Nita. Not her job and not even lunch with her father. After fifteen years of emotional exile, their slow reconciliation would have to wait another day.

She'd thought learning to run with a prosthetic and working her way back to the ATF's Special Response Team was the hardest thing she'd ever done, but the last twelve weeks had proved her wrong. Coming home every night to witness Nita struggle to balance her addiction and recovery from shoulder surgery was the ultimate test of patience. It was a trait Lexi had little of outside of defusing bombs. She'd wanted to pop the question every time Nita met a milestone in her rehabilitation, but somehow, she'd kept her eagerness in check.

Lexi poked her head into the break room on her way to the weight room. She spotted her former physical therapist tossing the wrappers from his lunch into the wastebasket. "I'm late. Did I miss it?"

Samuel released a lopsided grin. Lexi's medical records may have reflected that he was the therapist who got her running again, but even he knew Nita had done all the hard work before he took over. Technically, he was now Nita's therapist, but she was doing all the work again, planning and scheduling her own therapy. His role was to supervise. Sometimes. "No. She wanted to wait for you. She's still stretching."

"Thanks, Samuel. See you after we get back from Sacramento."

He offered her a flamboyant bow. "Hail to the hero."

"Give it a rest." Lexi gave him a dismissive wave. Nothing she did that day at the governor's mansion in Spicewood, Texas, was beyond her training. Receiving awards and medals for doing her job was unnecessary and embarrassing.

She strolled further down the hallway, stopping at the entrance of the exercise room. The room was busy with eight patients and their therapists. Well, except for Nita. She doubled as patient and therapist today. Lexi spotted her on a floor mat in the far corner, using perfect posture while performing her pre-workout stretches. Since her first day rehabbing, Nita had been the picture of determination to get back as much range of motion as the plate and screws in her shoulder allowed.

Nita looked up from performing an external rotation stretch with a stick and locked eyes with Lexi. An instant smile beckoned her over. While she closed the distance, Nita rose, taking care to not support her weight with the injured shoulder. Her tank top exposed the scar left behind from the surgery, and at its center was a quarter-sized blemish where a nightclub shooter's bullet had ripped through her flesh. Lexi's job of defusing bombs was inherently dangerous, and threats of violence came with the territory. But Nita's injury was proof that no one was safe from random acts or nutcases.

"I'm so glad you could make it today. Did Carlson throw a fit because you'll miss the monthly staff meeting?" Nita's slight grin meant Lexi had earned extra points by putting her needs first. Those meetings had become a colossal waste of time, serving only to make Carlson appear more involved than he was.

"He'll survive." Lexi winked, rubbing Nita's upper arms. "Ready?"

"For days." Nita released a breathy exhale. She'd kept to her slow and steady mantra to avoid injury, and today she'd savor her reward—weights. Her rehab had centered on stretching, counterweights, and bands until today. Yesterday, she'd finally hit the marks needed to graduate to free weights—the final exercise category for her type of injury. Since the bands had already rebuilt her strength to the five-pound level, she would double that to ten today.

Lexi retrieved a ten-pound weight from the stand against the wall mirror while Nita assumed the proper stance and posture. "You're sure you're ready for this? I don't want to be the one to set you back."

"Look who's cautious now about rehab." Nita narrowed one eye in her patented "I told you so" fashion.

Last year, Lexi had set her goals too high, despite Nita's warnings. She'd pushed herself too hard twice on her own journey to recovery, setting her back several precious weeks. "It's different when I'm responsible for someone else, especially you. I can't stand seeing you hurt."

"Now you know what I go through with every patient and what I especially went through with you."

"All right, smarty-pants, let's graduate you." Lexi lowered the weight to Nita's hand.

Nita kept her arm straight so her hand dangled at her hip and let gravity do the work when she gripped the weight. A smile appeared. "This feels so good."

Samuel approached. "Any pain?"

"Not yet, but I expect some when I start the routine." Nita cocked her head in his direction. "It was tight this morning when I woke."

"Keep an eye out for signs of a frozen shoulder after sleeping." His wink was a playful needle of the once student now teaching the teacher. When Samuel first stepped into the therapy office three years ago, Nita became his trainer. Now she was taking instruction from him. "You know the drill. I'll monitor you from over there." Samuel gestured his chin toward a row of chairs against a wall. "Have fun, but pace yourself."

Nita grinned, clearly relishing the coming workout. She then stepped through her week-twelve routine of stretches with the weight and transitioned into strength-building lifts. Surprisingly, she didn't grimace once. That was a good sign that her pain was under control. However, when Nita finished her thirty-minute workout and returned the weight to its resting place on the rack, she rolled her shoulder several times. Maybe her pain was still an issue.

"I'm so proud of you, Nita." Lexi kissed her forehead, tasting the salty sweat from her brow. "You're powering through your pain like a champ."

"Yeah, sure." The way Nita brushed off the compliment gave her pause. She hadn't been present for every physical therapy session, but she'd attended every one with a milestone. In those six instances, Nita had reached for a pain pill only twice, and with her history of addiction, that was something to be proud of.

"Let's get you changed and back to helping other patients." Lexi led Nita to the women's locker room and invited her to sit next to her on the wood bench.

Nita toweled off. "Are you packed for our flight tomorrow?"

"Not yet." Lexi let out a deep sigh. As if receiving the Public Safety Officer Medal of Honor wasn't enough for her role in saving the governor of Texas, she and Noah Black were featured speakers at the upcoming annual National Peace Officers Conference in Sacramento and guests of honor at the awards banquet that same night. Sadly, the real hero from that day wouldn't be on the stage with them. Simon Winslow was still recuperating following complications from the gunshot wounds sustained while saving Lexi's life. If not for his heroism, she wouldn't be here.

Nita rested a hand on Lexi's thigh. "I know you're not big on fanfare, but your peers are honoring you. You should be proud. I know I am."

"But Simon should be there, just like he should have been at the White House with us."

"He's bouncing back from the staph infection and should be released soon." Nita gave her leg a reassuring rub. "We should visit him soon. I want to thank him properly for saving your life."

Lexi interlocked her fingers with Nita's. "I'd like that."

"Hey, at least we're getting there a day early and get to see Noah tomorrow."

"Yeah." Lexi sighed deeper this time. Spending time with her friend somewhere other than behind a podium, on a stage, or shaking hands with government officials was a welcome change.

"Is your tux ready at the dry cleaners?" Nita asked.

Lexi slumped her shoulders. Organizers gave her the choice of wearing a cocktail dress or a tuxedo for the black and white event tomorrow. Since her first day of kindergarten, dresses hadn't been a part of her wardrobe, so her only choice was to wear the stiff tux she'd bought for the special events she now had to attend. "Yeah, I'll pick it up on the way home from the office." She let a smile grow. "Please tell me you plan to wear the little black number your cousin bought you for your birthday last month."

Nita rubbed her injured shoulder. "I'd love to, but the scars are still so prominent."

Lexi leaned back and kissed the surgical scar high on her shoulder blade. "I'm so glad the bullet missed your lung." She shifted again to get a better look at Nita. "How about I pick up your cousin's white lacey thing?"

Nita grimaced. "Ew. Her thong?"

"No, that thing she wears to the club on chilly nights."

"Oh, her scalloped lace shrug." Nita laughed. "That's perfect. I can pair it with my black and white heels."

"You'll look absolutely delicious."

"And you'll look ever so handsome. It should be a perfect trip." Nita scooted closer. "We'll fly to Sacramento in the morning, make love in the afternoon, and have dinner with Noah. Then, the next night, we'll dance under a disco ball."

Then, when the moment was right, Lexi would drop to one knee and propose to Nita with her grandmother's engagement ring. *Yep, this will be a perfect trip.*

3

"Shit. Shit. Shit." Zack gripped the steering wheel of his beat-up Corolla tighter, turning his pale knuckles a gnarly shade of white, almost alien-like. Running late to work was the last thing he needed. One more time, having McBean as a last name wouldn't matter. He'd lose his job.

Zack hated working as a grocery clerk, but he had no other choice. His inability to pass a drug test and no skills contributed to his unemployability since graduating high school three years ago. Then there was his mother. She'd threatened to kick him out of the house on his twenty-first birthday if he didn't have a job. She attributed the absence of prospects to his lack of initiative for anything but weed and video games. He agreed, but after three months of searching, his uncle was the only one who would hire him, not because he wanted to, but because he had to. An uncle by marriage, he was likely pressured into it by Zack's mother and aunt. After all, McBean's grocery store had been in the family for five generations, and any McBean who wanted to work there could.

He honked his horn at the towering Range Rover in front of him. The light had been green for three seconds, yet the ass behind the wheel had yet to stop thumbing through the Facebook feed on their phone. The idiot still didn't go, so Zack cranked his wheels left and punched it, crossing the yellow line and barely missing a postal truck. The soccer mom in the driver's seat flipped him the bird, which he gladly returned.

Skidding to a stop behind McBean's, Gladding's oldest grocery store, Zack pushed the driver's door open with both hands, kicking off the familiar loud creak. He grabbed his horrid brown work apron from the passenger seat before slamming the door shut with a powerful hip thrust and recreating the same thunderous screech.

Dashing toward the back door, he looped the apron over his neck and tightened the strings around his waist at the back. Then, slowing near the employee entrance, he straightened the button attached to the apron's upper bib to display the store's tiresome motto correctly: "Always clean at McBean's."

Rushing through the door, Zack threw on the brakes when he saw Riley stacking the banana boxes that had come in yesterday onto a flatbed cart twenty feet away. She was perfection in jeans and a McBean's apron, but her thin body was only part of what made her attractive. Riley's charming smile could bring traffic to a halt, and her wit could keep Zack entertained for decades.

Crap, he thought, rubbing his face stubble with a hand. He should have taken the time to shave before leaving this morning. Riley hated men with unkempt whiskers. She was way out of his league and never showed an ounce of interest, but stranger things had happened.

He let out a breathy sigh, punched in at the wall-mounted digital time clock, and slicked back his hair after wetting his fingertips on his tongue. Striding up to Riley, he put on a swagger reserved only for her. "I'll get that. I have fruit today."

Riley glanced over her shoulder at him, rolling her eyes. "You're late. Again. You were supposed to have these out before opening."

"My alarm must not have gone off." Zack stepped forward, hoping to get a whiff of Riley's intoxicating lavender shampoo.

"It hasn't gone off since the day you started. Nephew or not, I'm surprised you still have a job."

"I'm only ten minutes late most days." Zack shrugged, knowing if his last name wasn't McBean, he would have gotten the boot a long time ago.

But it was, which meant he had a job for life if he didn't steal from the till or do drugs in the store. "It's no big deal."

"One day, you'll push Biscuit too far." Riley turned her nose up. "When you do, I hope he shows you the door."

Zack snickered at his uncle's nickname. Every afternoon, he'd hunker down in his office and devour an entire package of English Tea Biscuits while reviewing orders, bills, and payroll. He must have had the metabolism of a teenager because he never put on an extra pound.

He looked past her and scanned the rest of the stockroom. "Where *is* Biscuit?"

"We don't know." Riley's narrowed brow meant she was concerned, a response he didn't share. Not in the least. "Bret had to use his key to let us in this morning."

Zack cringed at the mention of the assistant manager. Since his first day, College Man had been a thorn in his side. He insisted every item on every shelf be lined up perfectly before opening. "In that case, what's the rush?"

"You *are* a lost cause." Riley threw her hands up before pushing the cart through the double swing doors to the main floor.

"All righty." Zack patted his cargo pants pocket, hoping he hadn't forgotten to grab it. The bulge beneath the fabric said he hadn't. With Riley doing his job and Biscuit nowhere to be found, lighting up would start the day properly.

Retracing his steps, Zack exited through the employee door. He settled into his usual spot near the dumpster to mask the coming scent, retrieved his jar of Baby Jeeter, and pulled out a single pre-rolled blunt. One spark of his Bic and Zack was inhaling his stress reliever—Sativa. It had become his go-to drug in the morning to give him a boost of energy.

His mind drifted to everything that had gone wrong in his twenty-one years. Besides having a job he couldn't stand and a legacy he had no hope of living up to, he didn't know what to do with his life. He was a slightly above-average gamer with no hope of sponsorship, and the only other thing he knew well was weed. But budtender jobs were scarce these days. Every pothead in the region was vying for a handful of positions at dispensaries. So until one came open, he'd have to endure his daily dose of Biscuit.

An unfamiliar car turned the corner of the store at high speed, faster than Zack's typical panicked late approach. He harrumphed. It was more dented and beat up than his hand-me-down. The tires screeched against the pavement before the sedan abruptly stopped in the loading zone near the employee entrance. The driver's door flew open. His uncle stepped out, looking more jittery than usual.

Strange, Zack thought. That wasn't his uncle's car. He tried to make himself small by standing flat against the dumpster. He pinched out his joint against the metal siding, hoping he'd snuffed it before the smell wafted toward the door. When his uncle ditched inside the store, that was Zack's chance to sneak inside. He took two steps toward the door but stopped when it swung open and Biscuit reappeared, pushing a produce flatbed. Zack retreated to his hiding position.

Biscuit popped the clunker's trunk and moved at lightning speed, loading the flatbed with several metallic boxes. He always walked the store aisles fast, but this speed was off the charts. After closing the trunk, he opened a box, grabbed a canister the size of a baseball, and walked toward the dumpster.

"Shit," Zack whispered, stuffing the half-smoked blunt into his pocket. He was busted. On his first day of work, his uncle had told him if he ever caught him doing drugs, legal or not, on store property, he'd throw him out on his ear. Zack braced himself for an ass chewing as the appetizer and unemployment as the dessert.

Biscuit approached Zack but looked right through him as if he didn't exist. The armpits of his shirt were soaked through, something Zack had never seen before on his uncle. He worked hard but applied deodorant thick like a coat of paint. It worked better than a diaper. "Move," he ordered. Zack obliged. Biscuit then placed the container on the ground next to the dumpster. When Zack reached to throw it into the trash, his uncle pulled him back. "Leave it." He returned to the flatbed and pushed it to the door.

"Strange. Very strange," Zack mumbled, noticing the skin on his uncle's neck was blotchy. Something was up because he only got red when he was nervous or stressed. "Do you need help, Uncle Del?"

"No. I've got it." Biscuit disappeared inside.

Speechless, Zack caught the door before it closed and reentered the store. His uncle pushed through the double door onto the main floor without a single word. The only other time Zack had seen his uncle this off-kilter was when his father died. He'd said then, "The only thing that cuts me to the quick is family." Maybe he'd fought with Zack's aunt, or something was wrong with one of his kids.

The door swung open again, and Riley stepped through. She narrowed her eyes and gestured her thumb toward the door. "What's up with Biscuit?"

"I have no idea." Zack craned his neck before the door settled, catching another glimpse of his uncle. "He pulled up in some old beater, loaded up a flatbed with boxes, and went inside without giving me an ass chewing."

"That's strange." Riley joined his stare out the door. "Do you know what was in the boxes?"

"Not a clue." Zack shrugged. He couldn't care what his uncle was up to and grabbed another flatbed cart to load with other produce.

Riley wrinkled her brow. "We better keep an eye on him."

We? Zack thought. That was the first time Riley had offered to do anything with him. This was an opportunity he couldn't pass up. Maybe working together to solve the mystery of what had Biscuit flustered today might open the door to something more. Like a date.

"Sure. Why not?" Zack returned the flatbed to its proper spot and followed Riley onto the floor. Walking side by side, they scanned the aisles, looking for his uncle, eventually spotting him in the canned vegetable aisle. He placed a canister he'd brought in from his car on the top shelf and repositioned the stock in front of it. Sweat soaked more of his shirt. The red spots on his skin had expanded and stretched to his face.

His uncle looked like a man on a mission, moving from one aisle to the next, hiding canisters on the shelves. Then, pushing the cart to the hallway outside his office, Biscuit unloaded the boxes inside and came out carrying two small containers. He then doubled back to the storage area, reappearing a minute later with one less metallic cylinder.

"What do you think he's up to?" Zack eyed his uncle as he walked toward them.

"I don't know, but he looks unhinged." Riley turned her head, looking squarely at Zack. "Someone needs to talk to him."

"Not me." Zack took a step backward. Boldness was not his trademark. "He hates me on a good day."

"Fine. I'll do it." Riley touched Biscuit's forearm before he passed by, bringing him to a stop. "Are you all right, Mr. Beckett? Do you need help with anything?"

Biscuit darted his eyes back and forth. "There's no time." He continued to the front registers and spoke briefly to Bret at the manager's station. Bret then dug something out of his pocket and handed it to his uncle.

"He's acting really strange." Riley folded her arms across her chest.

"That's an understatement," Zack snorted. If his mother could only see Uncle Del now, she'd sing a different tune. "*Why can't you be more like your uncle?*" she used to say. Zack would rather be a stoner than a neurotic nerd.

Biscuit pressed a switch near the main entrance. The cashier and the two customers in line turned their heads simultaneously toward the door and ruckus as the overnight metal grate lowered, blocking the way out for customers. Biscuit padlocked it and attached a metallic cylinder to the grate. He then returned to the manager's station, ripped the landline phone from the podium, and pressed the microphone on the store's intercom system.

"Attention. This is an emergency. The store is locked down. I need everyone, including employees, to come to the registers immediately." Biscuit repeated the command and waited for people to filter to the front.

Zack counted twelve, including himself—five employees and seven customers. Their reactions ranged from confused to worried. He leaned into Riley and whispered, "Do you know what's going on?"

"I have no clue." Riley shivered. "But he's giving me the creeps."

4

Amanda Keene pulled her Range Rover into the shopping center, mumbling, "Asshole," without moving her lips. She glanced in the rearview mirror, confirming her son was still engrossed with his iPad. Since he'd become more adept at reading lips, she'd become the primary contributor to the family swear jar.

She mouthed the word again, still cursing the impatient idiot who couldn't wait an extra five seconds while she pressed send on her phone and safely stowed it in the center console cupholder. Amanda had become accustomed to it in California, just as she did in Manhattan when the FBI had stationed her husband there. It must have been a coastal, big city trait. Her husband's two assignments to "flyover country" in the Midwest, as he'd called it, were polar opposites. Drivers there were considerate and patient. Here, every other person in a beater or little imported sedan thought they owned the road. That everyone should make way for their inability to plan and leave on time.

Amanda coasted into her usual parking spot, halfway between the ice cream and grocery stores. Friday was her and Dylan's big day of the week, forgoing homeschooling in the morning. It started at seven-thirty with breakfast, continued with his weekly speech therapy session, and ended with his favorite ice cream cone. He got to suck it down while his mother did the weekly grocery shopping.

She'd timed their arrival just right again, one minute before Baskin-Robbins opened their door. She adjusted her rearview so Dylan could see her lips and waited for him to look up. He still had a way to go before he became proficient enough to rely on reading lips, but forcing him to practice was key to getting him to that point. "You did very good today. Ready for your treat?"

He grinned, exposing the newly formed gap of his two missing front teeth.

Once inside, Amanda waited patiently for the clerk to don her apron. "Good morning. It's good to see you back. What will it be today?" The plucky twenty-something clerk had served Amanda and her son for the last year, offering a glistening smile every time they walked through the door.

Amanda signed to her son as she spoke, "Chocolate again?"

He nodded and signed back, *On a sugar cone.*

Amanda repeated his order. Once Dylan was plied with enough sugar for a small army, she thanked the clerk and stuffed a few dollars into the tip jar on the way out. These places never paid enough to get by, but Amanda did her part by recognizing hard work.

She then checked the time on her phone—right on schedule. If the line was short at checkout, she and Dylan should get home in time for him to enjoy one episode of *Amphibia* before settling into their afternoon math lesson.

She couldn't spoil him enough on a speech therapy day. She remembered hearing his voice for the first time four months ago, and of all the words in the English language, he'd said the word "Mom." From that day on, he got every treat he wanted on Fridays.

Dylan grunted. One byproduct of speech therapy was becoming more vocal when he was frustrated.

Amanda glanced down. Two streaks of melted ice cream had made their way down to Dylan's hand. In his world, that was a disaster. Ice cream should never be wasted. She bent at the knees to his eye level, fumbling to stuff her phone into the hip pocket of her leggings. "Remember? Lick it in circles first until the ice cream doesn't flow over the edge of the cone." She reached into her pocket and wiped his hand dry with a tissue. "All good?"

He nodded.

Straightening her knees, Amanda glanced at the homeless man pawing through the curbside trash can as he pulled out four aluminum soda cans. She'd seen him before in the shopping center, each time appearing harmless, but she never as much as acknowledged him with a "good morning."

Since Dylan had the ice cream disaster under control, they continued to the next store. Once inside, Amanda grabbed a smaller-sized shopping cart and roamed up and down the aisles of McBean's, collecting the items on her list. The store was light on customers, but the manager was busy placing items and tidying up the shelves.

Amanda stopped at the bakery to place a special order. Waiting for the baker to finish shifting trays in the oven gave her time to consider whether the effort to make her husband's upcoming birthday special was worth it. Maxwell had made it clear he wouldn't change his work habits to lighten her load of homeschooling a hearing-impaired child while parenting two teenagers. His solution to every time-intensive home task was to hire someone to handle it. And when he suggested placing their son in a special boarding school, that was the last straw. Dylan's birth may not have been planned, but he was still Amanda's son. She refused to ship him off because he took too much of her time. But celebrating Maxwell's birthday wasn't for him. It was for the son who adored his father and insisted on a cake and candles for every birthday.

Amanda signed and said to her son, "What flavor should we order?"

He signed, *Chocolate*.

"Can you say it?" Amanda had discovered he was content in signing if she didn't encourage him to use his voice daily. While that was still effective communication, relying only on sign language defeated the purpose of taking him to speech therapy to learn to talk with those who couldn't sign.

Dylan opened his mouth but closed it quickly when the baker came to the counter. He was still self-conscious about talking in front of strangers.

"It's okay." She winked at him before turning to the Hispanic baker. "Good morning, Maria."

"Good morning, Amanda. And how are you, Dylan? I see you've finished your ice cream."

Dylan nodded. The chocolate smudges at the dimples in his smile were a dead giveaway.

"How can I help you two today?" Maria returned her attention to Amanda.

"We'd like to order a double-layer chocolate birthday cake for Tuesday." Amanda glanced at Dylan, signing the word "chocolate."

"Of course." Maria peeled an order from her pad and handed it to Amanda to fill out the details.

An announcement came over the loudspeaker. "Attention. This is an emergency. The store is locked down. I need everyone, including employees, to come to the registers immediately."

Maria narrowed her brow.

"What's going on, Maria?" Amanda's concern immediately went to her son.

The male voice repeated the command, prompting Maria to shut down her register. "I don't know, but we should go. That was the store manager's voice."

Amanda tugged on Dylan's jacket sleeve to get his attention. She signed and said, "There's some emergency. We have to go to the front." Her son wasn't the clingy type, preferring most days to be lost in his silent world. But when she took her first step toward the front, he grabbed her hand. She gave him a reassuring squeeze and followed Maria down the aisle.

A mix of employees and customers had gathered near the front registers. Everyone was staring at the manager with a microphone in his hand. Several employees whispered back and forth, but the customers remained silent in a thickening tension. Dylan acted like a champ, holding his mother's hand without complaint.

The manager pulled a pistol from his waistband to several gasps. Every set of eyes in the store widened, even his. "I've rigged the doors with motion-sensor explosives. Meaning, if anyone gets near the doors, the building will blow up."

Amanda instinctively hid her son behind her and reached for her phone in her hip pocket, but it wasn't there. "Dammit," she whispered. What a horrible time to lose a phone.

The manager pulled out a reusable plastic shopping bag from the supervisor's station. "I need everyone's cell phones and devices now. If you don't"—he pointed his weapon at the metal cylinder he'd attached to the security gate—"I'll blow us up." A chorus of gasps filled the room. Finally, he handed the bag to a tall, muscular employee who was the real-life version of a Ken doll. "Phones, now."

The employee approached each person, collecting cell phones, smart-watches, and an iPad from one customer. Amanda's heart pounded faster when he reached her. The manager would likely think she was holding out when she said she didn't have her phone with her. Would that earn her a pistol-whipping? A bullet in the chest?

Amanda patted down the pockets of her hoodie and the thigh pockets on her black leggings. She finally read Ken doll's name tag. "I'm sorry, Bret. I must have lost it in the parking lot."

Bret turned toward the manager. "She said she doesn't have one."

"Bullshit." The manager's anger built, turning his neck blotchy red. He waved the pistol in Bret's direction. "Search them."

"I'm sorry, ma'am." Bret dumped the contents of Amanda's small back-pack onto the register counter but didn't find a phone. He then patted her down gingerly, cringing when he reached her chest. "Sorry." He turned to search her son, but Dylan retreated behind her hip.

Resisting might be enough to push the unstable manager over the edge, so Amanda gently nudged Dylan out from behind her and spoke and signed, "It's okay. Let him touch you."

Dylan reluctantly stepped forward and endured the same humiliating search.

Bret turned toward the manager, extending the bag of devices. "This is all of them, Mr. Beckett."

The manager snatched the bag with a look of fear in his eyes. "I've placed devices around the store. You'll have access to the front aisle and a path to the bathroom. I'll detonate the bombs if anyone tries to break into my office. Stay put. If no one tries to be a hero, this will be over soon."

The ominous order left everyone quivering in silence. Even Amanda's son, who had a healthy fear of guns despite his father carrying one every day for work. This was the first time she was glad Dylan was deaf and couldn't hear how much danger they were in.

The twelve hostages—six women, five men, and Dylan—had divided into groups. The five employees huddled together—the two men were rubbing the backs of their necks in palpable frustration and the three women were comforting each other. The seven customers formed a loose group. An older couple, likely from the nearby senior community, joined Amanda and her son. Two women, one muscular and one young enough to be a student from Gladding High School, hovered close by. Finally, a man in his thirties who looked like he'd recently served in the military stood nearby, eyeing the aisles and looking like a trapped animal.

"What should we do?" The older woman trembled. Her voice was shaky too.

The older man wrapped an arm around her shoulder. "We do as he says, and we won't get hurt."

Amanda waved the women and the other man over. She then moved Dylan to her side so he could read the lips of everyone in the group. They appeared concerned but not overwhelmed. "Did anyone get off a message before the phones were taken?"

"I did." The young woman nervously bit her nails. "I told my mom about the bombs, and she's calling the police. The girl at the register ringing up my snacks texted too."

"That's good news." Amanda waved over the group of employees. They formed a circle, tighter than social graces would have dictated on any other day. The closeness was oddly comforting. "I understand one of you got off a text message." She gestured toward the high schooler. "She did too, so the police should be here soon."

"Thank goodness." A young female employee let out a deep sigh of relief. Her name tag read, "Riley." The others were Zack, Bret, Ally, and Maria. Amanda knew Maria from her frequent visits. *Funny,* she thought. She recognized their faces and had seen their name tags every week for over a year, yet she'd only bothered to commit Maria's name to memory. In fact, she couldn't recall the young lady's name at the ice cream store. That was a social oversight she'd need to correct in every store she visited regularly.

"That was the store manager, right?" Amanda asked.

"Yes." Bret rubbed the back of his neck, shaking his head in wonder. "I don't know what's gotten into him today. He seemed fine yesterday."

"Then something must have happened between then and now. How did he seem when he came in this morning?" Amanda never thought she'd think this but thank goodness she was married to an FBI agent. Nineteen years of listening to him talk about cases and how he solved most of them by understanding the subject. Strangely, the source of the stress in their marriage might now help her get through a harried situation.

"He was late." Bret crossed his arms across his chest, stressing his next point. "And that never happens."

"I saw him come in today." Zack wagged a thumb toward the corridor where she'd seen employees come through before. That must lead to where workers parked their cars. "He was acting really strange."

"Strange how?" Amanda asked.

"First, Biscuit didn't give a crap that I'd lit one up." Zack shoved both hands in his front pockets, hunching his shoulders when the high schooler snickered.

Amanda doubted Zack was referring to tobacco. "Biscuit?"

"Uncle Del, the manager," Zack explained. "He brought in a butt load of metal cases and cylinders, so Riley and I followed him around. We watched him drop off one or two on every aisle and take a bunch to his office. Then he left one in the back—I'm guessing at the rear door—and attached one to the front door."

Uncle? Amanda thought. Having family here might be helpful. Zack might know what would make his uncle go off the deep end. "Does he have a history of mental illness?"

"Uncle Del?" Zack smirked. "Not unless you count his obsession with rules and English tea biscuits."

"Something pushed him over the edge." Amanda conjured up several scenarios, the worst being that Uncle Del's family was lying dead in their house, and he intended to take more people out when he killed himself. "Until we or the police figure out what that is, we better do as he says."

"I'll check the back door." Bret took a step toward the corridor. "Maybe it's not locked."

"Are you crazy, dude?" Zack pulled Bret to a stop. "Biscuit left one of those metal cans in the back and said the bombs have motion sensors. If you get near that door, you could kill all of us."

"I agree. We need to stick to the areas he mentioned." Amanda moved her hands up and down in a calming motion.

"Who made you queen." Bret's sharp tone suggested he didn't like authority. Or maybe he didn't like women who took charge.

"Nobody. But my husband is an FBI agent. If there's one thing I learned from him about these types of situations, it's that people die if they don't cooperate."

"So you just expect us to do nothing?" Bret's dismissive tone was unmistakable.

"Until we know more about why Uncle Del is doing this, yes. We do nothing." Amanda then turned her attention to the group of employees. "Now, where's the bathroom?"

Riley pointed toward a passageway at the far end of the front registers. "Down that corridor."

Amanda glanced at the elderly couple. "Is there something to sit on? Some of us might not be comfortable on the ground."

"Yes. We have two disabled cashiers." Riley dipped behind a rarely used register and retrieved two folding stools. She then set them up for the couple.

Amanda considered their options—they had none. "Okay. We have everything we need—food, water, a bathroom, and a place to sit. I suggest we wait this out and let the police handle Uncle Del."

A loud explosion rocked the building, flickering the lights several times. Screams filled the air, and Amanda instinctively shielded Dylan with her body. She scanned the walls but found no signs of damage, suggesting the blast must have been outside.

"What the hell was that?" someone yelled.

Amanda squeezed her son tight. "A sign of things to come if Uncle Del doesn't get what he wants."

5

Returning to his hometown to round out a thirty-year career was never the plan, but neither was ending a twenty-six-year marriage. Nevertheless, Nolan Hughes strode down a hallway inside the headquarters building of the Gladding Police Department, juggling a laptop satchel and box of his office things. The label headquarters was a misnomer in his book. HQ would suggest this department had multiple locations. It didn't. With one hundred fifty sworn officers, not big but not small, the city had sprung for only one building. Thankfully, that structure was newer, equipped with modern technology, and laid out nicely for proper control of prisoners and visitors.

He tapped open his new office door with a foot and used a shoulder to hit the wall rocker switch to turn on the lights. He smiled. Hands down, this was the biggest office he'd had in his career. Coming from the Los Angeles Police Department, where he'd spent the last thirty years, office space for hostage negotiators was an afterthought. After all, they never negotiated from behind a desk at headquarters.

Nolan placed his box atop his modular desk and slipped the satchel from his shoulder. Scanning the eight-by-ten-foot room, he assessed the furniture was of better quality than anything he'd brought from LA after the divorce. Though, his crappy belongings didn't matter. After his mother passed last month, the house he'd inherited from her had more stuff than he knew what to do with. It would take him months to sift through every closet, cabinet, drawer, and box to figure out what to keep, toss, or donate. But, considering his recent life changes, staying busy was probably for the best.

An inspection of the desk drawers uncovered a perfectionist's dream. The office supplies were neatly arranged and spaced out. The rest of the room was filled with two guest chairs, an end table between them with a fake plant placed perfectly in the center, and a framed picture of some geometric shape on the wall. Nolan felt like he was in a doctor's waiting room, not a detective's office.

Turning on the department laptop, he was impressed with its sleekness. He'd have to stack five to equal the weight and thickness of the one he had at the LAPD. Before sitting, he unclipped the paddle holster with his department-issued SIG Sauer. He then laid it in the top desk drawer beside his new Gladding PD badge. It would take some getting used to carrying a star and not the shield he had for three decades.

Nolan spent the next hour navigating the employee section of the GPD internal website, familiarizing himself with personnel, department capabilities, and workload for the last five years. He quickly learned why his primary duty was investigating violent crimes and hostage negotiations were secondary. They had four detectives handling two hundred and fifty cases a year, and one recently quit. At the same time, the department needed to use a negotiator only twelve times last year. Eleven were domestic disputes, and one was a disgruntled employee who'd held his boss at gunpoint for two hours. The negotiator on each of those cases was the same one who had quit three months ago.

A knock on the open door drew his attention. His new boss, Captain Grand, was there. During Nolan's video interview two weeks ago, the captain was level-headed and professional. Working for him would be a pleasure. "Getting settled?" Grand asked.

Nolan had yet to touch the box of his personal items, but that was a project for another day. "Morning, Captain. Just getting the lay of the land."

"We're not that formal regarding rank around here, so call me Elliot. Have you picked up your badge and service weapon yet?"

"Yes. I did that first thing this morning."

"Good. Grab your things. We have a case."

"Wow. Okay." Nolan threw his office laptop into his satchel and unplugged the charger.

"Don't bother with the power cord. We have everything you'll need in the SWAT van." Captain Grand waved him along.

"SWAT? What's the case?"

"Someone at McBean's went off the deep end and has taken people hostage. The exits might be rigged with bombs."

Nolan grabbed his badge and service weapon. "Nothing like hitting the ground running."

Rolling up to the incident perimeter brought up a bucket of wonderful memories. McBean's grocery store was three blocks down from Gladding High School, Nolan's alma mater. Every teenager with a dime in their pocket since the store opening seventy-five years ago went there for lunch or after school. It was "the" place to go for junk food and Zig-Zags when he did weed as a sophomore. Nolan remembered Old Man McBean carding him to make sure he was old enough to buy smokes. *Ahh, the good old days*, he thought. The legal age to purchase tobacco was sixteen, gas was seventy-eight cents a gallon, and condoms were under a buck.

Nolan had gone into McBean's periodically when he visited his mother over the years after moving away, but he recognized no one who worked there—a byproduct of being absent for three decades. But if memory served, it was a family-owned and operated business, so he wondered which McBean was running it now.

"Who runs the place these days?" Nolan asked his captain.

"Delmar Beckett." Grand parked the shift commander's SUV just inside the entry control point of the two-block perimeter his patrol officers had established.

"Delmar Beckett? I haven't heard that name since high school." They had graduated the same year, were teammates on the varsity football team, and ran in the same circles, but they were by no means close. However, they'd shared some wild Friday and Saturday nights during parties at the old POW camp. "I thought a McBean always managed the store."

"He's the manager, not the owner. The McBean triplets own the store now, but none want to run it. Del married one of the girls, so he's part-owner by marriage."

Nolan replied with a nod. "Have you evacuated the high school in case this goes sideways?"

"It's underway. We don't want the perimeter to become a circus for students, so we're making parents show up in person and sign for their release."

"Smart move." The last time Nolan worked a scene close to a high school, getting a selfie with the hostages in the background had morphed into the latest TikTok challenge.

Exiting the SUV, Grand led Nolan by foot to the SWAT van located a hundred feet from the perimeter. They entered. The inside looked like something from a movie set with all the latest equipment and gear, even a restroom. Nolan issued a whistle to show his appreciation. "How does Gladding afford a tactical unit like this?"

"Covid was a godsend. The feds handed out funds like it was Monopoly money, so we sent the county our wish list. A year later, this came. We share it with Rocklin and Roseville and loan officers to each other to staff SWAT and the bomb squad."

Nolan shook his head. He was part of the LAPD during two windfall periods—the Great Recession and Covid—but never benefited one mechanical pencil from either. He decided that moving to a smaller department was the best decision he'd made in his entire career.

"Nolan Hughes, I'd like you to meet Craig Carver. He's our SWAT commander."

Nolan shook Carver's hand. He looked the part with above-average height, square jaw, and toned muscles and was decked out in a fully equipped tactical uniform. But he also looked too young to command a SWAT unit. In the LAPD, officers worked the streets for five years and another eight on the assault end of SWAT before being moved into a leadership position. This guy looked to be only thirty, with half that experience.

"Craig, this is Nolan Hughes. He's taking Schmidt's position and is our new hostage negotiator."

"Pleased to meet you, Nolan."

"Likewise." Nolan thought he'd have to get used to using first names. Unless he was partnered with someone, he never got close enough to other officers to bend formality, preferring rank or surnames. "Can you give me a rundown?"

"Thirty minutes ago, we received two 9-1-1 calls. The callers said they'd received text messages from their teenage children, one a customer and one an employee, saying they were locked inside McBean's. They'd said someone had placed bombs at the exits. The RPs said they tried to reach their children, but the calls went to voicemail. We dispatched an officer who reported that the security gate was down at the main entrance, and the employee door was locked. The only unobstructed window into the store is in the bathroom, but the room was empty."

"Do we have an identity on the hostage taker?" Nolan asked.

"No."

"Has anyone tried to make contact?"

"Not yet. That's your job." Carver's tone edged on dismissive, making Nolan think he held the negotiator's role in low regard. "We've had the phone company cut incoming calls to the store and have established a direct line whenever you're set."

"Great job, Craig." Nolan doubted the praise would melt Carver's frosty reception, but he'd learned a long time ago to drown pettiness in kindness. Eventually, the offender would give up. "You mentioned two hostages reported the exits were rigged with bombs. What do we know about the devices?"

"One texter referenced motion sensors."

"That takes a frontal breach off the table."

"Off the table?" Carver's reaction resembled Nolan's teenage son's when his mom took the car keys away from him for the weekend—shocked and mad as hell.

"Until I learn more about the devices, yes. We won't breach. Now, what do we know about the hostages? Do we know how many?"

"No," Carver said. "The only names we know for sure are the two texters. One is a student from Gladding High, and the other is an employee who graduated from there last year. Another caller reported their neighbors had gone to the store but had yet to return. We flew in a drone and snapped the license plate numbers of every car in the front and side lots. We have a list of the registered owners and have asked your dispatch to run down the names."

"How about the employees?" Nolan asked. "Has anyone called the McBean's to find out who was working today?" He glanced between Carver and Captain Grand. If memory served, the store didn't have too many people on staff in the morning, so the number of employees caught up in this should be low.

"Dispatch called the store's emergency contact number after receiving the first 9-1-1 call," Grand said, "but that was Beckett's cell phone. It went to voicemail."

"Okay. We're going in blind." This wasn't the first time Nolan had been asked to defuse a hostage situation with very little information to go on. He'd have to build a hook and trigger picture as he went. He scanned the van's interior, locating a whiteboard tacked above a countertop. "I'll set up there."

"But that's—" Carver started before the captain interrupted.

"Take whatever you need." Grand glanced at Carver, reminding him silently of the pecking order. He was on loan, not in command. "Until the scene turns hot, you're in charge."

"All right then." Nolan picked up the telephone handset, bringing it to his ear. The call started instantly. "Let's make first contact."

One ring. Two. Three. Four. Five. Finally, on the sixth, the call connected.

"Hello?" a man's voice said. Nolan grabbed a dry erase marker and wrote "shaky" on the upper left corner of the whiteboard. An unsteady voice could mean many things, ranging from drug withdrawal to a mental breakdown.

"Hello, this is Nolan Hughes of the Gladding Police Department."

"Nolan Hughes from Gladding High School?"

"Yes."

"This is Delmar. What in the hell are you doing here? I thought you were in LA."

Nolan wrote Beckett's name on the whiteboard. "I was, but I'm glad to be back in Gladding so I can help an old friend. Tell me what's going on, Del?" Starting with an open-ended question, let Del set the tone and direction of the conversation. The key to resolving any hostage situation was often revealed during the initial contact, so listening was more important than talking.

"I don't want to hurt anyone, but I will if I have to." Beckett paused, too long for Nolan to not fill the void.

"That's a good start, Del." Nolan wrote "reluctant" on the whiteboard. His mind went into overdrive, thinking of ways to leverage his personal history with someone he barely knew and hardly liked thirty-five years ago. "How can we get everyone out safely?"

"You can't. I'll only talk to ATF Agent Lexi Mills. You have six hours to get her here, or I'll set off the devices and kill people one by one."

"I can arrange for a phone call?"

"Just get Agent Mills here. She'll know what this is about. And to show you I mean business, here's a taste of what's to come if you don't get her." The phone went dead.

Nolan turned to Captain Grand. "I'll need a complete background on Delmar Beckett—family, financials, criminal record, job history, education, hometown. You name it. We also need to send a patrol to his house and talk to his family."

"I'll put another detective on it and notify dispatch." Grand pulled out his cell phone and gave Nolan the key fob to the SUV they drove here. "You'll need this."

A loud explosion rocked the area. Nolan tossed his stare to the wall-mounted monitors displaying live video feeds of the store. A white smoke cloud rose from the side of the building but quickly dwindled.

Sergeant Carver pressed the mic attached to his shoulder epaulet. "Somebody report. What the hell was that?"

"Charlie Three to Charlie One. We have detonation outside the store at the dumpster. Minimal damage."

"Charlie Three. Do we need Fire?"

"Negative. No fire."

Carver locked gazes with Captain Grand, adjusting his tactical belt to prepare for imminent action. "I think that qualifies as hot. We need to go in."

"That, Sergeant Carver, was a shot across the bow. He's gotten our attention, so now is not the time to escalate. It's time to locate Lexi Mills."

6

Middle seats should be outlawed, Lexi thought. No matter the airline, the middle seat, with little elbow and legroom on either side, should be labeled cruel punishment, which was why she always asked for the window. However, she gladly gave the precious seat assignment to Nita for the flight to Sacramento. A few extra inches of wriggle room and a balled-up jacket for cushioning behind her injured shoulder allowed Nita to get comfortable enough to fall asleep for several hours on the lengthy flight. All the while, Lexi fought her long-legged seatmate for every inch, leaping at every opportunity to reclaim her personal space.

The announcement over the cabin intercom alerted passengers they'd begun their slow descent, and attendants would come through to collect trash. Lexi reached across Nita's seat tray to collect her empty drink cup, pinching her side on the armrest—yet another penance for occupying the middle seat. A glance at Longlegs confirmed Lexi had lost every bit of ground she'd made in the last hour. Her seatmate had successfully shifted his elbow, claiming their entire shared armrest for himself.

"Dammit," Lexi whispered.

Nita stirred, wincing when she shifted. "Are we close?"

"We're beginning our descent, so we should land in about half an hour.

How's your shoulder?" Lexi had noticed Nita struggling to get comfortable earlier.

Nita straightened, closing her eyes to the unmistakable sigh of pain. "I'll be fine once I can move around."

Soon, the attendant came by with a plastic trash bag. When Lexi handed her some items, she leaned in. "Miss Mills, would you mind following me to the forward galley?"

"Of course." The request, while surprising, didn't alarm her. The flight was void of disturbances, so she doubted the crew needed a peace officer.

When Lexi undid her seatbelt, Nita placed a hand on her arm. "What's going on?"

"I'm not sure." Lexi gave Nita's hand a reassuring squeeze. "I'll be right back." She glanced at her space-stealing seatmate and smiled. "Do you mind?"

"Sure." Daddy Longlegs unbuckled. He then used the seat in front of him as leverage, pulling down hard to get up and exit to the aisle.

Lexi stood, sensing her residual limb slide some into the socket of her prosthesis. The replacement leg fit much better than the one she had when she first returned to SRT duty four months ago. And thanks to the generosity of Governor Macalister of Texas, the ankle was an upgraded model. It provided her a range of motion similar to a human one, allowing her greater agility and speed when running.

Following the attendant down the narrow aisle, Lexi stepped carefully to avoid several purse and backpack straps that had ventured from their cubbies beneath the seats. Once at the galley, she waited for the attendant to stow the trash before asking, "Is there a problem?"

"The captain has asked to speak with you in private. I'll tell him you're here." The attendant lifted the intercom handset and whispered a few words into it. Nothing about her calm expression suggested Lexi's status as an unarmed law enforcement officer was needed, but being called forward meant something was wrong.

The attendant handed the handset to Lexi before leaving the galley to continue her landing checklist.

"This is Lexi Mills." Her muscles tensed, wondering what in-flight event would require her attention.

"Agent Mills, this is Captain Lawson. We received a call from the FBI regarding a police emergency near Sacramento. Your immediate presence is required."

"What kind of emergency?"

"Details were sketchy, but there's an active hostage situation with a bomb threat. While we're taxiing on the ground, I'll make an announcement, instructing all passengers to remain seated after arriving at the gate to allow you to exit quickly. FBI agents will meet you at the gate and escort you to the scene."

"I'm traveling with my life partner." Lexi searched the rows of passengers against the windows for Nita, eventually locking eyes with her. She remembered the few lessons of American Sign Language Nita had taught her last month and signaled that she was fine. "Will she be able to deplane with me?"

"That's up to you. I've been asked to get you off the plane without delay."

"Got it. Thank you, Captain."

"Good luck, Agent Mills. Stay safe."

Lexi returned the handset to its cradle and retraced her steps to her assigned row. She smiled at Longlegs, who then unbuckled and repeated the awkward process out of his seat. Once Lexi buckled, she whispered to Nita, detailing the message Captain Lawson had passed along.

"Do you know where it's at?" Nita's body movements looked stiff, as if her shoulder was hurting her more than she'd let on.

Lexi shrugged. "I'll know more once I talk to the FBI agents. After we land, I'll ask an attendant to help us with your bag so you won't strain your shoulder." Sensing Nita's uneasiness, Lexi laced their fingers together. "Whatever this is, I'll handle it quickly so we can get to the hotel for our afternoon plans." She waggled her eyebrows at Nita.

"You're a naughty one, Lexi Mills."

"With you? Always."

Twenty minutes later, the plane's wheels skidded against the tarmac, bouncing only once in a near-perfect landing. The pilot's voice came over the intercom after the engines wound down and the aircraft settled into a comfortable taxiing speed. He announced a police emergency was ongoing, and the crew needed to escort a law enforcement officer off the plane first. Everyone around Lexi accepted the announcement in stride, except for Longlegs. He flapped his hands in the air, griping about a meeting he had to attend. "This had better be important."

Lexi snickered. "I'm sure they wouldn't have asked if it wasn't." She pulled out her cell phone and powered it on. Within seconds, it dinged and repeatedly vibrated, alerting on multiple missed messages. Entering the phone's passcode, she noted four missed text messages and two missed phone calls. One call was from Kaplan Shaw, a friend and ATF intelligence officer, and the other was from her SRT commander, Agent Jack Carlson. She dialed him, but the call went to voicemail.

A scan of the text messages revealed one from Carlson, Kaplan, her mother, and Noah. Noah had said he'd landed and would see her and Nita at the hotel later today. Lexi replied, *See you soon.*

Her mother had texted, passing along her congratulations for being the guest of honor at tomorrow night's awards ceremony. Lexi replied with a red heart emoji.

Carlson's text was brief, instructing her to call as soon as she landed. Lexi rolled her eyes. If his message was so damn important, he would have answered the call. She texted, *Returned your call. Will try again.*

Finally, Kaplan had texted, saying Lexi's name had popped up in a hostage situation at a grocery store in Gladding, California. She explained that the hostage taker had rigged the exits with motion-sensor activated explosive devices and had detonated one on the exterior to demonstrate his intent. She'd wished her good luck. Lexi mumbled, "Thank you, Kaplan." She'd have to buy that woman a drink for looping her in. Kaplan had a nose for intelligence and could ferret out the deepest hidden gems. She replied, *Thx for the intel. Will fill u in when I know more.*

Lexi returned her phone to her coat pocket, mulling over the information Kaplan had provided. Motion-sensor explosives were anti-personnel devices the United Nations had banned decades ago for their instability and indiscriminate nature. Anything, from a person to a moth floating through the kill zone, could set them off.

As they rolled up to the gate, an attendant reminded passengers to remain seated. Once stopped, she strode down the aisle with purpose.

Lexi unbuckled and stood.

"We're supposed to stay in our seats," Legs barked, his tone dripping with disdain for Lexi's inability to follow instructions.

"I know." Lexi offered her hand to Nita. "That's our cue." She then sneered at the space-stealer. "Do you mind? I have lives to save." Legs dropped his jaw. Once he was up, the attendant arrived. Lexi addressed her. "We have two carry-ons right above us. My partner is injured. Can you assist?"

"Of course." The attendant retrieved both bags, leaving one for Lexi. She expertly led the way down the aisle without hitting a single leg or elbow.

The distinct thud of the passenger door opening sounded when they reached the first-class section. The ground crew secured the door, clearing the way for Lexi and Nita to deplane. Once at the ninety-degree turn on the gangway, Lexi adjusted her bags, looking at the attendant. "We can take it from here. Thanks for your help."

"Best of luck, Agent Mills. I hope everything turns out okay." The attendant handed the bag to Nita.

Lexi acknowledged with a nod before leading the way up the gangway. Making the final turn, she spotted two men at the top. Their business cuts and tailored suits screamed FBI. The shorter one flashed his credentials and badge. "Agent Mills?" Lexi confirmed with a yes. "FBI. I'm Turner. He's Mitchell. We're here to escort you to the hostage scene."

Lexi glanced over her shoulder, hearing the wheels of Nita's suitcase rolling over a threshold divider on the gangway. "I'm traveling with my life partner. I need to get her to our hotel."

"There's no time, Agent Mills. Our orders are to take you directly to the on-scene command post."

Lexi released the handle of her carry-on, placed both hands on Nita's upper arms, and searched her eyes. She expected to find strength and understanding but found something disturbing. Her pupils appeared smaller than usual. While the changing light conditions could have been the cause, Lexi wondered if Nita had taken one of the two pain pills they'd put in her bag in case the pain had gotten worse.

"I'm worried about you. Can you call Noah when you get to the hotel? He landed a while ago and can hang out with you until I get there."

"I'll be fine, Lexi. You don't have to baby me." Nita's words came out sharper than they had in some time. The last occasion was when Lexi had forgotten to call after she'd safely disposed of a pipe bomb found near Tulsa.

Lexi couldn't blame her for being angry this morning, but she didn't have time for a proper apology. She then cupped her hands on Nita's cheeks and pulled her in for a brief kiss. "I love you. As soon as I figure out what's going on, I'll text you. And remember, you're stronger than you realize."

Before Nita could reply, the FBI agents whisked Lexi down the terminal and out to the arrival drop-off level outside. They guided her to the end of the curb, where a dark sedan was parked behind a police cruiser. After loading her carry-on bag in the trunk, Turner opened the rear passenger curbside door, gesturing for Lexi to enter before hopping into the front passenger seat. Mitchell jumped into the driver's seat and honked the horn. A second later, the overheads on the police cruiser in front of them came to life, its siren chirped, and then it lurched forward. They followed. A police escort meant time was critical.

Agent Turner shifted in the passenger seat to get a better view of Lexi in the backseat. "We have a hostage situation in Gladding."

"I know. Hold on. I need to make a call first." When Lexi pulled her cell phone from her jacket pocket, Turner pursed his lips. She dialed.

"Hey, Lexi. Have you landed yet?" Noah sounded perky. She'd gotten the impression at the White House last month that he wasn't much for ceremony either. But like her, he was looking forward to a paid vacation in California.

"We have, but there's been a change of plans."

They turned onto the highway. This was Lexi's first trip to California, so she tried to glimpse the scenery. She'd hoped to take in the warm weather and the beautiful rice fields that doubled as a waterfowl sanctuary but traveling at eighty-five miles per hour made that impossible.

"Is that a siren I hear?" Noah asked.

"Yeah, about that." Lexi told him about the hostage situation in

Gladding and the FBI pulling her off the plane. "I need you to take care of Nita until I get back. I think her shoulder has been bothering her more than she's letting on."

"Say no more. I picked up a rental an hour ago, but I'm not far from the airport. I can swing back around and take Nita to our hotel. I promise I'll keep her safe, Lexi. Just like I did for you."

"Thank you, Noah. I'll be able to concentrate knowing she's in your good hands. I'll do my best to make it for dinner tonight." Lexi finished the call and returned the phone to her pocket. She then redirected her attention to Turner. "I heard the hostage taker has rigged the exits of a grocery store with motion-sensor activated explosive devices and asked for me."

Turner narrowed his eyes at her as if sizing her up for handcuffs. "How did you learn that? Nothing about the explosives has been released to the press."

Lexi wagged her cell phone at eye level. "ATF intel got ahead of this as soon as my name was mentioned. Do we have a hostage count or know anything more on the devices?"

"Nothing on the devices. We have two hostage names." Turner further explained the frantic text messages sent from two hostages before communications stopped. "Another caller to 9-1-1 said their neighbors hadn't returned from the store yet. You should know that we found a body at the suspect's house."

"Wife?" Lexi asked.

"Maid. And the family is missing." Turner then detailed the city's SWAT initial setup. "They evacuated the outer perimeter to eighteen hundred feet and set the inner perimeter at five hundred feet."

"Geez. What are they expecting?"

"The worst."

7

Lexi's kiss, while reassuring, wasn't enough to persuade Nita that she'd ever acclimate to the demands of her job. She brought two fingers to her lips, still feeling them tingle as Lexi walked away under FBI escort. A small corner of her heart died every time Lexi received a call to defuse a bomb or clear a path for other agents to charge through. Nita never knew if she'd make it home. Watching Lexi disappear into the airport crowd, that same empty feeling found her.

Nita shook off her trepidation, gripped the handle of her carry-on, and took off in Lexi's direction. She waited at baggage claim for the suitcase containing her and Lexi's formal wear for tomorrow night's black-tie event. Familiar faces from their flight filled in around her as the carousel came to life.

While scanning the growing collection of circling suitcases, duffel bags, and backpacks, Nita felt her phone vibrate in her pocket. Pulling it out, she expected a sweet text from Lexi, telling her she'd be thinking of her until she made it to the hotel. Instead, she saw Noah's name. Clearly, Lexi had already rallied the troops. His message read, *Will pick you up in 15.*

Her reply read, *TY. Will txt when I'm out there.*

Nita spotted her bag and reached for the handle before it zoomed past. A sharp pain shot through her left shoulder when she lifted it from the carousel with her uninjured arm. "That was stupid," she mumbled to herself. Nita knew the bag weighed more than fifteen pounds, the maximum weight she should lift at this point in her recovery, yet she still heaved it. If one of her patients had done the same thing, she would have given them a lecture about recognizing limitations and not being afraid to ask for help.

Stepping outside to the pickup area for arrivals, Nita sent a one-word text to Noah, *Ready*. She rolled her shoulder several times, hoping to work out the new kink. She had little success, but the pain level was manageable thanks to the Norco she'd popped when Lexi talked to the flight attendant in the galley.

Soon, a white Nissan Versa pulled up to the curb where she was standing. A glance into the cabin revealed Noah's unique smile behind the wheel. The vitiligo around his mouth and eyes created a contrast of stark white patches against his light brown skin. Noah's distinctive appearance was the first thing Nita had noticed when she first met him, and it instantly made him more intriguing. Unfortunately, it was the source of prejudgment everywhere he went. But Nita's training as a physical therapist had her conditioned to view physical deviations as a facet of her patients, not as something to fear or look down upon.

The trunk popped up. Noah then dashed out and circled the car. He greeted her with a hug. "Let me get your bags. You shouldn't be lifting those by yourself."

"Thanks, Noah."

Once he'd loaded her bags, Noah darted to the passenger side and opened the door for her like a gentleman. "Do you need help?"

While Nita appreciated the extra attention, it was unnecessary. She'd been driving for six weeks. "Thanks again. I really appreciate you picking me up."

"It made sense for me to swing back around since we're staying at the same hotel." Noah hopped in and followed the instructions on the GPS screen to get to the highway. Once settled at a comfortable speed, he glanced at Nita. "Lexi told me about the hostage scene but was light on details. Do you know anything more?"

"Not really. The FBI whisked her away before she could ask questions.

So, we're both in the dark for this one, Noah." Nita patted him on the thigh. "I'm glad I got to go on this trip with Lexi. It's so good to see you."

He glanced at her and smiled, returning his gaze to the road ahead. "It's good to see you, too. It's been crazy since leaving Spicewood."

"Repelling an insurrection and saving the governor's life will do that." Nita laughed. Noah harrumphed. He clearly wasn't a fan of the attention swirling around his and Lexi's heroism, making them much alike in that department. "I guess you're as tired of the photo ops as Lexi is."

"I just want to do my job now that the shooting board has cleared me, but these events keep getting in the way."

"You got to meet the president." Nita waved her hands in the air, wincing at the tightness in her shoulder. She'd have to take another pill or stretch the hell out of it tonight. "I would have given anything to have been toured around the White House like a visiting dignitary."

Instead of shaking hands with senators, congressional representatives, and cabinet officials, Nita was recovering from a second operation to adjust the plate holding her shoulder blade together.

"You didn't miss much. Lexi and I were carted from one handshaking event to another. By the time we got to our hotel, we were exhausted. We never got to see the city other than the White House and the Capitol." Noah glanced again at Nita. "How about you? How is your recovery coming?"

"Slowly. Though, I've made better progress since the second operation." But if Nita were honest with Noah—and Lexi—she'd say the second operation had her back on opioids after she'd successfully weaned herself from them following the shooting. That she'd fallen into a cycle using the slightest twinge of pain to justify popping a Norco instead of stretching or reaching for a Tylenol.

Nita was riding the edge of dependency, but she was far from spiraling out of control. She was familiar with addiction, having hit rock bottom once before. Still, her Norco use was nothing like her experience with cocaine and meth. She was functioning well at work and at home, something she couldn't do if the opioids had a firm grip. They were nothing more than a crutch to get her range of motion back.

"I'm glad you're coming along physically. How about emotionally? Having gone through that horrifying experience with Lexi, Simon, and the governor, I know how facing certain death can screw with the mind. How are you holding up?"

"I'm okay." Nita thought a polite white lie was better than the truth. Every night was a crapshoot. If she numbed herself with Norco, she'd sleep comfortably for five or six hours. Otherwise, she'd toss and turn. And when she finally fell asleep, she'd relive that horrific evening at the nightclub. She'd dream of bullets flying around her and people to her left and right dropping like flies into puddles of blood.

"Then you're lucky." Noah signaled for a lane change. "I have nightmares most nights. I dream I wasn't fast enough on the trigger, and Lexi either blows up with that asshole's trailer or is shot by Calhoun's army."

Nita shifted her stare. Noah twisted the leather on the steering wheel wrap, turning his knuckles to a shade of white, matching his vitiligo. "You love her, don't you?"

"Yes, but not in the way you think. I grew up without siblings. As you know, in Hispanic culture, that's nearly unheard of. We rely on family and are often defined by them. My parents gave me up because they couldn't deal with me getting into fights every day. Don't get me wrong. I loved my life with my aunt and uncle, but other than them and Sister Agatha at the Catholic school, I was alone. No friends. No brothers and sisters. Lexi is like the sister I never had. We have each other's back."

Nita patted his thigh again. "Lexi thinks the same of you, Noah. She trusts you with her life, and I do too."

Turning into the hotel property, Noah parked beneath the portico. He shifted to look Nita in the eye. "Let's hope it doesn't come to that again."

A sense of dread formed in the back of Nita's mind. Bombs and hostages involving a madman who would only talk to Lexi Mills didn't sit right with her. Whatever situation Lexi was called out to, it sounded dangerous, and she was going there with no one she could trust. Nita had to fix that.

Noah turned the engine off to hand the key to the approaching valet, but Nita placed a hand on his forearm. "I fear it might."

"I have the same feeling." Noah twisted his hand tighter around the steering wheel.

"Are you thinking what I'm thinking?"

"Yes." Noah restarted the engine, put the car back into drive, and tapped his cell phone awake. "Siri... Get directions to Gladding, California."

8

On the biggest day of crime Gladding had seen since the murder-suicide forty years ago, Sergeant Melanie Thompson was diverting traffic while babysitting her latest rookie on his first day on the job. Despite the searing afternoon summer heat, it wasn't the worst assignment. That would have been taking meal orders for the tri-city SWAT and bomb squad guys and doing a drive-thru run. At least Gary Powell was more promising than her previous trainee. From the first day she shook hands with his predecessor, she'd assessed the badge was a power trip for him. He'd proved it on their first traffic stop and had washed out within a month.

Powell was a breath of fresh air. On the positive side, he was optimistic, bright, and had graduated near the top of his academy class. On the negative side, he cared. Too much. His intellect would serve him well in the community until some yahoo with a cell phone camera burned his career for putting his heart into the job.

For the third time in the last twenty minutes, a driver pulled up to the detour signs and rolled down the window. This one politely asked what was going on. Powell replied in his business-like voice. "We have a police emergency, ma'am. For your safety, we ask that you leave the area."

The elderly woman knitted her brow, thanked Officer Powell, and drove on. Mel snickered. Everything her trainee had said and did today was textbook academy training. She'd have her hands full loosening him up, but that was much better than the alternative. Being too loose on the job gave all cops a bad rep.

"Dispatch to one-two-four," Mel's tactical radio squawked.

Mel pressed the mic attached to her uniform at the shoulder epaulet. "One-two-four."

"Ten-fourteen approaching your twenty."

It was about time. Within ten minutes of their detective arriving on scene, word had spread that the hostage taker had requested to speak to a federal agent. Why it had to be in person was a mystery, but thankfully, that agent was reachable when the demand came through.

"Ten-four." Mel approached Officer Powell. He immediately snapped to attention. While she respected and appreciated his three years of military service, he had several habits she'd have to break him of. "The FBI is close."

"Yes, ma'am."

She shook her head, adding rigid formality to the list of things to work on.

A dark sedan rolled up to their location minutes later with its head-lights flashing. The driver's window lowered, and the agent displayed his credentials and badge from behind the wheel. Mel glanced inside the vehi-cle. Another suited agent was in the front passenger seat, and a woman in casual attire was in the back. She must have been the mysterious Agent Lexi Mills.

"Good luck." Mel waved them through before pressing her mic. "One-two-four to dispatch."

"Go, one-two-four."

"Ten-fourteen just rolled through."

"Ten-four," the radio squawked. "Dispatch to one-two-four, sending relief to your twenty."

"Ten-four," Mel replied. She glanced at Powell. He rocked back and forth on his heels and toes with a pained expression, making it clear he was unaccustomed to standing for hours on end. "I recommend getting inserts for your shoes. Some days, this job is nothing but standing."

"I'm getting that impression." Powell rocked again.

Staffing a roadblock for three hours was tedious. It was boredom stacked upon boredom, especially when all hell could break out at a moment's notice just two blocks away. The only locals seeing action were the shift commander, the detective-slash-negotiator, and the few assigned to SWAT. Anything beyond an evacuation was beyond the capability of their small department. That meant Gladding cops were on traffic control, and their more extensive sister department officers were on the tactical response. In turn, that meant outsiders would get all the glory or all the blame when this thing concluded. In the current climate of tension between the police and the public, Gladding was on a sound footing no matter how this turned out.

When their relief came, Mel suggested to Powell, "If you're hungry, we should eat. There's no telling how long this scene will be active."

"Yes, ma'am. I thought you'd never ask." He hopped into the driver's seat of their cruiser. Mel joined him.

"We gotta work on the ma'am thing. Call me Mel or Sergeant Thompson. You're making me feel ancient."

"It's a hard habit to break."

"If it's your worst one, we'll get along just fine." Mel glanced at the speedometer from the passenger seat, checking Powell's first performance behind the wheel of a cruiser. She snickered. Driving thirty-three in a thirty-five zone was overboard. "Do you drive this slow in your POV?"

Holding his hand pristinely at "eight and four" like a driver's ed instructor, Powell briefly shifted his stare from the road toward Mel with confusion in his eyes. "No, why?"

"Then drive as if you were off duty. Nobody likes an uptight cop. Just don't overdo it."

"Yes, ma'am. I mean Sergeant Thompson." Powell picked up speed and glanced over again. "I have a question."

"Fire away."

"If we drive over the speed limit, how can we issue tickets for it in good conscience?"

"That's a good question. In short, we use discretion. Giving someone a ticket for going three over the limit does no good. It pisses off the driver and gives cops a bad name. If they're not being dangerous or committing other crimes, we learn to let it go."

"Got it."

Mel tapped on the dash-mounted tablet, bringing up the shift change notes. Their assigned section of the city wasn't a hotbed of crime. Still, it had its share of drug-related crime, domestic issues, and tomfoolery. One vehicle had been reported stolen this morning, another was broken into in the owner's driveway, and graffiti was reported at the abandoned World War II German prisoner of war camp remains slated for historic preservation. Without drilling down to the case, Mel already knew the specifics. Two decades on patrol had taught her to review the previous day's end-of-shift reports before starting the engine of her cruiser. Now Powell was about to get his first test.

"Can you tell me what's special about the car in front of you?"

"It's a white Toyota Camry." Then, without skipping a beat, Powell continued, "One was reported stolen from Ranch Road last night, but the license plate doesn't match."

"Very good." Mel let a smile form. Powell was the real deal. She'd love to end her career by starting this man on his.

She'd had a good run—ten years as a patrol officer and ten as a training officer—but after two years of being spat on, Mel had concluded she'd been serving a citizenry that no longer appreciated her protection. But, of course, it wasn't always like that, and she wasn't always this jaded. When Mel was Powell's age, police were respected, and she was idealistic, just like the ball of putty she was supposed to mold. But when she crossed the twenty-year mark last month, her tolerance for working a thankless job had bottomed out. Retirement looked like her best option to hang up the badge before she was forced out. For that reason, Officer Powell would be her final trainee.

Fifteen minutes later, following bathroom breaks, Mel and Powell were parked in a virtually empty commuter lot, eating sub sandwiches in their cruiser. Patrolling had taken a back seat to the volatile scene at McBean's, but dispatch had held back one unit from traffic control to allow for meal breaks and unforeseen calls.

Thankfully, Powell didn't have a thing for small talk and had limited their discussion to the job. He'd grown up twenty miles away and knew the area well, so questions about the town centered on crime patterns, not the layout.

"The lower-income part of town between First and Fifth Streets receives the lion's share of the drug and disturbance calls, but the HOA community gets the load of the theft calls. That's where the money is in town," Mel explained. "The casino on the edge of town generates a lot of DUIs, so you'll get a lot of practice performing field sobriety tests."

"Dispatch to one-two-four," their car radio chirped.

Mel nodded at Powell to respond.

The corners of his lips turned up when he lifted the mic for the first time. "This is one-two-four."

"Report of a suspicious person at the POW site. Proceed code one."

"Ten-four, Dispatch. Will advise on code one."

Mel silently thanked JoAnne on the other end of the radio. They'd been friends since JoAnne came on board eight years ago, and her sending Mel on a code-one call on a day like today was her way of giving Mel a well-deserved break. That meant she and Powell could go at their convenience.

Mel stuffed down one more bite and two swigs of soda. "Let's go check out that suspicious person."

Powell put their cruiser into gear and drove north out of town. He picked up the mic. "Dispatch, this is one-two-four. Rolling code one to the POW site."

The drive allowed Mel to assess Powell's driving. He'd remained alert and set a commonsense pace on the single-lane, low-trafficked highway by going a few over the speed limit. Powell turned off the thoroughfare eight miles out of town, continuing on a gravel road marked by a simple sign with "POW Camp" and a painted arrow.

"You don't know how many times I drove down this road as a kid." Powell's coy smile meant those trips weren't for sightseeing.

He *is* a kid, Mel thought. Powell was twenty-six and young enough to be her son, but she had to not think of him as a child. He was a grown man with a badge and a gun. "It's supposed to be paved in a few months."

"That's right." Powell nodded a few times. "The camp was bought up last year. I feel bad for the high schoolers."

"It's your own fault," Mel chuckled. This abandoned site had been a teenage hangout for decades, but the crops in the last ten years had taken good care of it. "Your generation had the unspoken code of leaving the last remaining hut untouched during your Friday night drunken parties. It wouldn't have been on the Preservation Society's radar if you'd destroyed it like the others had before you."

As Powell pulled up to the cyclone perimeter fence, he harrumphed, clearly proud of the legacy he and his like-aged friends had left. "This is new."

"Yeah." Mel unbuckled, preparing to exit. "A homeless man moved into the hut last month, so the Society put up the fence to keep him out. He's been seen here several times. When someone complains, we send him on his way and ask him not to trespass."

"Why don't you arrest him and get him some help?"

"He doesn't want our help and just wants to be left alone. So as long as he doesn't cause a disturbance, steal, or destroy anything, we just let him go where he wants."

"Drugs?" Powell asked.

"Maybe at one point, but the times I've seen him, he appeared to suffer from mental illness. So, there's not much we can do other than keep an eye on him. I think he's ex-army like you."

"Maybe I can help, then." Powell unbuckled, too.

"Maybe you can," Mel said. "Call us in." Powell reported they had arrived at the POW site and would search the area.

They exited the cruiser, grabbing their sunglasses. The sun was bright, radiating a brutal afternoon heat. Mel glanced at Powell's web belt and placed her hand on her own, ensuring her expandable baton was in place. That was the most versatile piece of equipment they carried. It not only was a nonlethal weapon, but it was also a pry bar and a search tool. Mel had lost count of the times she'd used her baton to open stuck doors and sift through trash and debris.

Mel rolled her neck once, putting herself into training mode. Every call, every traffic stop, and every contact with a citizen was a training opportunity. Though this call was to check on a suspicious person in the area, Mel considered using the chance to train Powell on proper building search techniques.

"What are you thinking right now?" Mel asked, knowing his answer would tell her how much work was ahead of her before letting Powell loose on the streets solo.

"That I might find someone I can help in there," Powell replied.

"And that will get you killed. I put the thought into your head that we might find an army vet in need. We don't know who or what is in there. Always think tactically and think survival. Assume an armed confrontation every time you enter a building." His deflated expression meant she'd driven the point home. Hopefully, the lesson might save his life one day. "Now, step me through your observations."

Walking up to the gate, Powell scanned the fence and the area inside. The padlock and chain were on the ground, but the gate panels were pushed together to appear closed. The ruins seemed to be unoccupied. However, they couldn't see inside the intact prison hut. "The chain has been cut, but the fence appears undisturbed."

"What does that tell you?"

"The intruder likely isn't kids. They rarely carry bolt cutters. However, homeless men often steal them from home improvement stores to break bike chains, and bad actors have them."

"Correct. That tells me to grip my pistol, not my Taser." Mel liked his silent nod. He was listening and learning. "Let's walk the hut's perimeter and see what's there."

Powell pushed the cyclone gate open, resting his right hand on the grip of his holstered service weapon. A gridwork of foundations and the rubble of ninety-nine prison huts in ten rows of ten lined the weed-laden field in what once housed a thousand WWII German prisoners of war. Near one corner of the former compound was the last remaining hut. That was their destination.

It appeared the Preservation Society had done some work, laying out plywood between the former rows of prison huts. A pathway had also been laid to the one remaining structure. Footprints suggested workers were supposed to remain on temporary wooden tracks. However, considering a suspicious person call had brought Mel and Powell out there, following such a path bothered her. She wanted to see what she was walking on, so she stepped to one side of the platform. Powell followed her example.

Following the pathway's edge, Mel noted a mix of footprints in terms of size and freshness—another teaching moment. She slowed her pace and pointed to a newer print highlighted by the red clay soil Gladding was known for. "It looks new. How many different prints could you make out?"

"Three or four. Different sizes, too. They could be from the workers or from a group of intruders."

"Good. Never assume signs are benign."

Stepping within thirty feet of the one concrete hut, Mel stopped, thinking she heard something. "Stop." She also used a hand signal to bring Powell to a halt. She drew her weapon. Powell did too. "Did you hear that?"

Powell stilled, listening intently. His head shifted at the same time Mel cocked hers toward the hut. She thought she saw a small red dot near the entrance but was sure she heard multiple moans. If they were low and slow, she'd suspect an injury. However, these were rapid and higher-pitched, suggesting a different type of distress. Mel glanced at Powell. His prominent Adam's apple bobbed once. His first day on the job wasn't halfway over, and he'd already drawn his weapon from his holster. If Mel were in his shoes, she'd be nervous too.

"Just keep your eye on me and follow my lead, Powell. You'll be fine." Mel pushed forward, lighter on her feet to minimize approaching noise. She signaled for Powell to swing slightly wider to give a subject targets from multiple angles, not two that were tightly grouped. He acknowledged with a nod, keeping his weapon close to his body. He'd been trained well.

The noises increased in volume and frequency, making it easy for Mel to determine they were coming from inside the hut. If memory served, the prison structure had a concrete foundation and roof. It was divided into ten smaller cells, five on each side, with a corridor running down the center. Cinder block walls separated the cells, so she and Powell would have to clear each individually.

Nearing the hut entrance, Mel noticed a section of plywood path had freshly disturbed dirt on both sides. Those mounds gave the impression that digging had occurred there recently. It seemed odd. She then signaled for Powell to stop, but he didn't have his eyes on her and took an extra step onto the platform. A click sounded.

"Stop," Mel yelled. A sense of doom washed through her. Every instinct told her they'd stumbled into a trap. The moaning continued, adding to the confusion. "Don't move, Powell. Don't shift your weight."

"Sergeant?"

"I think you've tripped an IED. Just be still." Thankfully, the moaning from inside the building slowed, allowing Mel to think more clearly. "I'm going to get a better look at what's beneath the boards."

Mel dropped to her knees and slowly brushed away bits of dirt from the pathway's edge to where Powell had stepped, revealing a gap between the ground and wood. She grabbed her flashlight, lowered her head, and shined the light into a dark hole. An object resembling the shape of a two-by-four came into view. She then spotted a wire and followed its path. In an instant, she recognized the familiar form of a pipe bomb. Her stomach knotted. Powell had put his life in her hands this morning, and now it looked as if it might suddenly end.

Mel lifted her head. "Powell, you've definitely tripped an explosive. Don't move."

"I'm screwed, aren't I, Sergeant?"

"Listen to me, Powell. I'll get you out of this, but you have to trust me. Can you do that?"

"Do I have any other choice?"

"Not really." Mel rose to her feet. "I don't know what kind of trigger this has, so I'm going back to the cruiser to call this in. I'll be right back."

When Mel turned to retrace her steps to the gate, Powell forced a chuckle. "I wish I'd listened to you about those shoe inserts. My feet are killing me."

"You'll be fine, Powell." Mel stepped away, knowing she'd lied, but false hope was the only thing she could offer.

9

The police escort peeled off when the FBI sedan rolled down the highway exit. That was Lexi's clue that they were close to the hostage scene. Thirty miles northeast of Sacramento, the town of Gladding wasn't on her radar until Kaplan had mentioned it over the phone earlier. Nothing about the city rang a bell.

When they reached the bottom of the ramp, a Gladding police cruiser picked them up and led the way further into town. The city looked like a typical upscale bedroom community, where a good swath of the residents commuted into the city. It had the usual shopping and fast-food suspects, but what made the downtown interesting were the local shops and refurbished main drag with nineteenth-century gas streetlamps.

Traffic veered toward the curb to let them pass. Soon they reached the intersection where an officer had diverted the flow of vehicles. That meant the incident scene was a few blocks away. Once at the roadblock, a sergeant peered into their sedan, confirming the driver's identity in seconds. "Good luck." She waved them through.

The driver stopped at the end of the block at the inner perimeter. The location was a circus more chaotic than the tunnel bombing in Nogales that had garnered national attention. Police, fire, SWAT, bomb squad, and media vehicles were parked haphazardly. Two dozen first responders milled about, and a dozen reporters had formed a loose line in the street.

"You're needed in the SWAT van." Mitchell reclined the driver's seat to a relaxed position. "Our orders are to stick around while this unfolds. Holler if this becomes a federal issue."

"I'll be sure to let you know." Lexi forced a smile. It was bitter. Arms folded behind his head, Mitchell acted as if catching up on sleep was more important than freeing a store full of hostages held by a potential madman.

Lexi stepped toward the SWAT van, taking extra-long strides to work out the distaste of indifference and the kinks of travel. If this thing escalated to federal jurisdiction, she wouldn't trust those two to tie her shoes, let alone have her back.

A tall man was leaning against the van's side, reading through several papers in his hands. His civilian attire suggested he was a detective, not part of the tactical units waiting to be put into action. He rubbed his jaw with an upturned palm, hinting the information in those papers was perplexing.

She approached. "Excuse me. Where can I find the on-scene commander?"

The man looked up, his eyes shimmering with recognition. "You're Lexi Mills. You look just like your official ID."

"You have me at a disadvantage."

The man extended his hand. "I guess you're looking for me. I'm Detective Nolan Hughes, the hostage negotiator. We've been waiting for you."

"Can you tell me what's going on? All I know is that someone took over the store, wired it to blow, and asked for me."

Hughes thumbed through the papers in his hand, pulling out one with a California DMV photo. "Do you know this man?"

The driver's license information identified the thin man with glasses as Delmar Beckett, age fifty-two, of Gladding, California. Lexi studied the man's face, but he didn't look familiar. "No. Is he the hostage taker?"

"Yes, and for the life of me, I can't figure out why." The confused look in his eyes said he and the suspect had a history. "Nothing makes sense."

"What can you tell me about him?"

"I knew him in high school. We were teammates on the football team. He had one hell of a leg back then." Hughes ran a hand across the back of his neck. "I haven't seen him in thirty-four years, but I understand he married one of the McBean triplets and now manages the store."

Lexi glanced up at the storefront with McBean's blazoned in large red channel letters across the top. "So this is a family-owned store. Is that a source of contention, having an outsider running things?"

"McBean's has been a staple in this town for seventy-five years. I've been doing some catchup today. As far as I can tell, Del is the first non-McBean to manage the place. But neither of the triplets was up to running the store. Their older brother did until five years ago when he dropped dead from a heart attack."

"So this isn't likely a family squabble." Lexi probed. "What about Del? Does he have a record?"

"Not even a parking ticket." Hughes shook his head.

"What about his personal life? Is his marriage stable? What about kids?"

"As stable as it can get being married to a McBean girl. Those three were wild growing up." Hughes flipped through more of the papers. "He has two teenage kids—a girl fifteen and a boy thirteen. We can't track either of them down. The kids never showed up for school today, and his wife isn't answering her phone. No one has seen them since school let out yesterday. The only one we found was the maid, shot dead in the kitchen."

"This sounds like a breakdown. A dead body doesn't bode well for the missing family." Every time Lexi was called to a scene to disarm a device set by a distraught husband or father, it ended in tragedy. Instinct told her the family was already dead and Delmar Beckett was on a mission to take out everything he hated about his life, ending with the grocery store. "Was social media any help?"

Disappointment infused Hughes' head shake. "Del and his wife aren't on it. His daughter has Instagram and TikTok, but nothing suggests an unstable family life. I don't get it. Del has no history of mental illness, and everyone we talked to suggested they were a typical mildly dysfunctional family."

"This doesn't leave us with much." Lexi hated going into a scene blind, but it appeared that was the case. "What exactly did he say when you made first contact?"

"He said he didn't want to hurt anyone but would if he had to. Then he asked for you, saying you would know what this is about. So what is this about, Agent Mills?"

"I have no idea." Nothing about their conversation hinted what the hostage taker was talking about. "I've never met Mr. Beckett. This is the first time I've been to California. The only reason I came was to attend the National Peace Officers Conference in Sacramento."

"There's no need to be modest, Agent Mills. I looked you up. You're one of the honorees tomorrow night for preventing that homegrown terrorist group from killing the Texas governor. Could today's events be associated with that incident or another case you've worked on?"

"That terrorist group was the Red Spades. We took them down, but they were part of a bigger plan to create a revolution in the country." Lexi thought back to that day in Spicewood, Texas, and how things might have turned out if she and Noah hadn't persisted. She got that same vibe of determination from Hughes. "We linked them to the Aryan Brotherhood and the Gatekeepers."

"I'm familiar with the Aryan Brotherhood, but Delmar doesn't fit the profile. His mother is Jewish." Hughes scratched the light stubble on a cheek as if solving a puzzle. "Who are the Gatekeepers?"

"They intended to start a revolution by unseating the government that had betrayed them. This is a nasty group. We know they stole two shipments of nitroglycerine but haven't found any of it."

"Let's hope Beckett has nothing to do with them. Let's introduce you to the rest of the team." Hughes opened the rear door of the SWAT command van and invited Lexi inside. "Lexi Mills, this is Sergeant Craig Carver. He's the on-scene SWAT commander."

"It's a pleasure." Lexi shook Carver's hand. "Has your bomb squad been able to make an assessment?"

"Not yet. We've been sitting on our hands." Carver's tone contained the bitterness of resentment as he gave Hughes the side-eye.

"It's probably for the best. I understand the devices might have a motion-sensor trigger," Lexi said. "In my experience—"

Carver interrupted, "Let's leave bomb disposal to the experts, Agent Mills."

Lexi raised her eyebrows but quickly reeled in her ire, remembering why she'd been called here.

"If you'd bothered doing your homework, Sergeant Carver"—Hughes emphasized his title and name as if giving him a virtual swat on the butt—"you'd know Agent Mills is one of the ATF's top explosives specialists and likely has more training and experience than your entire team combined."

"Your job is to know the people and talk someone down. Mine is to know the lay of the land and take someone out." Carver turned his attention to Lexi. "We have no line of sight into the store, so we have no intel beyond what a hostage passed along before communications stopped. I'd like to send a man up to the roof and get a camera through an exhaust vent."

"We've been through this." Hughes' heavy sigh showcased his frustration. "Let's see if we can resolve this peacefully before taking risks. Beckett wanted to talk to Lexi Mills. She's here, so let's first see what he wants. If this stalls, then we can send in a camera."

"Fine." Carver rested his elbows on the equipment belt over his tactical uniform, a not-so-subtle reminder he was the last resort. "I'll make sure we're ready to go." Carver went to the other end of the van and consulted with another SWAT officer.

"Is he always like that?" Lexi wagged a thumb in Carver's direction.

"I have no idea," Hughes said. "This is my first day on the job. I came up here after thirty years with the LAPD."

Lexi was instantly reassured. Los Angeles had an excellent reputation for using cutting-edge, world-class tactics. "Nothing like a baptism by fire."

Hughes invited Lexi to sit in a folding chair in his work area marked by a whiteboard. The far-left side listed three descriptive words: shaky, reluctant, and cagey. Two other columns contained only one word beneath their titles "Hooks" and "Triggers"—family and family.

"Do you have any experience as a hostage negotiator, Agent Mills?"

Lexi recalled her failed attempt to talk down David Lindsey of the Gatekeepers, but that ended in Noah putting a bullet through his temple. "Just the basic FLETC course." She glanced at the whiteboard again. "So I understand your hooks and triggers. I take it your research told you that family is important to him."

"You're very observant." Hughes grinned. He clearly felt their level of trust growing, as did Lexi.

"It goes with the training." Lexi studied the board. "I take it those were your observations from your initial contact with Beckett."

Hughes nodded. "His shaky tone was that of a man at the end of his rope, but when he said he didn't want to hurt anyone, I'd hoped today was just a call for help. But when he wanted to get you here, not just talk to you, I suspected something else was at play."

"Like what?"

"I don't know, but I'm sure it has to do with your work. He asked for Agent Mills, not Lexi."

"How should I play this?" Lexi asked.

"Use open-ended questions at the start. That will get him talking. Hopefully, we can learn why he's doing this, the number of hostages, and what weapons he has."

"All right, let's talk to him." Lexi would soon find out if she'd asked the right questions.

Hughes gestured toward the desk phone. "It's a direct line. It will ring automatically."

Lexi placed her hand on the phone. The feeling that this was the start of something dangerous tingled her skin. She lifted it and waited for Beckett to answer. "This is Lexi Mills. I'm right outside, Mr. Beckett. Why did you ask for me?"

"Hold on." Several moments of silence passed before Beckett returned. "I have her on the store line. Okay, I'm putting you both on speaker. Lexi Mills, I have someone who wants to talk to you."

This just got confusing, but Lexi was committed to resolving the standoff. "Okay. This is Lexi Mills. Who is this?"

"This is the hand of God." The cold male voice radiated chills through Lexi, prickling every hair on her arms. She'd only heard Tony Belcher's voice on a poorly recorded cell phone video. Still, she'd never forget his low rasp and slow, rhythmic cadence that had his disciples glued to every word. It was as if he'd perfected a resonating tone to bring home the point that he was the chosen one.

"Tony Belcher." Just saying his name made Lexi's skin crawl. She'd been after him for nineteen months, but this was the closest she'd come.

"That's right, Lexi Mills. Judgment day has arrived. Your antics in Spice-wood have forced my hand, and now I want something from you, or those people will die, and their blood will be on your hands."

"What do you want?" Lexi asked. Whatever Belcher had in mind, she was sure he didn't intend for her to survive.

"The world may think you're a hero, but I know better. You cost your partner his life."

"You did that, Belcher. That was your compound and mine."

"But it was your recklessness that sent him to his death." Belcher's ugly accusation wasn't too far afield, but how in the hell could he know that? No one outside the ATF and her small circle of people knew what happened the night Trent Darby died.

"Get to the point, Belcher. What do you want?" Lexi's frustration pumped through her neck veins, proving that guilt from that night had yet to heal.

"I'll give you a choice to be a hero or prove to the world you're a fake."

"And what's my choice?"

"I can tell you what I want, but I will kill Mr. Beckett's family if I do that."

Sobs in the background confirmed the gravity of the situation.

"What's my other choice?" Lexi knew the other option was just as grave.

"Pass a test of skills, during which you will either end up a hero or the dead poser I know you to be. I will tell you where they are, but I'm watching them closely. If someone other than you tries to free them, everyone dies, there and at the store."

"Where are they?"

"Where else would I keep my prisoners but at a prisoner of war camp? I hope you like the little surprises I've left because I have one catch for you."

"What's that?"

"No protective gear. You will live if you're skilled enough. Otherwise, you'll die with them." The smugness in Belcher's voice clarified which outcome he hoped for. He wanted Lexi to die in an explosion of his making. But, even if he had another demand, it was secondary to seeing her dead, and that thought sent a chill down her spine. She'd worked with a partner on every call she'd been on to help with her gear and walk her through the dangerous steps. But she was going this alone with no one to back her up. She had a sinking feeling that this call might be her last.

"You have one hour, Lexi Mills." Belcher added an evil laugh. "And if you're quick, you might save the lives of two unsuspecting brethren."

"Please, Lexi Mills," Beckett pleaded. The pain in his voice was palpable. "You have to save them. They're all I have."

Lexi couldn't promise to save them, but she could give him some assurance. "I'll do everything I can, Mr. Beckett."

"Make sure she goes, Nolan. You owe me for what you did after the state championship game."

Seeing the confusion in Nolan's eyes, Lexi gave him a reassuring nod. Beckett's family wouldn't be in this mess if it wasn't for her. Now she had to do what she did best—disarm a bomb or two.

"We'll get them, Del, and get you out of this." Nolan Hughes pounded his hand against the desk when the call went dead.

10

Returning from the ladies' room, Amanda Keene scanned her fellow hostages. Everyone had shared a little background after introducing themselves. She was right about the elderly couple being from the retirement community and the high school girl. Similar to Amanda, the other woman had said she was a soccer mom, running errands before school let out.

Only the thirty-something male customer remained a mystery. His high and tight haircut suggested a military history, but nothing about his casual clothes and Nikes gave away more about who he was or where he was from. All he'd said was that his name was Hunter, and he'd come to the store to buy a loaf of sourdough bread. His quietness made him difficult to read. Amanda couldn't tell if he was plotting a way out of this horrifying situation or considering what food he'd snag next for lunch. The others had been an open book, sharing their opinions, worries, and food preferences.

Employees had gathered food and drink together from the end caps without endangering the group by going down the aisles. The picnic atmosphere they'd created was a sweet gesture but did little to ease everyone's anxiety. Some reacted by crying periodically, and some remained silent, but thankfully, only one had burst out in anger. Amanda attributed his fit to a sense of responsibility and couldn't attach an ounce of blame. As the assistant manager, Bret was akin to a ship's first officer whose captain had gone mad and taken the passengers and crew off course and headfirst into a deadly storm. If Amanda didn't have her son to consider, she would have joined him.

Amanda sat with Dylan on the floor, noticing he hadn't touched his food. Instead, Dylan had his head buried in his arms atop his upright knees. He hadn't moved from that position in the last twenty minutes. Hours of waiting had taken their toll on the hostages, but it was especially tough on him. Dylan's deafness had made him more acutely attuned to the emotions of those around him, and the tension emitting from everyone in the store clearly overpowered him.

Learning speech the past year had brought out Dylan's bubbly personality to a handful of people outside of the home. His speech therapist had become his giggle partner, and the boy across the street had become the closest thing he'd had to a friend. Week by week, Amanda had watched her son evolve from a scared child who sought shelter in his mother's arms to an independent little boy who was no longer afraid of the world. Now, all that hard work was wasted. Dylan had withdrawn back into his shell, breaking Amanda's heart.

She scooted closer, tapping an arm to get his attention. She mouthed and signed, "Are you sure you don't have to use the bathroom? It's been hours." When Dylan signed that he'd try, Amanda rose to her feet and announced to the group, "I'm taking my son to the bathroom. Does anyone else need to go?"

Riley, the female floor stocker, stood. "I'll go. Strength in numbers, right?"

Amanda held Dylan's hand tight and linked arms with Riley. "Absolutely."

Simple gestures like Riley's were something Amanda's husband hadn't offered in years. That lack of politeness hadn't bothered her, or so she'd thought. But with her and her son's lives at risk, it irritated her like nails on a chalkboard. If she and Dylan got out of this alive, things would change in their home and marriage.

Reaching the public restroom corridor, Dylan tugged on his mother's hand, encouraging her to take him into the men's room. At a time like this, social observances didn't matter, but they did to her son. Since starting grade school, he'd refused to follow her into ladies' rooms.

Amanda pressed her lips into a small smile. "We'll be right back, Riley."

"I get it. My little brother is the same way." Riley then disappeared into the other restroom.

Dylan forced the door open with both hands. Then, too short for the urinals, he went directly toward the toilet stall. When he pushed the metal door open, a small horizontal picture window high on the cinderblock wall above the toilet came into view. The glass appeared pitted. It didn't open and was too small to fit an adult, but Dylan might if his head could slide through.

Amanda let her son finish. Then, while he washed up, she climbed atop the toilet with one foot on either side of the seat and peered through the dirt-smudged window. It provided a view into the side parking lot. Several cars were pitted, similar to the window, and the dumpster appeared misshapen with signs of explosion damage. That solved the mystery of the blast they'd heard a few hours ago.

Amanda strained to see further left and right and spotted police tape at the parking lot edges and a large police van across the street. Her mind ran through Dylan's possible escape. First, she'd have to break the glass and lift and lower him to the ground. That would take nearly a minute. Dylan would then have to dart across the lot to safety. He was good at running but sending a deaf boy into a police cordon was risky. However, staying was more life-threatening, and she had to save her son.

Dylan tugged on her hoodie sleeve, signaling he was done.

Amanda visually measured her son's head and then the window. It would be tight, but he could fit. She clutched him by both upper arms and bent at the knees so he could see exactly what she was saying. "You know we're in danger, right?"

He nodded slowly, tightly.

She pointed at the window until he looked in that direction. She then drew his head back with a hand under his chin. "You can fit through the window. I can break it and lower you to the ground outside. The police are right across the street."

He signed, *You come too.*

"I can't fit, but you can." He shook his head so hard that Amanda feared he might give himself a concussion. To stop him, she clutched his arms tighter and spoke slowly so he could read her lips. "Listen to me, Dylan. I need you to be safe and tell Daddy I'm here. Can you do that for me?"

He nodded with tears shimmering in his eyes.

Amanda scanned the room, looking for something to break the glass, but had no luck. Then she remembered a janitor's closet across the bathroom hallway. "Wait right here."

Amanda dashed out the door, discovering Riley leaning against the wall next to the supply closet, nervously biting her fingernails. A conundrum formed. Should she tell Riley her plan? If she did, would she try to stop her? Then she thought through the mechanics of getting Dylan out the window. He weighed fifty-two pounds and would have to go through the window feet first. Unfortunately, she wasn't strong enough to boost him up while teetering atop a toilet seat.

"Riley, I need your help." Panic must have been in Amanda's eyes because Riley flinched. "There's a window in the bathroom."

"I know, but it's too small even for me." Riley had a slight build, but she was right. Her head would get stuck.

"But not for my son. We can get him out, but I'm going to need help. I can't get him through the window by myself."

"Bret could help. He tosses around those gigantic bags of dog food like they're paperweights." Amanda pivoted on her heel toward the front of the store, but Riley stopped her. "Wait. How do we know Mr. Beckett didn't rig the window to blow?"

"If he did, it likely would have gone up when the dumpster blew."

"That's what we heard? My car is out there. I hope it's all right." Riley ran both hands down her face. "Zack saw Mr. Beckett arrive today. He should know if there are more bombs out there."

Following a confirming nod, Amanda dipped into the men's room. She pulled her son out, explaining they'd need help for him to escape. When they returned to the main floor, Amanda called the group's attention and had them form a tight circle so her voice wouldn't travel. "I have an idea." Amanda detailed her plan to get her son through the bathroom window.

"Are you nuts?" Bret's raised voice suggested he'd be hard to convince. "What if it's rigged?"

"I only saw him put something behind the dumpster," Zack said.

"That blew up," Riley added, "and maybe some of our cars."

"But what if the manager sees him?" the teenage girl asked. "That might piss him off enough to blow us up."

"What happened to waiting this out and letting the police get us out of this?" Hunter's point marked the most the mysterious man had said since the beginning of this ordeal.

"That was before I knew there was a way out for one of us." Amanda reined in her frustration with the opposition. She needed their help and would never get it by acting haughty. "Look, the police have no idea how many people are in here nor the type and quantity of devices they're facing. By sending my son out, he can give them that critical information. Then, maybe they can get us out of here."

"Let's put it to a vote," the senior woman said. "We're all in this together, so we should all decide. But once we vote, we live by that decision."

Her husband placed a reassuring arm over her shoulder. "I agree. We vote."

"Yes," the muscular soccer mom added. "We vote."

Amanda could have hugged these people. "All right then. All in favor of getting my son out?"

One by one, hostages raised their hands. When Zack remained still, Riley slapped him on the shoulder. "Fine." Zack raised his hand reluctantly. The teenage girl followed, leaving Hunter as the final holdout. All eyes settled on him.

"I think this is a suicide mission. He'll be seen and will get us killed." Hunter lowered his head, refusing eye contact with anyone.

"He's wrong," a gravelly male voice said from the direction of Amanda's back. All heads turned. The voice belonged to the homeless man Amanda had steered clear of earlier in the parking lot. His earthy scent preceded him by five feet.

"Where did you come from?" Bret asked in an uncertain tone.

"The soda display at the front. It's cool in there." The man shrugged with the confidence that anyone would agree it was the best place in the world to escape the heat.

"Is there anyone else with you?" Hunter asked.

"Hell no." The man drew out his words before looking left and right as if searching for spies or aliens. He then placed an index finger over his lips. "That's my secret spot."

"Do you have a phone?" Amanda asked.

"What in the hell would he be doing with a phone?" Bret's dismissive expression deserved a slap across the face. Homelessness didn't mean being completely cut off from the world. The state offered programs to provide those on the fringes of society a lifeline to medical and emergency services.

The man reached his hand with leather-like skin into the pocket of his soiled, tattered light jacket. When he pulled it out, a three-inch pocketknife fell to the floor. He picked it up, causing Amanda to take a step back. The man then returned the knife to his pocket and handed Amanda a cell phone with several scrapes on the metal back. "Yours."

Adrenaline rushed through Amanda's veins at the possibility of reaching the outside world and not having to put everyone's life at risk with Dylan's escape. Then she turned the phone over, revealing a shattered screen. Her cell phone looked as if a gravel truck had run over it and dumped its load on it for good measure. Unfortunately, facial recognition didn't register, and pressing the screen failed to bring the smashed mess to life.

"I found it after you went inside. If I'd been faster on my feet"—the man shuffled like a tap dancer—"I could have gotten fifty bucks for it." He then shifted his attention to Dylan. "How was your ice cream, little man?"

Dylan took shelter behind his mother's leg, peeking his head from around her butt. Amanda wrapped an arm around her son, mildly ashamed of herself that he'd had such a strong visceral reaction to the man's interaction. If she got out of this, she'd have to examine her own response to others experiencing homelessness.

"He enjoyed it. Thank you for asking," Amanda replied. "What's your name?"

"Clarence." He winked.

"Hi, Clarence. I'm Amanda. You said that Hunter was wrong. What did you mean?"

The man scratched his overgrown, scraggly beard. His smell became more pungent when he leaned into the group, looking left and right again as if he were about to reveal the nation's top-secret war plans. "Everyone knows a camera can only see what's in front of it."

"No shit, Sherlock." Bret's scowl suggested his irritation had graduated to loathing, and it wasn't a good look on him.

"No, he's right." Zack gave Bret a dismissive look. "The camera on the roof is pointed at the dumpster to deter the bums." He shifted his stare to Clarence, giving him an apologetic smile. "Sorry, dude. If Dylan went in the opposite direction, he wouldn't be on camera."

"All right, then we're in agreement." Amanda bent at the knees. She spoke and signed to her son, explaining the plan and the need for him to run in the direction opposite the dumpster and find a police officer. "Do you understand what to do?" she asked.

He nodded.

Amanda wanted this message to be only for him, so she limited her communication to sign language. *I've never been prouder of you. I know you can do this.*

Dylan threw his arms around his mother's neck and used his voice for his following words. "I love you, Mom."

Amanda squeezed him tight, letting several tears escape her eyes. Most parents wait twelve months to hear their child say their first word, but Amanda had to wait for nearly seven years with Dylan. She wasn't supposed to have a favorite child, but how could she not hold a little extra love in her heart for this courageous boy? She couldn't stand by without doing everything possible to save his life.

Amanda pulled back, kissed his forehead, and signed, "I love you to the moon and back." She then looked at the group. "Bret. Zack. Can you help us?"

"Let's do it." Zack smiled. Under that simple facade lay the heart of a hero.

Once in the men's room, Zack held a jacket over the small window to muffle the coming blow. Meanwhile, Bret heaved a fire extinguisher over his head with sufficient force to break the glass without creating an echoing sound that might alert the store manager in his office. Zack then used the jacket as a glove and punched out the remaining jagged edges to create a safe pass-through.

"All right, little man." Zack got Dylan's attention and spoke slowly to allow for lip-reading. "When you get down, run opposite the dumpster and find a cop. Got it?"

He issued Zack a nod before signing to his mother, *I got this.*

Amanda resisted the urge to give her little boy one last hug because this was the moment he'd become a man. That was the memory she wanted to carry forward. If something went awry, she needed to think of Dylan in terms of his full potential and good heart.

Bret and Zack then lifted Dylan over their heads and shoved him through the window feet first, face down. His slim body slipped through easily. As his head reached the casing, he looked up and gave his mother a wink, mouthing, "Love you."

Amanda blew him a kiss, and he disappeared. The only things visible of her son were his little hands. Then Zack said, "Let go on three. One. Two. Three." And Dylan was gone.

11

"One-two-four to Dispatch. Eleven-eighty-seven. Officer needs assistance at the POW site," came over the radio.

Lexi's mind was still spinning over the mess her feud with Tony Belcher had created, but she was concentrating enough to cue on the word POW. "Isn't that where Beckett's family is being held?"

"Yes." Nolan Hughes picked up his radio and keyed the mic. "Command One to Dispatch. Belay sending units to POW site. It is a secondary location for my eleven-eighty-seven. Set up a perimeter at eight hundred feet. I'm sending EOD."

"Dispatch to Command One. Ten-four. Perimeter only."

Lexi easily deciphered the local ten code. "That's what Belcher meant by unsuspecting brethren. A patrol had stumbled upon one of his traps. Can you put me through, so I'll know what I'm walking into?"

"Sure. Hold on." Hughes used his cell phone to contact the Gladding dispatch and connect him to the patrol officer at the POW site. He put the call on speaker. "Sergeant Thompson, this is Detective Hughes. I have you on speaker. You discovered a part of the incident we're working at McBean's."

"Hughes? You're taking over Schmidt's job, right?" Thompson asked. "This is one hell of a first day."

"It's been quite the welcome. Do not approach the POW hut. I have ATF Agent Lexi Mills with me. Walk us through what you found."

Thompson detailed her observations regarding the plywood walking paths, the clicking sound when her trainee stepped on it, the two-by-four, and the pipe beneath the wood. "Officer Powell is stable for now, but it's his first day on the job, Hughes. We need to get him out of this."

"Sergeant Thompson, this is Lexi Mills. It sounds like your partner stepped on a modified bar mine. It can be detonated in three ways: by a second instance of pressure, handling it, or removing pressure. I won't know which kind it is until I see it. You did the right thing by having him remain in place. I know who planted the device, so the pipe bomb likely contains nitro or TATP, a homemade substance. Both are deadly and unstable."

"How do I get Powell out of this in one piece?"

"You don't," Lexi replied. "Your location is being monitored by the bomb maker. He'll detonate if anyone but me goes in. I'll get there as soon as I can."

"Hurry, Lexi Mills. I don't think he can last much longer." More than worry cut through Thompson's voice. Guilt did too. It was an emotion Lexi knew too well. She'd put Trent Darby in the situation that killed him, and that guilt had stayed with her like a dysfunctional old friend who refused to leave her side. Mel Thompson was already experiencing remorse for a foreseeable outcome. If this went sideways, she'd feel responsible for the rest of her life.

The call disconnected. Lexi asked Hughes, "How long will it take to get there?"

"Twenty minutes."

"That gives me fifteen minutes to gather some tools from your bomb squad."

Sergeant Carver stepped forward. "What do you need?"

Knowing the configuration of the exterior mine was helpful, but Lexi didn't know what was waiting for her inside the prison hut. Without time to go back for tools, she would be limited to what she could carry, so preciseness and flexibility of her choices were vital. "A flashlight, hand shovel, telescoping mirror, plunge saw with an extra battery, wire cutters, electrical tape, duct tape, scissors, seatbelt cutter, and a five-gallon bucket."

"I'm on it." Carver rushed from the van, clomping down the exterior stairs.

"You'll need a car." Hughes dug into his front pocket and tossed Lexi a car fob. "Take my command SUV. Give me your phone, and I'll bring up directions to the site."

Lexi pulled her phone from her hip pocket but first noted a text message from Nita. *Noah n I coming to Gladding. Will wait this out nearby. Love you.* Under any other circumstance, having her girlfriend show up to a bomb call would have Lexi rattled. But considering she was about to disarm multiple devices without her equipment and protective gear, having Nita and Noah close was oddly comforting.

"I need to send a text first." Calling would tug on Lexi's emotions when she needed to remain detached, but a text was the next best thing. She typed: *Glad you're coming. This might take a while. Love you.*

The moment Hughes returned her phone, the radio squawked in his hand. "We have movement on the west side."

"Launch drone," a voice said over the air. The tone sounded like Carver's, but Lexi couldn't be sure.

She shot her gaze to the wall-mounted monitors. Impressed by the number of feeds providing three-hundred-sixty-degree coverage, she located the screen showing movement. A body was dangling from a narrow window. Then it dropped to the pavement, falling to all fours. The person was likely a seven- or eight-year-old boy based on size and clothing. He pushed himself up and scanned left and right. He pivoted to go left but kept his stare facing right. Another video feed showed a SWAT officer waving the boy to him from the inner perimeter. The boy hesitated, looking in the opposite direction again, but eventually ran toward the officer through the side parking lot.

Lexi picked up the action on the next screen. The officer ushered the boy further away toward the outer perimeter and waiting paramedics. Hughes flew out the door. Lexi followed him across the street to the EMS rig, where medical personnel were examining the boy. He waited a respectable two minutes before inching forward.

"Is he injured?"

A paramedic craned his neck toward Hughes. "He has a few scrapes from crawling out the window. Otherwise, he's fine."

"Can he speak to us?"

"Do you know American Sign Language? The boy is deaf and has minimal vocal skills."

Hughes' deflated expression provided his answer. He whipped out his phone and dialed. "Captain, a hostage escaped. A boy. He's deaf. Do we have an ASL translator on call?... When can we get them here?... Send them." He returned the phone to his pocket and rubbed his free hand down his face. "They're an hour out."

"I have an idea." Lexi pulled out her phone and sent Nita a text, asking when she and Noah should arrive in Gladding. Seconds later, a reply said they should be there in twelve minutes. If they didn't run into traffic, they might come before Lexi had to leave for the POW site. She silently hoped that they did. *One more kiss*, she thought. If she had the opportunity for just one more kiss, she'd make it more memorable.

"My girlfriend knows sign language and should be in Gladding in twelve minutes. She could translate for you."

"That should get us started, but we still need an official translator."

"I understand," Lexi said. Every agency rightly had policies about translators to protect the interests and rights of everyone involved. She then typed a text to Nita while she spoke. "I'm telling her we need her ASL skills and to check in at the control point." Once Hughes called in Nita's name, Lexi remembered the trick Nita had used with her patient until she became proficient with sign language. "I have an idea, Hughes. The boy might be too young for this, but if he reads lips, he could answer questions by typing into a phone or tablet."

"Great idea, Mills. It's worth a try." Hughes stepped closer to the boy on the gurney and got his attention by tapping him on the arm. "Can you read lips?" The boy offered a tentative nod before shrugging. That likely meant he was still learning. "My name is Nolan. What is yours?" Hughes then handed him his phone with the notepad application open. "Can you type your name?"

The boy typed a few letters and returned the phone.

"Hi, Dylan. I'm a police officer. Who were you with in the grocery store?"

He typed, *Mom.*

"What is your last name?"

Keene.

"So your mom is Amanda." Hughes paused at Dylan's nod. "How many other people are in the store?"

The boy counted, using his fingers before typing the number thirteen.

"Did you see any of the bombs?"

Dylan nodded.

"How many are there?"

Dylan shrugged.

"All right, Dylan. You've been helpful. Let's get you inside our van and something to drink."

Dylan shook his head hard and snatched the phone from Hughes' hand. He typed, *Get Dad.*

"What is your Dad's first name?"

Dylan typed out *Max.*

"Do you know your dad's phone number?" Tears welled in Dylan's eyes when he shook his head no. Hughes placed a hand on his shoulder. "That's all right, Dylan. We'll find him." He then walked him toward the command van.

Lexi followed. "How did you know his mother's name?"

"License plates. We have a list of the cars in the lot and their registered owners, and one came back to Amanda Keene. Unfortunately, a stretch by the street is the town lemon lot, so the list doesn't help much until dispatch contacts every RO. Most haven't returned our calls."

"That's good police work," Lexi said.

"I can't take the credit. The SWAT commander sent in a drone. He got the plates and checked for IEDs inside and below each vehicle. Nothing looked suspicious."

"I'm impressed." Lexi glanced to her left. Sergeant Carver was approaching with a bucket of supplies. *Damn, that was quick,* she thought. Carver may act like a jerk and be singularly focused on brute force, but he was a brilliant law enforcement tactician who got things done.

They joined up near the stairs leading to the SWAT command vehicle. "We have everything you requested, Agent Mills." Carver placed the bucket at her feet before handing her a tactical radio, an earpiece, and a clip-on camera. "I tossed in a pair of tweezers in case you need to do any delicate work. The earpiece will allow you to go hands-free while staying in communication with us. Clip the camera to your jacket. That way, we can be an extra set of eyes."

"Thank you. Those are great additions." Lexi didn't want to admit her doubts, but going in without someone to bounce ideas off made her nervous. The radio and camera weren't the same as having Trent Darby or Noah Black there, but it was the next best thing.

"My bomb squad and EMS will follow you to the site. They'll stage a quarter mile down the road and will only come in on your order. We'll be on Tac Two if you want to talk through anything. We'll have an army of first responders just minutes away, Mills. What you're doing takes guts. Know that SWAT has your back."

Lexi inserted the earpiece and clipped the radio to her waist and the camera between the top two buttons of her light jacket. "Thanks. I appreciate the backup."

She checked her watch. If Nita didn't arrive in the next five minutes, Lexi would have to leave without seeing her. That bothered her not for herself but for Nita. If something went wrong, Nita's last memory of Lexi would be her irritation that she'd babied her at the airport. She didn't want that for Nita. She wanted Nita to remember their final encounter as being without tension and filled with love.

Lexi glanced toward the FBI sedan and the traffic checkpoint in the distance. "Come on, Nita. We need one last kiss," she whispered.

Lexi and Carver followed Hughes inside the SWAT van when he ushered Dylan inside. Once he settled Dylan into the seat at his workstation and gave him a Coke from the mini-fridge, he returned to Lexi. "I feel like I'm missing something Beckett said to us earlier. Want to sit with me while I review the tapes while we wait for your girlfriend?"

This might be Lexi's only chance to empty her bladder and get her head straight before stepping into Belcher's trap. "I need to use the bathroom first."

"Sure." Hughes pointed toward the center of the van. "We have one on board."

Once Lexi finished her business, she took in the woman standing at the sink in the mirror. She'd been an explosives expert with the ATF for ten years. She could identify any bomb in the world and figure out how to disarm it without injury in the time it took to fry an egg. She'd rendered forty-two devices safe with only one blemish on her record—Trent Darby. But it wasn't her lack of skill that caused her partner's death but her drive to bring Belcher to justice. Now she was facing Belcher again, but she couldn't let her hatred drive what she did in the next hour.

The stack of accommodations and awards in her desk drawer said she was as good as they came. Lexi was the ATF's best, yet doubt floated in her eyes. She could blame it on not having a partner or going in without her protective gear, but she knew that was a lie. Maybe Belcher knew it, or maybe he didn't, but Lexi's greatest fear was that she was a poser. She was book smart and superior at doing things by a checklist, but she never considered herself imaginative. The only time she had to get creative was during the escape from the Red Spades at the Texas governor's mansion. Lexi wasn't sure what Belcher had waiting for her, but she was sure she wouldn't find the solution in a damn list or book.

Lexi pressed her palms against the sink counter and leaned closer to the mirror. "You can do this," she told herself. She was the reason Belcher planted those devices and took Beckett's family, and now she had to fix it. Backing out wasn't an option.

Adjusting the camera on her jacket, Lexi swung the door open and stepped into the main compartment. More people had gathered at the far end of the command vehicle, but Hughes' large frame hid most of them. Then Lexi recognized a voice. How could she not? It had seduced her regularly for a year, but most importantly, it had made her whole.

As she stepped down the center pathway, Nita's voice grew louder. Correspondingly, Lexi's heart beat harder. Her breathing shallowed more on each step. Then Hughes shifted position, bringing Nita into view. Their gazes met, and Lexi felt the worry in Nita's glossy eyes.

Lexi mouthed, *I love you.*

Nita mouthed it back.

Reaching the group, Lexi nestled herself between Nita and Noah. She grasped Nita's hand, lacing their fingers, and rubbed Noah's back with the other. "Thank you for bringing her, Noah. Did Detective Hughes fill you in?"

"You're welcome." Noah added a friendly wink. "Partly."

"I don't have time to stay for the full briefing." Nita and Noah narrowed their brows, but Lexi didn't have time to explain twice, so she turned her attention to Hughes. "Are we ready to roll?"

"The bomb squad and EMS are waiting," Hughes replied.

"All right, then. I'll keep my comms open."

Hughes shook Lexi's hand. "Godspeed, Agent Mills."

Lexi turned to Nita, tugging her hand. "Come with me." She led them out the door and down the stairs, stopping at Hughes' SUV. She silently pulled Nita into a tight embrace, feeling her chest expand and contract with each breath. Squeezing tighter, Lexi drew strength from the woman who was the essence of toughness. She'd clawed her way back from addiction to dedicate her life to healing amputees like Lexi. It had been a daily struggle since her gunshot wound, but Nita had dug deep to keep her demons at bay.

The virtual ticking clock blared in Lexi's head. She had to go, so she pulled back, looking Nita in the eye. "Belcher is behind what's happening here, so I have to do my thing."

"I hate that man." Nita lowered her stare.

"That makes two of us." Lexi lifted Nita's chin with a hand. "I need to do this."

"I know you do." Nita's eyes pooled with tears, drawing Lexi's closer examination. Her pupils were still like pinheads.

"Are you in pain?"

"Not now." Nita's response troubled Lexi. It translated into she was managing her pain chemically.

"Are you okay to translate for Hughes? If you aren't, you need to tell him."

Nita's eyes narrowed to a breathy huff. "I'm fine, Lexi."

"Okay." Lexi swallowed her thick, choking worry. This was not the time to pick a fight. This wasn't how Lexi wanted to leave things between them, so she pressed their lips together in a deep kiss. This time, Lexi took stock in its warmth, moistness, and encompassing effect on her. If she were in the privacy of their apartment, she'd let arousal build until it culminated in their making love. But here, on the precipice of her deadliest mission yet, Lexi let it fill her heart with the promise of eternity together.

Lexi broke the kiss. "I love you, Anita Flores."

"I love you, Lexi Mills."

Lexi exhaled, hopped into the driver's seat, and rolled down the window. "When I get back, I'm claiming a raincheck for our afternoon plans." She winked and drove off, hoping that kiss wouldn't be their last.

12

The feeling that he could throw up at any minute hadn't left Delmar Beckett since the moment he received the demanding call from the kidnapper yesterday. Del was never a religious man, so he had no basis for comparison, but the last twenty hours had been hell on earth. When he'd picked up the phone and the kidnapper put his wife on, the fear in her voice told him the lives of his entire family were in danger.

The quagmire that had ensnared him necessitated lots of liquid courage to get through. He reached into his lower desk drawer, pulling out his last package of English tea biscuits. Stuffing one into his mouth, he searched deeper in the drawer, bypassing the glass tumbler. Instead, he retrieved the Scotch bottle he'd kept there since he knew he was in over his head managing the store—his first week two years ago. He'd gone through a bottle every few weeks, so this must have been his fiftieth.

Unscrewing the cap, he chugged down three stomach-burning gulps and chased them down with another tea biscuit. He chuckled at his guilty pleasure, knowing it was the source of his nickname at the store. There were worse things his employees could have called him, so when he'd overheard his nephew referring to him as Biscuit, he had to laugh. He figured it was better to be known for a habit his British grandmother had instilled in him than for his lack of leadership skills.

Del took one more gulp before continuing his analysis of the phone call he'd put through to Lexi Mills. At least now he had the name of the man holding his family hostage—Tony Belcher. Not being privy to the specifics of their rivalry, he'd pieced together that Mills had been chasing a nutcase extremist. But nothing in that conversation explained why Belcher had brought Del into the feud to do his bidding. Nor did it explain his endgame beyond Lexi Mills' death. Whatever Belcher wanted, Del had to rely on a stranger to save the lives of his wife and two children. He had to bide his time and ensure his hostages stayed put until he got word from Mills.

Del stuffed more biscuits into his mouth after returning the bottle to its hiding place. He then resumed his watch of the black-and-white security monitor on the corner of his desk. He counted nine hostages huddled together near the front registers. He then clicked on the computer mouse to scroll through the live camera feeds to locate the other three but found no one. They were likely in the bathroom, so he continued to scroll until motion on a feed caught his eye.

Del spat a mouthful of cookie mush onto his desk and sprang from his chair. "What the hell?" The exterior camera focused on the blown-up dumpster showed a young boy running into view and then across the parking lot and into the waiting arms of a police officer. The boy looked exactly like the one he had Bret search for a phone. "No, no, no, no, no!" he yelled, pulling at his hair with both hands. "He's going to get my family killed."

Del paced the small section of linoleum between his desk and the door, running through how in the hell this happened. One minute the hostages were all gathered at the front registers. The next minute the little runt was running through the parking lot.

Del returned to his desk and scrolled through the camera feeds, confirming that the front and back doors were still closed and had the magnetic explosive devices with the red lights attached. That left the sliver of a window in the men's room as the only means of escape. He rested a little easier, knowing it was too small for the rest of the hostages to fit through, but the damage was already done. Every awful thing Del had done up to this point to protect his wife and kids was for nothing if Belcher had his eyes glued to the store's live video feed he'd hacked into. Maybe, just maybe, Belcher hadn't seen the boy. Or, if he did, perhaps he thought the boy was an innocent bystander who had wandered into the area.

"That's it," Del mumbled to himself. "Belcher won't put two and two together." The idea wasn't completely unrealistic. At least, that was what Del told himself.

Then the flip phone the kidnappers gave him rang, making Del jump. The timing of the call couldn't be coincidental, deflating his only hope. On instinct, he picked up the phone from the desk. He hesitated opening it to debate his molten hot options if Belcher knew a hostage had escaped.

Belcher might make him do something unspeakable if he answered, like shoot a hostage as punishment. Killing another person was something he doubted he could bring himself to do, even if it meant saving his family. But if he didn't answer, Belcher might think Del was incapacitated. But Del had to consider the impact of either option on his family. He couldn't undo the boy's escape, so Belcher would be furious. Accordingly, his best option was to do nothing.

Del returned the phone to the desk on the second ring, releasing it abruptly as if his burning decision was too hot to handle. It continued, vibrating on the metal desktop through five nail-biting rings. The cycle repeated four times until the phone finally lay quiet, foreshadowing the silence ahead for Del if he'd chosen incorrectly. He considered breaking the damn thing in half and adding it to the pile of phones he was told to destroy when this ordeal began but thought better of it. It might come in handy.

Unable to control his shaking, Del ran his hands through his hair again. There was no going back. He'd likely sealed everyone's fate, from his family to the people in the store, including himself. "What have I done?" He reached into his desk drawer, snagging the Scotch again. He downed three more gulps, one each for his wife, son, and daughter, praying he'd done the right thing.

He sat in the stillness for a half-hour, maybe more, hoping his old friend had picked up on the clue he'd given him so Lexi Mills could safely extract his family from the POW hut. If he didn't, all of them were dead.

A light knock on the door startled Del, causing his heart to race suddenly. He grabbed his pistol and pointed it at the noise. His hands shook, him fearing the hostages had figured out the path he'd left clear of devices and had come with pitchforks to kill him.

"Go away, or I'll blow us up."

No one answered. There was only silence. Then a folded slip of paper appeared from beneath the door. Suspecting a trick, he waited several moments before moving forward. He cautiously bent at the waist, picked up the paper, and scurried back to the safety of his desk to inspect it. Slowly opening it, he discovered a handwritten note. *We are watching you. Answer the phone the next time it rings, or every hostage will die.*

Del slumped in his chair, realizing Belcher had planted one of his people inside the store and had been watching his every move. It had become clear. He could no longer hold off Belcher. Then, the flip phone buzzed, making Del's hands tremble more at the thought of being forced to make an untenable choice. He picked it up, opened it, and brought it to his cheek. "Yes?"

"You have failed me, Mr. Beckett."

"It's not my fault. I did exactly as your man said to the letter. I couldn't have known a boy small enough to fit through that window would be in the store. And once I'd taken them hostage, I couldn't board up the window on both sides. I guarantee no one else can get out."

Silence. Belcher's heavy breathing was the only sound, each exhale dripping with rage. "You have one chance to make this right. Is the phone in your office a portable?"

"Yes. Why?"

"I can't have this unraveling too soon. Someone must pay the price to show my resolve." Belcher's bitter tone made Delmar think that person was him.

"What do you mean?"

"You need to pick which employee to sacrifice and shoot them in front of the other hostages while you're on the phone with the police. This will serve two purposes. First, it will teach the hostages the consequences of not complying. Second, it will show the police that this won't end until I get what I want."

"I can't. I can't shoot someone in cold blood."

"If you don't, I will have my operative in the store pick off the hostages one by one until you do as I say. The choice is yours, Mr. Beckett. Either one will die, or all of them. You have five minutes to decide." The call went dead.

The liquor in Del's stomach churned and bubbled like a volcano about to blow. When it crept up his throat, he bent over his trash can and unleashed the guilt from the gut-wrenching act he was about to commit. Wiping the corner of his lips with a sleeve, he nearly hurled again from the sour taste in his mouth. He then picked up a water bottle from his desk, unscrewed the cap, took a swig, and spat it into the can.

Reality sank in. Del had to become a killer to save the lives of another ten. He grabbed his gun and the two phones, pulled the door open, and prayed to God he could go through with it. But then, the store phone rang.

13

Lexi was accustomed to taking the lead in a tactical caravan. In nearly every operation she'd been assigned, explosive ordnance disposal was the first step. Thus, her vehicle had to be the first in. But going in alone was foreign. She didn't have her partner sitting next to her in the front seat, running through scenarios and deciding whose turn it was to buy drinks afterward. Talk about what came after a job kept Lexi's nerves down.

Today, Lexi had only her phone's mechanical computer voice spitting out directions, which made her more anxious, so she turned on the car's radio. Surprisingly it was tuned to a country station, blasting the Cody Johnson song that had convinced her to stop wasting precious time and propose to Nita. She sang along utterly out of tune, patting the ring box hidden in her cargo pants pocket to the fast beat. It didn't matter who was listening on the other end of her microphone because she was going to take her chance, chase her dream, and hold the woman she loved while she still could.

When the map on her phone showed the turn to the abandoned POW site was rapidly approaching, Lexi twisted her neck several times to work out the rest of the kinks. However, she discovered her muscles were already relaxed. Thinking of Nita always had that effect on her. She then turned off the radio to focus on the now, not tomorrow.

Slowing her vehicle, Lexi made the turn onto the gravel access road, noting the sign that showed the POW camp was straight ahead. Then her tactical radio crackled in her ear. "Mills, we're staying back just off the main road."

"Copy," Lexi said. "I'll let you know if I need anything."

"I wish you steady hands, Agent Mills," the voice added.

"Tango. Copy," Lexi replied. Clearly, whoever had said those words was from the bomb squad. Most explosive technicians didn't believe in luck, and Lexi was one of them. Disarming a device came about through skill, knowledge, and steady hands.

Soon a cyclone fence came into view, as did a police cruiser parked at a gated entrance. A female officer was standing near the front fender with both forearms resting on the gear attached to either side of her duty belt. She must have been Sergeant Mel Thompson. The mirrored aviator glasses hid much of her features, making it difficult for Lexi to assess her state, but her relaxed posture and the tone of her voice earlier over the radio suggested she was a seasoned officer with a calm head. Lexi let out a sigh of relief. The last thing she needed was an anxious partner breathing down her neck.

Pulling up behind the cruiser, Lexi searched the SUV's console, eventually finding what she wanted—a pair of wraparound sunglasses to combat the powerful glare of the late afternoon sun. She then exited, grabbing the bucket of tools and supplies Carver had assembled.

After one step, the throbbing in her residual limb reminded her she hadn't adjusted her prosthetic since landing. She'd learned through experience that the effects of flying in a pressurized cabin often made her limb swell for several hours. As a result, she had to reposition the socket several times to relieve the pressure. So she dropped the bucket, leaned against the car door, and pushed back her custom pant leg with the side zipper. She didn't have time to doff the prosthetic properly and check her liner, but she did the next best thing and shifted it, using both hands until she felt the suction give a little. That should be enough to get her through the next task. Finally, after she lowered and re-zipped her pant leg and retrieved her bucket, Lexi realized the officer had been watching her. Displaying her handicap in public no longer bothered Lexi. However, she was sensitive to the idea that it could bother others, especially a veteran cop who depended on her to save her partner.

"You must be Sergeant Thompson. I'm Lexi Mills." She shook her hand.

"Call me Mel." She glanced at Lexi's leg. "On the job?"

"Yes, and it's a constant reminder of what's at stake every time I get called out." Lexi hoped the hard truth put Mel at ease. "What is your partner's name?"

"Gary Powell."

"It's his first day, right?" Lexi continued at Mel's affirmative nod. "How is Gary holding up?"

"Emotionally? Better than I'd be at this point. But physically? He's fit and as strong as an ox, but he's been on his feet all day with traffic control, and his feet are killing him. I'm afraid he'll give in and shift his weight."

"I understand you heard sounds from inside the prison hut. I know you couldn't search it, but did you see anything that might tell me what kind of explosives might be in there?"

"I only glanced in that direction once." Mel closed her eyes as if trying to pull out a stubborn memory. "I thought I saw a red dot near the entrance closest to the pathway."

"Thank you. That's very helpful." A red light likely meant a motion sensor. If it was a laser detector with dual sensors, she could overcome it by not breaking the beam. But if it was infrared, she could set it off by merely walking into its sensor range. Not knowing its reach would complicate entry. But first things first. Lexi needed to rescue Officer Powell.

She patted Mel on the upper arm. "All right then. Let's get Gary home tonight." When Mel joined Lexi in walking toward the gate, she stopped. "You have to stay here, Mel."

"He's my partner and trainee. I need to be there."

"I understand the instinct, but the area is under surveillance by the man who planted these devices. He warned that he'll detonate if anyone else but me goes in." Lexi pointed to her earpiece and then the camera attached to her shirt. "The bomb squad is my extra pair of eyes, and I'll be in radio contact every step of the way."

Mel rolled her neck. "He's just a baby, Lexi, but Gary is the real deal."

Lexi replied with a stiff nod and a second pat on the arm before stepping through the gate with her bucket in tow. She was confident on the outside, but self-doubt had made an untimely appearance on the inside. Every call unearthed a variety of insecurities, but this time it was accompanied by a sense of dread she needed to kick to the curb. She glanced over her shoulder and winked. "Then I guess he's buying afterward."

Lexi stepped a little more confidently toward Officer Powell, avoiding the wooden walking path. "This is Mills. Making sure everyone can hear me. Bomb squad, are you there?"

"We're here, Mills, and your video is coming in clear."

"Good to know. How about you, Hughes?"

"I'm here, Lexi. We'll be with you every step of the way."

Having an open comm link to someone she knew during a disposal was always comforting but was doubly so without the benefit of her blast suit. "Everyone's here. Let's get the party started."

Lexi scanned the gridwork of pathways and rubble, thinking each pile of rock and board was a possible hiding place for a mine or a tripwire. In essence, she had entered her worst nightmare. Mirroring the path, Lexi walked beside the wood planks toward Powell on the side closest to his foot on the wood. She then carefully placed her bucket on the ground five feet away.

"Hi, Gary. I'm Lexi. I'm here to get you out of this."

Gary let out a long, breathy sigh. "You're very popular today, Lexi Mills. Please tell me you know what you're doing."

"I'm a trained explosives expert with the ATF. Normally I don't brag, but when the President gave me a medal last month, he said I was the best at what I do."

"Oh shit." Gary forced a laugh. "I read about you. You're a national hero. Aren't you the one who saved the governor of Texas?"

"That's me. And I'm here to do the same for you. We'll both walk away in one piece if you do exactly as I say."

"That sounds like an excellent plan." The strain in Gary's voice suggested Lexi would have to hurry things.

"All right then. I'm going to look at what's below the boards, so I need you to be very still. Can you do that?"

"I haven't as much as twitched my nose for the last twenty-five minutes."

Gary's statue-like posture confirmed it. "At this point, moving will be the problem if you told me to run for it."

"Then let's see if we can avoid that." Then, for the benefit of the bomb squad, she added, "There's loose dirt here, so I'm going to dig around the device and try to expose it."

"Copy, Mills," she heard in her ear. "Most of the soil here is hard clay, so anything loose is a fresh dig."

"Thanks." Lexi retrieved the flashlight and hand shovel from the bucket and knelt beside the wood planks where Powell was standing. She then eased the fresh dirt from the edge until she unearthed a small gap between the wood and the device. After removing her sunglasses, she peered into the hole. The mine appeared to be positioned at an angle beneath the board, so she'd have to go to the other side to estimate its length and composition. But first, she cleared more dirt away, hoping to find the end of the device. Seeing that would give her a better idea of which type of bar mine she was facing.

Removing the dirt was a tedious process, but caution was essential. If Lexi dug too deeply, she might send a pebble tumbling toward the mine and trigger it. She followed the device's angle to where it would terminate on her side of the plank but had to stop when she got close to Powell's foot. Unable to see the end of the mine, she had to move.

"I couldn't see much from this angle, so I'm heading to the other side." The bomb squad acknowledged her. She then replaced her sunglasses and rose to her feet. "How are you doing, Gary?"

"I'd do a lot better if you told me I can move."

"Give me a few more minutes. I need to get a look from a different angle." Lexi scanned the area, locating the end of the walkway. She grabbed her bucket and circled the pathway, glancing at the prison hut twenty yards away. Something caught her attention. She raised her glasses and spotted the red dot Mel had mentioned. It was a single red vertical light about one inch long. That told her the sensor was likely an infrared motion sensor, but she still didn't know its range. Approaching it head-on would be too risky.

Lexi continued to the other side of the walkway, stopping near Gary and positioning her bucket within reach. "A little more digging, Gary, and hopefully, I'll know what we're dealing with."

"And if you don't?" Harried nerves cut through Gary's voice.

"I'll have to saw out a section of the board." Cutting was Lexi's last option. She didn't know how sensitive the mine's pressure plate was, and she feared vibration from the saw might detonate it. Though, of all the power saws at her disposal, the plunge saw she'd brought had the smoothest motion, causing only minor shaking.

Wiping perspiration from her brow, Lexi wondered how much longer Officer Powell could hold out. She was already sweating, and Powell had been out here for a half-hour and was likely becoming dehydrated. Giving him a water bottle would alter the weight on the pressure plate, so that idea was off the table. She would have to hurry.

Lexi located the spot where Mel had dug out a small section of dirt and used that as her starting point. Removing her glasses again, she shined her flashlight into the hole. She had a better view of the mine's structure and determined she was definitely facing a British bar mine with three external pipe bombs wired to it. Now, she had to ascertain which type. Was it the kind that would trigger when pressure was released or the type that required a second pressure?

There were two ways to make that determination. Knowing the model number was the most definitive, but the numbers were stamped on the top and bottom of the mine, two locations she couldn't access. Alternatively, she was limited to a visual inspection of the mine casing. She could determine the model if she could locate and see inside the pass-through slot for the wires connecting the external charge.

Lexi used the spot where Mel had dug as a starting point and slowly shoveled dirt and rock out of the way. Within minutes, she'd exposed the shear wire slot. She had a decent view of it, but it wasn't perfect, so she had to get creative. Retrieving the extendable mirror, Lexi lay flat on the ground and positioned it to see its reflection, but she still couldn't be sure. She then shined the flashlight into the hole, moving the beam until it hit the slot. Bingo. She had the perfect view and had seen what she needed to know what type of mine Powell had triggered. "I've identified the mine and am heading back around," she whispered into her mic.

Lexi rose and brushed herself off. "I'm coming back around, Gary." She then collected her things and circled the wooden pathway to the other side. After placing the bucket down, she considered Powell's condition and how quickly he could move. His muscles were likely tight and might cramp if he moved suddenly. That gave her no other choice. She had to help him off.

Lexi reached her hand out. "Grab my hand."

Gary looked confused and leery. He'd stood entirely still in the heat for the better part of an hour, facing sure death if he as much as sneezed. Sweat rolled down the sides of his face like an open faucet. If she had to guess, Gary was about to hurl or pass out.

Lexi extended her hand further. "Trust. Me." He tentatively raised his hand until it met Lexi's, and then he clutched it. "Now step off. I'll make sure you don't fall."

"Wait. That's it? Just step off?"

Lexi smiled. "That's it." She dropped the corners of her lips to stress that they weren't entirely out of danger. "But whatever you do, don't step on it a second time."

When Powell tentatively lifted his right leg and swung it backward, Lexi steadied and pulled him back into her waiting arms. He then fell to his knees from sheer exhaustion and threw up.

Hoots of jubilation came through Lexi's earpiece as she rubbed Powell's back in small circles. "Are you okay, Gary?"

He raised an index finger, gesturing for Lexi to give him a minute. "How did you know what to do?"

"Once I was sure we were dealing with an anti-tank bar mine, I needed to know which model it was. If it was the L89, it would have exploded when you lifted your foot. But it was the L90. If you'd stepped on the board with your other foot, you would have been in trouble on the second step. So it's a good thing you listened to your training officer, or you'd both be dead."

"But how did you know what kind it was?" Powell asked.

"That was simple. I looked through a small slat on the side of the mine. Once I saw the pivot pin for the trigger wasn't touching the pressure plate, I knew this was an L90. It was waiting for the second pressure. So, all you had to do was step off."

"That's some real hero stuff, Lexi Mills," someone announced in her earpiece. But Lexi didn't have time to celebrate.

Lexi offered Powell a hand and pulled him to his feet. "I'd love to sit and chat, but my work isn't done."

14

Nita ran her fingers across her lips to an eerie feeling that the toe-curling kiss she and Lexi just shared might be their last. She watched the SUV pull through the police control point into traffic, unable to shake the awful sense that Tony Belcher had Lexi right where he wanted her. "Come back to me, Lexi Mills," she whispered.

A hand fell on her back, and then Noah spoke softly. "She's the best at what she does. She'll be back."

"I'm not so sure this time. Belcher is evil." A chill went down Nita's spine when she said his name.

"I know what he's capable of, but Lexi knows her stuff and can think her way out of anything. I saw her make a bomb out of candy wrappers and drain cleaner. If anyone can save the officer and family and make it out alive, it's her."

"It's the *if* part that scares me." And it had Nita wanting to pop another Norco to not feel like Lexi was driving off to her death. Coming here was a mistake. She'd rather be in the dark and wait for Lexi to walk through their hotel room door like she did for her other SRT calls than sweat this out with her.

"Detective Hughes was asking for you, but I'll tell him you'll be right in if you need a minute."

"No, I'd like to help." But Nita really meant that she needed the distraction.

Noah led her inside the SWAT command van, where the young boy was drawing stick figures on computer paper. Detective Hughes was sitting close by, listening to an audio recording. He replayed the same thing three times: "Make sure she goes, Nolan. You owe me for what you did after the state championship game."

Nita tapped Hughes on the shoulder to get his attention. He turned around.

"Oh, hi. Anything you can get out of Dylan about the hostages, the store manager, or the explosive devices would be of great help. He said there were thirteen people inside. We know two teenagers are there and think an elderly couple is too. We tried having him type out answers on the phone but couldn't get much out of him."

Nita glanced in the boy's direction. "He looks like he's in first or second grade, so his writing skills must be rudimentary. I've had patients his age who couldn't read the rehab instructions, so we used picture boards for everything."

Hughes placed a second chair next to Dylan. "Do you mind giving it a whirl?"

"Not at all." Nita sat beside Dylan, admiring his drawing for several beats before tapping him on the shoulder to get his attention. She signed and spoke. "Hi, Dylan. I'm Nita. Can we talk?" He nodded. "Do you prefer to sign or read lips?"

Sign. Reading lips is hard.

"I know. I tried but failed miserably. I thought my girlfriend was saying bye, but she wanted pie."

Dylan laughed. *That's an easy one,* he signed.

"Maybe you can help me someday, but I need to ask you some questions about the grocery store." Dylan nodded again, but this time more expressively. Nita had clearly put him at ease. "Earlier, you told the officer that thirteen people were in the store. Do you know any of their names?"

Dylan picked up the pencil he'd been using to draw stick figures and what resembled a store shelf with boxes and cans on three levels. He then wrote letters below several of the figures, pressing hard on the paper at the start of each letter. When he finished, he'd written the names: Mom, Zack, Riley, Bret, Maria, and Train. Six others near the shelves had no names. Three had long hair. Finally, one figure in the corner, holding a gun, read, Bad Man.

"Excellent, Dylan," Nita signed. She then pointed to the ones with long hair and no names. "Are these women?" Dylan circled two but put an *x* through the third. "Is this a man with long hair?" Dylan nodded. "Very good. We know there are two teenagers in there. Can you point to them?" Dylan circled two women figures. "Are there any old people? Old like grandparents?" Dylan circled one man and one woman, leaving two men unidentified.

Country music came over the police radio on the shelf above Nita's head, drawing her attention. The next second, a familiar voice sang along, making Nita chuckle. Lexi could do many things well, but singing wasn't one of them. Though, her inability to carry a tune never stopped Lexi from belting out a song in the shower. Now the entire Gladding Police Department was privy to that little-known fact.

When the song ended, Nita glanced over her shoulder at Hughes. "I think that's all we'll learn about the hostages. What else should I ask him?"

"This is very helpful. Can you ask him about the explosive devices? How many? What do they look like?

"Sure." Nita tapped on Dylan's arm again, and said and signed, "Can I ask you about the bad man?" Dylan nodded, but timidly this time. "He put things at the doors to make you stay in. Did you see them?" Dylan used both hands to demonstrate an explosion. "I know it's scary, but can you draw one of them for me?"

Dylan grabbed another sheet of paper from the nearby shelf and began recreating the object he'd seen inside the store.

Meanwhile, Lexi's voice over the radio had captured Nita's attention again, and despite a churning in her stomach, she couldn't break herself from it. Nita feared every word from Lexi would be her last and hung on every syllable. She made out that the officer's name was Gary and that Lexi would have to do some shoveling to see what type of bomb he'd stumbled onto.

Nita's legs had become so restless that she stood. She placed her ear nearly against the speaker to hear everything coming from the radio. Even the scraping of the shovel against the ground was a welcome sound. It was a sign that Lexi was still alive.

Then when Lexi said, "Trust. Me," Nita's breathing increased to a pace that matched her racing pulse. Nita's heartbeat reverberated in her ears so loudly that it drowned out what Lexi was saying. She couldn't hear past, "Whatever you do..."

Dylan tugged on Nita's arm, but she slapped it away, unable to catch her breath or concentrate on anything other than Lexi's impending death if she'd done any of a myriad of things incorrectly while assessing that bomb. "Not now," she yelled.

An arm fell on Nita's shoulder again, and she instantly recognized Noah's comforting touch. He remained silent but kept his hand there, preserving their connection. The contact was a reminder that she wasn't alone. That they were going through this nerve-racking event together.

Then, Lexi's voice came through loud and clear. "Are you okay, Gary?"

Those four words broke the dam of emotion Nita had been holding back. She slumped in her chair, letting a river of tears streak her face. Lexi had completed the first hurdle, but the danger wasn't over yet. She still had to save the store manager's family being held there.

Nita buried her face in her hands, wondering how she could make it every day, waiting for Lexi to come home now that she'd gotten a taste of the intense nature of her job. But, deep down, Nita knew herself, and the answer was that she couldn't remain sober.

Dylan's chair scraped against the metal floor, causing Nita to look up. Dylan had drawn his eyebrows together in apparent worry and signed, *Are you okay?*

Nita signed back, *I'll be fine.*

Do you need a hug? Mom says hugs fix everything.

"Yes, please." Nita opened her arms and drew Dylan into a tight embrace. This poor little boy had been through a harrowing experience, being taken hostage and nearly blown to pieces by a madman he'd never met. Yet, here he was, comforting Nita at one of her lower moments in recent years. She'd have to do the same for his mother when this was over and thank the woman for raising such a sensitive, intuitive boy.

She released Dylan to hear Lexi talking to the officer, explaining how she defeated the bomb. Dylan then handed her a drawing of a door with grates running horizontally across the front. Near the center was a circular object with arrows pointing to it and the word red below it.

"Is this what the bad man put out?" Nita asked and signed.

Dylan nodded before handing her a second sheet of paper. On it, he'd drawn sets of parallel lines. First, two were close together, then there was a space, and two more were close together. This pattern repeated five times. He'd also placed arrows in several of the broader spaces.

"What is this?" Nita asked.

The store, Dylan signed.

Nita cocked her head, inspecting the drawing closely. Then she realized each arrow pointed to a device the manager had left, leaving Nita with a sinking feeling. The entire store was booby-trapped with explosives. The odds of Dylan's mother making it out alive were nearly impossible. Then Nita gasped. If Belcher lured Lexi into it, she wouldn't make it out alive either.

The radio crackled with Lexi's voice again. "I'm heading to the prison hut."

That was all Nita could take. She signed goodbye to Dylan. Then, unable to breathe, she rushed toward the door and burst out into the blazing late afternoon sun. Her demons were calling her. They'd crept back into her head after the first taste of opioids following her shoulder surgery. Now they were starving for another helping, a stronger, more substantial one.

The door to the SWAT van slammed closed again, but Nita didn't have to look over her shoulder to know that Noah had followed her. Instead, she felt his support from behind. "I can't do it, Noah. I can't listen to her facing death again."

"Then don't. I'll take you anywhere you want to go. Name it. So, what will it be?" Noah asked.

Nita turned, seeing genuine concern in Noah's eyes. She was certain no matter the state she was about to put herself in, he would make sure she was safe. And if the worst happened to Lexi, he would be there to pick up the pieces. "Take me to a bar."

15

Once Lexi grouped several rocks to mark the area where Officer Gary Powell had tripped the buried anti-tank bar mine, she returned him to Sergeant Thompson's safe hands. "Make sure he gets lots of water. He was sweating buckets out there."

"Let me get you one too." Mel went to her trunk and retrieved two plastic water bottles, tossing one to Lexi. "We can't have you getting shaky."

"Thanks. You might want to have three more ready. The Beckett family has been in that hut since last night. I'll be right back." Lexi winked and stepped inside the cyclone fence line.

"I'm heading to the prison hut," she announced into her mic. Lexi then retraced her way up the middle path, carefully placing each step beside the wood planks and avoiding rock groupings. "I'll do a walk-around first."

Coming even with the area where Officer Powell was trapped, she took a few steps closer to the hut, but not so close that she might set off a motion sensor. She stopped to study the device she'd seen earlier and pulled out her cell phone. Opening the camera app, Lexi pointed it at the entrance, zoomed in close, and took several pictures. She discovered four red laser beams and eight devices, four on each side of the opening. They were positioned so that no one could crawl or hunch through without breaking a beam. Lexi then scanned the roofline. At the corner seams, she spotted two infrared motion sensors. Those were likely positioned to detect strong vibration to protect against breaking through the cinder block walls or roof.

"It looks like the entrance is rigged with multiple laser wires. There's no way I'm getting through that. The structure is also wired for vibration, so we can't break through the walls. I'm heading around to the other side."

A chorus of groans came from inside. They had to be from the Beckett family.

Lexi spoke loudly to penetrate the cinder block walls. "I'm a federal agent. I'm here to get you out." The groans stopped. "The place is rigged with explosives, so I need you to remain still. I'll let you know when I'm coming in."

Lexi released a breathy sigh. If the Becketts hadn't already realized the magnitude of their imprisonment, they were now terrified. If they had, Lexi now had them hoping they would soon get out of there alive, which was far from a certainty.

She circled the small building, maintaining a twenty-foot buffer in the event Belcher had laid proximity sensors too. The single-story block structure had only one entrance. It appeared to be thirty feet long by twenty feet wide with five evenly spaced tiny openings on each side six feet from the ground, each guarded by rusted metal bars. But a conundrum was building. The windows weren't large enough for an adult man to fit through, but a slender woman or teenager could, just like Dylan had at the grocery store. However, Lexi had been so focused on selecting the right saw to cut through the plywood that she hadn't thought about the prison structure. The plunge saw she had was rated to cut through non-ferrous metals but not iron.

Lexi lowered her head in disappointment. She didn't bring the right tools, but she had to try. "The only other way in is through a cell window. I'm going to try cutting through the iron bars."

Lexi placed the bucket on the ground and pulled out the extendable mirror. She wanted to work from the west side of the building, where she would have the most light before sunset came in the next hour, so she circled back around to the other side. Closely inspecting the area between her and the structure, Lexi didn't spot signs of sensors or tripwires but proceeded with caution. Stepping gingerly, she avoided any rock that appeared out of place or had been recently moved.

Once at the side of the building, she called out, "I'm looking for a way in. Hold tight." She extended the mirror and held it up to a cell window, squeezing it between the rusted bars. The first two cells were unoccupied. Then, when she peered into the third, she located the hostages. The three were lying on the ground a foot apart on their sides with their hands and feet bound. From their positions, she couldn't be sure if they had explosives attached to their bodies. Lexi then scanned the entire cell but found no signs of another device or sensor.

"I'm right outside your window," Lexi called out. "I can see you. I need all three of you to lay flat on the ground so I can see your chests. I need to make sure there are no surprises."

The hostages whimpered but complied. Once they shifted, duct tape on their mouths came into view. Their torsos appeared normal without bulges or wires. That was an excellent sign.

"I'm going to try cutting through the bars to get you out. Sparks might fly, so I'll need you to get far away from the window without leaving your cell. I repeat. Do not leave your cell. There might be other tripwires."

The hostages shifted to another short round of whimpers.

Lexi returned to her bucket, dumped the contents onto the ground, and grabbed the handle, the plunge saw, and the extra battery. The three hostages appeared thin enough to fit through the window. However, Lexi would need to remove all three bars to make that happen. That meant she'd have to make six cuts—the top and bottom of each bar—to create a wide enough escape hole.

Not tall enough to reach the top of the bars, Lexi placed the bucket on the ground directly below the window and stepped on top of it. She then positioned the power saw close to the bar on the right to make her first cut. The shape of the saw and the closeness of the bars made it impossible to cut the first bar flush, so having a short nub was better on a side, not the center. The hostages could shimmy through with minimal obstruction.

Lexi pressed the power trigger and revved the saw to a low-pitched whine. Pressing it against the top of the bar, the friction screeched and sent sparks flying in multiple directions. Several arced back at her face, but thankfully her sunglasses absorbed them. She made a mental note to buy Hughes a new pair because these were toast. The blade hung three times, requiring as many restarts. Each time, the motor sounded strained. She wasn't sure how much longer the blade and motor would last.

After finishing the first cut, Lexi changed plans. She tugged on the cut bar with as much strength as she could muster, bending it an inch to enable her to position the saw better to move on to the second bar. If she could nurse the saw through three cuts, she could then hang from the bars, using her weight to bend them enough for the hostages to pass through.

Lexi started the saw again and pushed the blade against the middle bar. Sparks danced in the air again while the metal grinding assaulted her eardrums. Seconds later, the blade caught, causing the motor to hiss. Then something inside the casing clanked, sending a sense of dread surging through Lexi. She un-wedged the blade from the partial cut and pressed the start trigger, but nothing happened. She repeated, but still nothing. Hoping she'd drained the power, Lexi hopped down and changed the battery. Nothing.

"Damn it." Lexi slumped her shoulders. She'd blown out the motor and the Becketts' only means of escape with it. "Carver, I have a problem."

"What do you have, Mills?" SWAT Commander Carver said through her earpiece. "My team can walk you through it."

"I don't think they can. I blew out the power saw." Lexi fell to the ground on her butt, knowing her failure had sealed that family's fate. "I have no way of getting the hostages through the cell window in time."

Her head throbbed at her horrible blunder. Then her residual limb did, too. Every muscle ached like her heart did for that innocent family. They'd done nothing to deserve Belcher drawing them in as pawns in their long, deadly feud. The children were only teenagers and likely had yet to experience their first proper kiss. They'd never know romantic love because Lexi had failed to plan. Belcher was right. She was a fraud.

Lexi placed a hand on either temple to hold back an avalanche of guilt when a voice came through her earpiece. "Mills, wait. I have an idea."

16

Feeling defeated, Lexi looked up from her seated position on the dirt, hoping to see a circular saw magically waiting for her at the base of the prison hut, but all she saw was clay soil and rock.

When the radio squawked again in her earpiece, she recognized Detective Hughes' voice. "Something Del said stuck with me, but I couldn't figure it out until now. He said that I owed him for what I did to him after the state championship game. I hated high school and had forgotten most of it until you said you had to get them through the window. When we were kids, the football team came here after losing the big game. Del was getting it on in a cell with a McBean sister, and we wanted to catch him in the act. The prison hut had a metal door at the entrance back then, and it was louder than cats fighting when it opened. Since we couldn't go that way, one kid said that a cell had loose bars that were only wedged in place. You can probably get through that way."

The possibility of getting inside shot adrenaline through Lexi. She'd only have to clear a path for the hostages to get out. "Which cell?"

"I'm trying to think. It should be the cell on the northeast side."

Not knowing what she'd find, Lexi stuffed the flashlight, wire cutters, electrical tape, duct tape, scissors, and seatbelt cutter into her cargo pockets. She then grabbed the telescoping mirror and bucket and headed to the other side of the building. Standing atop the upturned bucket, she tugged on the middle bar, and with some convincing, it came out.

Lexi let a smile sprout. "It worked, Hughes. I have the first bar out."

"Glad to help." The relief in Hughes' voice was palpable.

Lexi removed the other two bars from the cell window with considerable effort. Then, the tricky part came—hoisting herself up and through a narrow hole while balancing atop a Homer bucket. Luckily, she was dressed for it. With a prosthetic, she only wore sneakers with excellent grip.

Lexi called out to prepare the hostages, "I'm going in through another cell." She placed her hands on the gravelly windowsill, barely reaching the other edge. Then, using her natural foot as leverage, she put it knee-level on the wall and strained to do a pull-up. The odd angle required more leverage from below. She maneuvered her prosthetic leg upward, but the rigid foot refused to bend enough to get traction, causing her to fall.

"Damn it." She would have made it up if she had two natural feet, but she couldn't surpass this hurdle because of Belcher. He'd limited her abilities by planting the landmine that took her leg. Consequently, for the first time since Lexi learned to run again, she felt handicapped.

"Are you okay, Mills?" a voice asked over the radio.

"Yeah, I just have to figure out a way to get up and through the window." If she only had more leverage. Lexi went through the list of supplies she'd brought with her, ruling out one at a time. But when she got to the hand shovel, an idea came to her. The telescoping handle was made of steel. If she used it correctly, it could provide more leverage. "I might have something."

Lexi darted around to the other side of the building, retrieved the shovel, and returned to the open hole. Stepping atop the bucket again, she pushed the fully extended mirror through, letting it dangle before letting it go. After expanding the shovel to its full length, Lexi put it through the window, holding onto it with one hand. She then angled it vertically and, in one swift move, yanked it hard against the interior wall and raised her right foot on the exterior. Next, she shimmied her foot against the cinderblock surface until it was at the optimal height to launch herself upward. Finally, Lexi pushed and pulled hard until her head and shoulders were through the open hole.

Dangling from a prison cell window headfirst, face down, six feet off the ground, Lexi had maneuvered herself into a dilemma. How was she supposed to get down without breaking a wrist or an arm? Breaking her fall seemed like the best option. She scooted out the window, bending at the waist until her body hugged the wall, and extended the shovel toward the floor. Hooking her right foot outside the window, she continued scooting, but her prosthetic caught on the sill. She then shifted her weight to her right side, lifting the prosthetic a fraction, and continued her slide until the shovel touched the concrete floor. Finally, she released her foot and transferred pressure to the shovel, breaking most of her fall as she rolled to the ground. She never wanted to do that again, but she might have to do the same thing on the way out, only without the bucket.

Before getting up, Lexi checked the prosthetic she felt shift during her ingress. Running her hands up and down the socket, she didn't sense any cracks, so she rocked it back and forth until her residual limb felt it was in perfect position.

Once on her feet, Lexi noted the cell was musty and smelled of animal waste. She called out, "I'm in. Hold on. I'll be right there."

Compacting the mirror to its shortest length, Lexi stepped up to the edge of the cell doorway. The doors and hinges had been removed, leaving only the cinderblocks forming the frame. She then inched the mirror out slowly until she could see down the center corridor between the two rows of cells. A dual laser tripwire had been set up two feet off the ground, running the length of the passage.

Following wires leading from one of the laser sensors, Lexi discovered a cache of pipe bombs large enough to destroy anything within five hundred feet. If she had to guess, she'd found a good portion of the stolen nitro she'd been chasing before leaving the Kansas City ATF Field Office last year. Lexi had faced this much explosive material before. The quantity never mattered when working up close, only the proximity. While handling it face to face, any amount could leave her maimed or dead.

Putting the explosives out of her head, Lexi low-crawled in the corridor and to the center cell entrance on the other side. Once she crossed the threshold, the hostages all squirmed. She then rose to her feet. "Hi, I'm Lexi. Let me get the tape off so you can breathe better." She moved to the girl first and peeled off the duct tape in a single hard tug. Doing it gingerly would have only prolonged the pain of it coming off and wasted more time.

"Ow!" the daughter screamed. "I'm Brittney. This is my brother, Chase, and my mom, Kathy."

"Hi, Brittney. I'll get you out of here soon." Lexi brought the girl to a sitting position. She then removed the boy's tape.

"Where's Dad," Chase asked. "Is he okay?"

"Hi, Chase. He's at the grocery store, but he's in danger." Lexi did the same for the boy and moved to his mother.

"Why are they doing this," the mother asked after Lexi removed her tape.

"The man behind this won't tell us what he wants until I rescue you." Lexi brought the mother upright.

"This is insane." The mother appeared frazzled but unhurt. "We've never hurt a soul."

"Let's get you out of here." Lexi retrieved her seatbelt cutter. "Then we can debate the man's sanity." She released the woman's hands and feet first. "There are more tripwires in the corridor, so I need everyone to do exactly as I say."

Once everyone was free of their bindings and worked out the kinks from being tied up for hours, Lexi got their attention. "There's a laser beam sensor about two feet high in the corridor. So we'll have to low-crawl on our bellies."

"Will hands and knees work? I have big boobs," the mother asked.

Big was an understatement, but this wasn't the time to critique the wisdom of breast enhancements. "No. You'll trigger the explosives. There's enough nitro out there to blow up a city block. I'll lead the way. Crawl exactly the way I do and take the same path. Do you understand?"

Everyone nodded.

Lexi first took out her cell phone and snapped several pictures of the laser devices and collection of pipe bombs. Documenting what was inside would help the waiting bomb squad and might help her assess what was waiting for her at the grocery store.

Lexi slithered across the corridor and down two doors on her belly and forearms to the correct cell. She then stood and called back, "Chase, let's have you go first. Stay low and keep your head down. It's just like playing army man in your backyard."

Chase and Brittney had done an excellent job and joined Lexi. Now it was Kathy's turn. "Take it slow, Kathy. Keep your head down, for heaven's sake." Lexi watched her struggle to keep her chest flat. She cringed every time Kathy bobbed her head up to check her direction of travel. One arch of the back, and they'd all be dead.

"These damn boobs. I never wanted them in the first place, but Delmar thought I would look sexier with double Ds."

"When this is over"—Lexi cringed again—"I'll take you to the reduction appointment myself."

"I'll hold you to it." Kathy inched her way to the door.

"Wait until your feet have cleared before you get up." Lexi estimated she had another two feet to go.

"Honey, I couldn't get up from this position if I wanted to."

Once she was through, Lexi and Chase helped Kathy to her feet. "We're not out of danger yet," Lexi warned. "We have to crawl out the window, but the compound is rigged with landmines. So everyone needs to stay put until we're all out. Is that clear?"

Everyone nodded.

"Chase, you look the most flexible. Let's have you go first. It's a six-foot drop, so it might hurt when you hit the ground."

"I've fallen from a tree taller than this and walked away without a scratch. I'll be fine."

"Good. Then you can help your sister and mom on the other side." Lexi laced her fingers together, preparing a foothold for Chase. "I'll boost you up and will hold your feet until you're ready for me to drop you. But, whatever you do, don't step on any of the wood boards out there. That's where the mines are."

"Holy shit."

"Language, Chase," his mother scolded.

"I think he deserves a pass, Kathy." Lexi hoisted Chase to the open window and dangled him by his feet. "Say when."

"Go."

Lexi released Chase's feet. A thump. She waited for a scream or groan but heard nothing. "Are you okay, Chase?"

He coughed. "Yeah. I'm fine. I landed on my head."

"Are you sure?" Lexi asked. "That was quite a drop."

"Trust me," Brittney snickered. "He's hit his head a hundred times. He's fine."

Brittney followed easily. Now, it was her mother's turn. Lexi boosted her up. Kathy grabbed the ledge of the windowsill and shoved her head inside. "Oh, this is a tight fit." Kathy wriggled, wedging her chest through.

"Think of it as mammogram day." Lexi shifted position to grab her feet. "A little flattening, but they'll go back." She gave a good push, and Kathy was into the waiting hands of her children.

Now it was Lexi's turn. Her arms were weak from lifting three people to safety. Even if the kids shoved the bucket through for extra height, she wasn't sure if she had enough strength to lift herself up the same way she did coming in. That required every ounce of power she had. She placed her hands on her hips, arms akimbo, thinking the window looked as high as Mount Everest. It was impossible to scale in her tired state.

"Are you coming, Lexi?" Chase called out.

"Give me a second. I'm a little tired. I'll need that bucket to stand on."

Moments later, the bucket came through the window, but Lexi's arms still felt like limp noodles. Next, the sleeve of a hoodie appeared and dangled a few inches below the sill.

Chase yelled, "Hold on to my sweatshirt, and we'll pull you through."

"That's genius, Chase." Lexi positioned the bucket and stepped on top. She then pressed her right foot high against the wall and gripped the end of the sleeve. "Pull!"

Lexi kicked upward while Chase pulled, giving herself momentum to the opening. Ducking, her hands went through first. Then her head. She let go once her belly reached the sill. Chase and Brittney were there, reaching for Lexi's hands.

"We got you, Lexi." Brittney gripped tightly.

Lexi grabbed both hands. "Don't pull. I have a prosthetic leg. It might get caught. Just steady me." Lexi shimmied her torso through, shifting her weight so her socket would make it over the lip. When her head reached the kids' shoulder level, they grabbed her by the underarms and eased her out until her feet hit the ground with a thump.

Brittney and Chase refused to let her go, giving her a bone-crushing group hug. "Thank you, Lexi." Next, Kathy joined the fray, pressing her big boobs against her.

"Great job, Mills," Lexi heard in her earpiece.

Lexi broke the group hug. "Let's get you out of here and some medical attention." She led the Becketts single file safely through the compound to Sergeant Thompson and Officer Powell outside the cyclone fence. She then announced into her mic, "The family is secure. Bring up EMS and the bomb squad."

Minutes later, Lexi stood by while paramedics examined the Beckett family. Besides dehydration, their only injuries were a few cuts and scrapes sustained from their bindings and escape. She then chugged down an entire water bottle, said her goodbyes to the family, and approached the squad leader. She showed him the pictures she'd taken inside the compound. "I suspect every pipe bomb in there contains nitro from a stolen shipment last year. You'll need to sweep every inch of those wood planks for bar mines. I'd appreciate it if you preserved one of those exterior pipe bombs for analysis." Next, Lexi flipped to the interior pictures. "I recommend controlled detonation of the building. The vibration sensors at the roofline make another approach too risky."

"Great analysis, Agent Mills. We'll take it from here." He shook Lexi's hand. "That was one hell of a rescue."

Lexi thanked him and returned to the police cruiser. "I need to return to the grocery store. Can you give me an escort?"

Sergeant Thompson pushed her mirrored sunglasses further up the bridge of her nose, releasing a broad smile. "With pleasure."

17

One block from the police cordon in Gladding, The Salt Mine smelled of stale grease and was packed tighter than the Beebo Club on a Saturday night. According to the man sitting next to Nita at the bar, "It's like rubber-neckers on the freeway. Everyone in town wants to see what's going on at McBean's, but this is the closest they can get." It seemed that every Gladding resident of drinking age had tired of standing on the street corner to glimpse the biggest event the town had seen in decades and wandered into the bar to swap rumors and opinions.

Nita wanted no part of it. All she wanted was to drown out thoughts of Lexi getting blown to bits and The Salt Mine police scanner junkie rumor mill. Moments earlier, the same man sitting next to her had pointed to the other end of the bar. He'd said, "Ray over there said he heard on the scanner that some ATF agent is in the thick of this, and Old Biscuit had asked for her by name."

"Is that right?" was Nita's evasive reply. He needn't know that the ATF agent in question was the love of her life, nor that the criminal mastermind behind the siege was the evil extremist the agent in question had been chasing for two years. The crowd might turn on her or pelt her with never-ending questions about something she desperately wanted to put out of her mind.

Where in the hell was Noah? Nita asked herself. It shouldn't take this long to park a car in a town of only sixty-five thousand. If not for this crazy hostage scene, the only full parking lots should be at the church on Sunday or the shopping center with the In-N-Out Burger she and Noah had passed on the way into town.

The squirrelly bartender approached, placing a white paper napkin on the countertop in front of Nita. She'd been watching him for several minutes while he served other customers. His appearance and behavior checked every box. Thin, pale, unshaven, jittery, and bouncing around like the Roadrunner behind the bar. Without a doubt, he was an addict with a taste for uppers.

"What will it be?" he asked, not knowing the significance of his question.

It had been six years since Nita had ordered anything other than soda or water at a bar. Still, she wasn't worried about breaking her streak of abstinence. Alcohol was never an addiction, so she couldn't label her lack of drinking sobriety. Instead, it was a stepping stone into a world she'd already returned to when she took her first opioid not for pain but for the buzz. That was also the day she realized she and Lexi were drifting apart, and she needed the escape. One more step in that direction wouldn't matter. The world of drug-induced highs was now a place of refuge. At least she felt she could still control it.

Nita didn't have to think about what to order. She reverted to her drink of choice from grad school. "A double shot of Grey Goose on the rocks with a twist of lime."

"That's top-shelf. Tito's is half the price." He leaned in closer, waiting for a response.

"Did I ask for Tito's?" Nita wasn't usually that snippy, but Lexi's hero complex and Mr. 4-1-1 at the next stool had worn down her social politeness. She regretted coming across as a bitch but refused to take it back.

"Grey Goose it is." The bartender walked away unfazed, as if witnessing Nita's surly behavior was part of his daily routine.

She glanced up at the two large flat screens mounted on the wall behind Squirrelly. Both were tuned to local news stations, with reporters on the scene one block away. One screen displayed pictures of four unconfirmed hostages with their ages and occupations. Two were high school students, and one was a retired executive from Matson, a shipping and navigation company. The other was his wife, a former belly dancer. Why that tidbit was an essential part of the story was a mystery, but Nita figured it fed into the local lore.

The other screen broke away from the live shot at the store, flashing a "Breaking News" banner. Another live feed popped on with a different on-the-ground reporter. Behind her was a SWAT bomb squad van and an EMS rig. The text crawl at the bottom of the screen read, "Second bomb at abandoned POW site."

Nita turned her head away, closing her eyes. She couldn't watch, waiting to hear a loud explosion or see a plume of smoke rising in the background. Doing so would make her insane. Instead, she listened to the hum of the crowd. Dozens of conversations blended in the small bar, making not one decipherable.

Something clanked in front of her, followed by Squirrelly saying, "Your very expensive double."

Nita chuckled and turned toward him, opening her eyes. "Sorry about earlier. I've had an awful day."

"Maybe this will take the edge off."

"Alcohol rarely does it for me, but I'm from out of town." Nita lifted her glass, tipping it toward him in appreciation. "So this will have to suffice." Without thinking twice, she brought the glass to her lips, took in the pungent odor briefly, and swallowed a generous portion, savoring the potent taste as it tingled every nerve ending in her mouth. She'd forgotten about the luxurious smoothness of expensive straight vodka and wondered why she'd bothered with anything else.

Squirrelly parted his lips as if to say something but stopped. The next moment, a hand fell to the small of Nita's back. She turned, discovering Noah's uniquely kind face. "Sorry that it took so long, Nita. I had to park several blocks down, and the traffic is at a crawl with the police activity and media frenzy."

"I figured as much." Nita wagged her thumb in the direction of the television screens without turning her head. "I can't watch."

"Then let's find a table." Noah shifted his stare over Nita's shoulder toward the bar. "I'll take a lager on tap." He returned his attention to Nita. "We can order a burger or something."

"That would be great. I haven't eaten since the plane." Nita wasn't hungry but figured eating would be a good idea if she moved on to the second round of drinks. At least with nothing in her stomach right now, she'd feel the effects of the first double within minutes.

"I'll be right back."

Moments later, Squirrelly returned with Noah's beer. He leaned in, gesturing with his finger for Nita to do the same. "If you're looking to party, I can hook you up. Name it."

Squirrelly's offer had her conducting a mental inventory. She had three Norco pills left in her carry-on bag in Noah's trunk that she intended to save for tomorrow and the flight back. Lexi knew of two, but Nita had doubled her stash before leaving their apartment. She then tossed the idea and mentally patted herself on the back. Yes. She wasn't so far gone down the road of addiction to consider mixing opioids and alcohol. But that rational thought made room for Squirrelly's offer, which made her realize she'd slipped further than she'd thought. Her only craving until now was for the opioid buzz, and some Grey Goose, but that didn't count in her book. Booze had never been a problem before.

Pressed for an answer, she dug deep. "I'm good." When he turned to walk away, she felt herself slip and called out, "Wait. Maybe later." A hollowness stuck in her gut for saying those words, and she knew the reason she did. She'd rather feel nothing than go through losing someone she loved again. Losing her father nearly destroyed her.

Noah returned. "All the tables by the windows are taken."

"Everyone wants to rubberneck at the chaos," Nita scoffed.

"There's one by the bathroom if you don't mind the foot traffic."

Nita wagged her thumb behind her again. "It's better than staring at those for the next hour." She got Squirrelly's attention, signaling that she and Noah were moving to the table. He acknowledged with an exaggerated nod.

Drinks in hand, Noah led Nita to the only unoccupied table in the joint. She picked the seat that didn't face the bar and the constant reminder that

Lexi was somewhere in the distance of those live shots, risking her life to save the family of someone she'd never met.

"I hope you don't mind"—Noah pulled out Nita's chair—"but you looked like you were starving. I thought I'd save some time, so I asked the waitress to send over two cheeseburgers with fries."

"That's perfect." Nita felt her stomach growl. She couldn't remember the last thing she ate more substantial than pretzels on the plane. "I don't mind at all."

"Good. Let's get some food in you. Then you can decide whether you want to stick it out here or have me take you to the hotel."

Nita reached across the table, giving Noah's hand a tight squeeze. "Thank you."

"This can't be easy on you. I've seen what Lexi does for a living. I'd pee my pants if I had to do it."

"This isn't helping, Noah." Nita sucked down the rest of her double.

"Maybe knowing how good she is at her job could help you accept the dangers that come with it."

"I know she's driven by perfection. When she was rehabbing from her amputation, she pushed herself harder than any patient I'd ever seen. She was determined to get back to the ATF's Special Response Team within a year, and she did."

"From what I've seen of her, she has that same drive in every aspect of her job. She is a walking encyclopedia for explosives. She's innovative and can think her way out of anything."

"But she's also headstrong and thinks she's the only one who can get the job done."

"Based on the calls she's sent out to, she *is* the only one with enough expertise and technical skill to avoid tragedy. But it's not only her training that makes Lexi special. It's her sense of calm. I listened while she stood in the kill zone of a bomb and reasoned with an unhinged man with his finger on the trigger. She nearly talked him down."

"Was that the incident in Bowie? Lexi didn't tell me any specifics. She never does."

"That sounds like her. Besides protecting you, she's protecting herself."

"Herself?" Nita cocked her head back when Noah averted his eyes.

There was likely a story behind them. "Why would she need to protect herself?"

"Because she needs a clear head to do what she does. If she thought about how you would react every time she had to perform something dangerous, she'd make a mistake. It's better to leave you in the dark than to have that image of fear on your face in her head."

Noah's explanation for Lexi's secrecy made sense, but it still didn't ease the root cause of her anxiety. Nita had never learned to grieve loss in a healthy way. She was sure if the worst happened while she and Lexi were life partners, she'd break with no chance of putting herself together again.

Their food arrived, prompting Nita to roll up her sleeves above the elbow to prevent getting grease on them. "Wow. I see leftovers in my future." Her plate contained a burger big enough to feed her for three meals. After devouring half, she circled around to their earlier conversation. "You mentioned that Lexi nearly talked down that guy in Bowie. What happened?"

Noah wiped the corners of his mouth with a napkin but waited to speak. The lengthy pause made Nita think he was choosing his words carefully. "I did the one thing she told me not to, but I'm not sorry I did."

"I don't understand." Nita narrowed her brow.

"I was her over-watch, meaning I had a high-powered rifle with a scope trained on the man ready to take him out if I thought he might trigger the bomb. She told me to hold off until he told her where to find Belcher."

"I hate that man." Nita recalled the file Lexi kept on their dresser that contained everything she'd compiled on that horrible man. She'd look at it weekly, studying every detail. It had become an obsession, and now he was behind today's events. Nita had surmised months ago that Belcher would be the death of Lexi, and now that prediction might become a reality.

"I do too." The stern look in Noah's eyes said Belcher had also become his obsession.

"I'm guessing you took the shot."

"I did, and I'd do it again if it meant saving Lexi's life. That's how much she means to me." Noah downed his beer and scanned the room for their waitress.

"Let me." Nita rose from her chair, leaving her cell phone on the table.

"I need a refill, too." She couldn't go quickly enough. Lexi may have needed to keep Nita's fear out of her head, but Nita needed to keep Lexi's bravado out of hers.

Stepping up to the bar, she flagged down Squirrelly. "Another round for us." A minute later, he returned with their drinks. Nita pressed her hand over his before letting go of her glass. "I've changed my mind."

"What will it be?"

"White lady."

18

Sergeant Thompson and Officer Powell led the way to Gladding with the siren blaring and the red and blue lights glowing in the darkening sky. Traffic parted the entire route, giving the short caravan a clear path to the grocery store. Lexi waved out the window at the control point, thanking them before rolling through. She parked Hughes' SUV in the same spot but remained in the driver's seat. Reclining against the headrest, she finally let the totality of the last hour soak in.

The lives of four people had rested on her years of training and ability to think her way out of a deadly box. And if not for Hughes' attention to detail, she would have failed because she'd let the ticking clock guide her thinking. As a result, she had forgotten the cardinal rule of envisioning the entire disposal process from beginning to end before stepping foot into the kill zone. That was a lesson she'd never forget.

Her mind drifted to the last time she was in this exact spot. She'd given Nita what might have been their last kiss and had put every ounce of passion behind it. That kiss and the thought of facing certain death had solidified her earlier decision to propose. She needed to make Nita her wife. Living together had gone a long way in making her feel whole, but committing their lives to each other would finally complete her.

Lexi squeezed the ring box in her pocket through the fabric of her cargo pants before exiting the SUV. She anticipated holding Nita in her arms again when she entered the SWAT command van. Ascending the stairs, Lexi felt her lips tingle at the thought of repeating that heart-pounding kiss. She opened the door but stepped inside to instant disappointment. Nita and Noah weren't there.

All heads inside the van turned toward Lexi, followed by a chorus of cheers and applause. She'd returned the hero, not a dead poser as Belcher had predicted. But accolades and pats on the back weren't what she needed. She wanted to feel Nita's warm body to recharge her strength to move on to Belcher's next hurdle.

Once the commotion died down, Lexi approached Detective Hughes. "Where's Nita?"

"She was great." He shook her hand and offered his congratulations. "We got what we needed from Dylan. She took off with Noah after listening to your rescue operation. I gotta say that she looked frazzled."

"I should call her."

"That can wait." He gestured toward his work area, where Dylan was still sitting in the same chair before Lexi had left. Beside the boy was a man Lexi hadn't seen before. "This is Dylan's father, Maxwell Keene. He's an assistant deputy director with the FBI and the regional Joint Terrorism Task Force Commander."

Lexi shook his hand. For a tall man, he had a weak handshake. She trusted no one with a badge who didn't have a firm grip. She'd discovered that they were more politician than cop and typically folded under pressure. "It's a pleasure, Agent Keene."

"What can you tell me about this Belcher character who has my wife hostage?" he asked.

"Excuse me a second." Lexi pulled Nolan Hughes deeper into the van for privacy. "What is a family member doing here? Is it wise to read him into the situation? He's obviously biased."

"I don't like it either, but my chief cleared him. Keene has some pretty big pull in the state."

"Is there anything you want me to hold back?" Lexi asked. Having a family member present was great for gathering insight into the hostages but not deciding whether to breach a building or give in to demands.

"Revealing details of the explosives or my connection to Belcher might overwhelm Keene and start him down a path of using his political power to influence the outcome of this standoff."

"I appreciate your insightfulness, but my chief said to give him full access."

"All right." If Lexi read Hughes' tight expression correctly, he was as unhappy with this as she was. Returning to the work area, Lexi briefed Agent Keene on her history with Tony Belcher, the Gatekeepers, and the Red Spades, highlighting the stolen shipments of nitro. "I believe a good portion of that missing nitro is in the pipe bombs at the secondary hostage site. And there's a good chance it's also in the proximity devices in the grocery store, where your wife and a dozen other hostages are being held."

"You've really stirred a hornet's nest, haven't you, Agent Mills?" Keene's prickly tone was about as welcome as a case of hemorrhoids after the day Lexi had. She considered throwing it right back at Keene but bit her tongue. Instead, she attributed his brusqueness to the pressure of his wife's life hanging in the balance.

"That was out of line, Agent Keene." Hughes' chivalry was surprising yet welcomed. She'd only known him a few hours but had already considered him a man of honor. She'd gladly work with him any time. "If you're in this business long enough, you're going to make enemies. That doesn't make Mills a reckless agent. In fact, it makes her a damn good one in my book. She didn't have to put her life on the line to save our officer and Beckett's family. She chose to. Lexi Mills is a real-life hero."

"I know exactly who Agent Mills is. I'm slated to introduce her at tomorrow night's awards banquet." Keene rolled his neck before acknowledging Lexi with a nod. "All right, then. Let's hear what Mr. Belcher has to say."

Hughes lifted the phone handset to the grocery store direct line and pressed a button to activate the speaker. "Del, this is Nolan. Your family is safe and unhurt. EMS is checking them out and should release them soon."

"Thank goodness." Beckett released a heavy sigh. "Tell Lexi Mills thank you."

"Del, I need you to get Belcher on the phone, so he can tell us what he wants," Hughes said.

"Hold on." Del then whispered, "I hate talking to that man." Moments later, he returned to the phone. "Put Lexi Mills on. I'm putting you both on speaker."

The stage had been set. This was between Lexi and Belcher.

"Hello, Tony. British anti-tank mines weren't that creative." Lexi nearly believed her own taunt. But if she were honest, they were brilliant devices for upping the casualty count. Someone unfamiliar with the sound made by landmines when triggered wouldn't know that anyone within fifty feet of the next person to step on it was a goner. Gary Powell was lucky to have such an attentive partner. "Neither was leaving me a way inside. You're losing your touch."

"Now where's the fun in giving you an unsolvable puzzle, Lexi Mills?" Belcher's cold voice told her their cat-and-mouse game was far from over. "I enjoy a fair game."

"Risking innocent people's lives isn't a game. It's evil."

"Oh, we've only begun, Agent Mills."

"I've passed your test. Now tell me what you really want."

Several seconds of silence passed, making Lexi wonder if he had more games in store for her, but then Belcher let out a heavy breath. "Amadeus."

Lexi sucked in a deep breath, biting the inside of her cheek and drawing the familiar coppery taste of blood. Spilling blood was a familiar theme with the Belcher brothers. While Tony was the inspiration behind the revolution to prepare his followers for the return of God, his brother, Lyle, was its composer, earning him the nickname Amadeus.

If Tony was evil, Amadeus was the devil personified. If not for a partial fingerprint found at the scene of an execution of a twelve-year-old Texas Aryan Brotherhood member who had crossed him, Amadeus would have been free. And if he were, Lexi was sure the attempted assassination of the Texas governor would have had a different outcome. With Amadeus, there were no rules. Nothing was off-limits, not even killing children. But after today, it appeared Tony had taken a play out of his brother's book. Lexi was grateful that she could stop it.

"There's no way we're letting your brother out of prison."

"Then the people in the store will die, and I will do this again until you free him. I want him on a US Forest Service plane stationed at the Castle

Airport outside Atwater Penitentiary and bound toward Las Vegas within the hour. Today, a package was delivered to my brother at Atwater, containing a sat phone. I'm sure it's being held. That phone is to accompany him on the plane. Once he's in the air, he's to call me to confirm he is en route." The certainty in Belcher's voice left no doubt he was telling the truth. He would go to any length to get his brother back.

"Even if I wanted to release him, it's not up to me." Even if it were up to Lexi, she'd never let that evil man loose on the world. "I'll have to run it up the chain to the attorney general."

"Then I suggest you make that phone call, or I'll blow up the store, and we'll do this all over again. I suspect by now that Amanda Keene's husband has arrived. I'm sure he'll have enough pull to make this happen. You two have one hour, or his wife dies first."

The call went silent for several moments before Delmar Beckett returned to the phone. "Do as he says, Agent Mills. He wants me to shoot one of my employees to prove how serious he is."

"Don't do it, Mr. Beckett. Belcher needs his leverage until he gets his brother out."

"But he has someone on the inside. If I don't do it, they will kill them one by one until I do."

"Who is the inside person?" Lexi's stomach soured at how twisted this situation had become. Belcher had planned this to a T. He'd added so many layers to this operation that she didn't know what to expect next. He must have known she'd be in town for tomorrow's conference and banquet. But how did Belcher realize she'd be here today? The fact that he did sent chills down Lexi's spine. Belcher had a direct line to someone who knew her travel plans. But who? She could count on one hand the number of people she'd told.

"I don't know. Someone left a note under my office door." Beckett's voice cracked. "I have no choice. I'm supposed to have you listen."

The sound of a door slamming shut meant Lexi had failed to talk him down. Someone in the store was about to die.

19

Amanda had sat on the floor, leaning against the soft drink cooler, one checkout stand away from the group. She knew the store manager had seen her son on the security camera, and it was only a matter of time before he did something about it. However, it didn't matter what happened to her next because Dylan was safe. But thinking the manager might take out his anger on the rest of the hostages had Amanda swimming in guilt. Her son's mistake might have cost every hostage their life.

She glanced at the others, and like her, they were waiting to die. The two women and the elderly couple had paired off, holding each other. Zack and Riley had done the same. Clarence had disappeared, likely returning to his home among the soda display. Meanwhile, the rest had lined up shoulder to shoulder, holding hands. The periodic sound of sobs broke the silence, accentuating the gravity of their circumstance.

Amanda closed her eyes and replayed the scene of her son's escape after she'd shoved her way past Zack and Bret in the bathroom. First, she focused on what he looked like, searing that memory into her brain. He'd worn clean jeans and a new hoodie today—a radical departure from his usual attire replete with the previous day's playground dirt. He was long overdue for a trip to the barber with his brown hair reaching halfway down his ears. Next, she focused on his motion. Dylan's arm-flailing running style made her laugh. It always did. However, despite Zack's instruction, Dylan ran in the camera's direction and into the arms of a waiting police officer. He'd made a horrible mistake, but her son was safe, which was all that mattered.

Soon, the distinct smell of burning marijuana wafted past Amanda's nose. She craned her neck, following the scent, discovering Zack had lit up a joint. Why didn't that surprise her? He handed it off to Riley, who then handed it to the elderly woman. Next, Zack encouraged the others close by to reform their circle, lit up a second joint, and passed it around. Finally, he waved Amanda over.

"Why not?" Amanda happily obliged.

Everyone except for Bret partook. Some handled the joint with considerable expertise, inhaling and exhaling as if they'd been doing it for years. Others held it gingerly and inhaled, instantly bursting into a coughing fit. The rookies earned giggles and smirks from their counterparts. Amanda harkened back to her college days and used a well-practiced technique.

It was a welcome moment of camaraderie. Fate had put a dozen strangers in the store at the exact time when Biscuit went off the deep end, but a few joints brought them together. They finally had something else to share besides their impending death.

When the effects finally kicked in, Amanda thought, *Why haven't I done this sooner?* Though it was legal in California, she hadn't done this in years. Decades. Not since becoming pregnant with her first child. She was sure her husband would have a thing or two to say about her choice, but screw him. She was the one facing death, not him, and if this was the end, she wanted to die with one less regret.

Then it came.

A door slammed shut and echoed throughout the building, causing every hostage to flinch, including Amanda. She glanced quickly at her fellow hostages, one by one. Each of their chests rose and fell to a rapid cadence. Clasped hands gripped more firmly after footsteps started and grew louder with each passing second.

Moments later, the wiry store manager appeared from the end of an aisle, holding the pistol in his right hand and a cordless phone in his left. Beads of perspiration dotted his forehead and streaked the sides of his jaw.

His complexion seemed paler, a disturbing sign he was on the verge of falling off a psychotic cliff. He kept his distance but focused his attention on the group with Hunter and several employees. "The boy escaped. Now I have to shoot one of you."

Amanda stood, trembling for the lives she and Dylan endangered. "This is my fault. I had to make sure my son was safe. He's only a little boy, for God's sake. If you have to shoot someone, shoot me."

"I don't want to do this, but I have no choice." Biscuit rapped his phone-toting fist against his temple before wagging the gun toward Zack and Riley. "Get up, Zack."

Zack squeezed his arm tighter around Riley's shoulder. "But I'm family, Uncle Del."

"Which is why it has to be you." Biscuit wiped a drop of sweat dangling over an eyebrow.

Amanda positioned herself between Zack and Biscuit. "You don't have to do this, Mr. Beckett. Zack did nothing wrong. I did. I'm the one who came up with the idea to push Dylan out the window. If anyone should be punished, it's me."

Biscuit grabbed at what little hair he had with both hands. "You don't understand. It has to be an employee."

"But why? It wasn't Zack's decision. It was mine." Amanda remembered her husband once regaling others with stories of a hostage standoff he'd responded to, during which the negotiator had worn down the suspect by asking questions and getting to the suspect's underlying fears. That tactic might work here.

"It just has to be, or more of you will die." Biscuit's statement made no sense unless he was an unwilling participant. Someone else must be pulling the strings. But why hadn't he said as much? Maybe whoever was making him do this had Biscuit over a barrel. Perhaps his life or family had been threatened if he let on that he wasn't in control. Amanda would have to play this carefully.

"I get the impression you really don't want to do this. You don't have to listen to the voices in your head, Mr. Beckett. Those voices only have power over you if you let them. You can stand up to them. I can help you. We all can."

Beckett eyed the hostages one by one as if judging if he could trust them to have his back. "You can't. I can't. If I choose the wrong person, more will die. It has to be him." He then pressed a button on the phone. "Nolan, my hands are tied. Are you listening?"

"You don't have to do this, Del," a male voice said through the phone.

Motion appeared from the aisle from where Biscuit had come. Whoever it was, they moved at a fast pace. It took Amanda a second to decipher Clarence's shape barreling toward Biscuit with his extended pocketknife in hand. His growl caused Biscuit to crane his head in that direction. Then simultaneously, Clarence lunged with the knife, plunging it into Biscuit's arm, while Biscuit turned and fired a single shot. Screams pierced the air. Both tumbled to the floor, creating a loud thud with Clarence lying atop Biscuit. Blood appeared on the linoleum, but Amanda was unsure whose it was. Both lay still.

20

After hearing Delmar Beckett say he was off to kill a hostage, Lexi's head throbbed from the nonstop spinning since stepping off the plane. So much had happened in the last several hours. Unfortunately, it was all circling around in her skull as if she were stuck in a high-speed blender. Her greatest nemesis was taunting her with those skill tests. She'd passed them, but at what cost? Nita wouldn't have taken off if she hadn't reached a breaking point. And that was on Lexi. She shouldn't have brought her girl-friend into this, knowing she was already on shaky ground with her addic-tion. At the very least, she should have asked Noah to ensure Nita didn't listen to her unnerving bomb assessment play-by-play. Now Lexi had to clean up her mess.

Dialing her phone, Lexi listened to it ring until it went to voicemail. Leaving a message seemed impersonal and insufficient, but she had no other choice until this crime scene was rendered safe. "I'm okay, Nita. I'll call again when I get a chance. Love you."

Lexi then punched in a text message to Noah. *Cleared the POW site. Returned to store scene. Take care of Nita. She needs a shoulder tonight. Will call when I can.* Pressing send, she knew Nita was in good hands.

Lexi slid the phone into her hip pocket in time to hear Agent Keene lose his temper with the Deputy Director of the FBI over the phone. "Dammit,

Jeff. He has Amanda. At least get the ball rolling... No, I don't plan on letting him escape custody. I just need him on that damn plane to buy us time until we can get the hostages out. Once Amanda is safe, we can throw him out the window for all I care. Thank you, Jeff. Let me know when he's at the gate."

Keene ended the call, turning his attention to Lexi and Detective Hughes. "Lyle Belcher is being processed for release. If his brother thinks we're cooperating, we have time. What do you have in mind?"

SWAT Commander Carver's wry smile and raised chin telegraphed his satisfaction of finally being called up to bat. "Belcher's plant inside the store complicates our options. It means any rescue plan will have to include stun grenades and rapid ingress and egress. That limits our options to the ground level. The weakest point is the wall with the window the kid escaped through. In the event of an escalation, we've also planned an emergency explosive breach through the front door."

"What's holding you back?" Keene asked.

Carver shifted his stare to Detective Hughes. "Ask him. He's in charge."

Delmar Beckett's voice came over the radio. "Nolan, my hands are tied. Are you listening?"

"You don't have to do this, Del," Detective Hughes pleaded.

A loud animal-like grunt came over the air, followed by the unmistakable crackle of a gunshot. Blood-curdling screams rang but were suddenly cut off.

Silence. The sound of death.

Then came one of the worst sounds the police could hear during a hostage negotiation—the dial tone of a disconnected call. Belcher's game of cat-and-mouse had suddenly changed.

Carver threw off his bulky headphones, reached for his tactical radio, and pressed the mic. "Cut the power. Cut the power."

Hughes snapped his head in Carver's direction. "What the hell are you doing?"

"My job." Carver stood, puffing his chest. "We now have an active shooter. That puts SWAT in command."

"Just wait a damn minute." Hughes raised a hand in frustration, forming a fist. "We have no idea what happened. Let me try to raise Del on the phone."

"You have one minute." Carver checked his watch as if starting the clock.

Hughes picked up the direct line, putting it on speaker. It rang, which was a good sign. That meant the phone connection inside the store was still intact. Two rings. Three. Four. Five. Six. Hughes let it ring twenty times until Carver made the call.

"That's it. Comms are out. Negotiations are over." Carver returned his attention to his tactical radio, engaging the mic again. "Prepare for breach."

"Breach?" Lexi couldn't believe what she'd heard. What in the hell did Carver cook up while she was gone? Any breach at this juncture was premature and dangerous. "We don't even know what charges are inside."

"You're a little behind, Mills." Carver handed her a drawing from Hughes' workstation. It appeared to be something Dylan might have drawn, showing a round device and marking a dozen locations. "My bomb squad leader estimates a kill radius of fifteen feet with these proximity devices. The boy showed the hostages huddled near the cash registers. They should be safe."

"Your bomb tech is basing his assessment on a child's drawing? I saw the devices up close at the POW site, and the kill radius was a lot bigger. Your guy is likening those devices to a fragmentation grenade. I guarantee you that those aren't it. A simultaneous explosion could bring down the building if those bombs are daisy-chained via a remote signal."

"We're out of options with that gunshot. Protocol says we breach." Carver's textbook-quoting tone was both grating and unnerving.

Lexi rolled her neck at the commander's narrow thinking. "At least try to ascertain the location of the hostages before you give the order."

"How do you propose I do that?" Carver's curt tone suggested he didn't expect a reasonable answer.

"Do you have a small drone that can fly through the window Dylan escaped from? If you do, put an earpiece on it and turn up the volume so someone can hear you."

Carver's eyes lit up. "Yes, we have one. That's a great idea." He pressed his mic again, explaining the mission to his SWAT element. "Send in the micro-drone... Put the feed on screen one."

Two minutes later, the main screen flickered. The static image of the storefront disappeared and was replaced by the moving live feed. If the drone was anything like the type the ATF used, it weighed less than a half-pound and could fit in Lexi's palm. It was an excellent surveillance tool but had limited flying time and range. Adding the weight of a fragile earpiece would lessen that time. Even if SWAT flew it inside, there was no guarantee it would have a clear path into the main store or broadcast its video through the cinderblock walls.

The drone flew at breakneck speed toward the building, slowing when the dumpster came into view and hovering when it reached the window. It jigged up and down and left and right until it lined up with the opening. Since the drone was too delicate to carry an infrared night vision camera, an onboard light switched on, showing the way inside. Once past the windowsill, the surroundings became apparent. The window led to a bathroom.

The drone rose a foot, escaping the toilet stall, immediately running into a stumbling block. The exit door was closed. Since this was a last-ditch effort to establish communication with the hostages, remaining unnoticed wasn't imperative. The remote pilot bounced the drone off the door, creating a clanking sound. Again. And again. It repeated so many times that Lexi was concerned the drone had reached the end of its flying time.

Finally, the door opened, and a woman came into view. She appeared fatigued and bloody. The microphone picked up her voice. "What the hell?"

Agent Keene called out, "That's my wife. That's Amanda."

A voice came over the radio. "This is the police. What's your situation?"

"We're—"

The screen filled with static, confirming Lexi's fear. Their one opportunity to make contact slipped through their fingers.

"What happened?" Keene yelled. "What in the hell just happened?"

"We just lost our last chance to establish communications. We need to go in through the back." Carver pressed his mic. "Prepare to breach."

Lexi turned her attention to Agent Keene. "That's a bad idea. They've set explosives to blow the door. That can set off a catastrophic explosion. You can stop this."

Keene rubbed the stubble on his jawline with a hand. "Belay that order. I'm declaring this a terrorist attack. It's now a federal crime, which puts the FBI in charge." He turned to Lexi. "What do you suggest?"

"I'm not sure yet, but I'm positive if SWAT breaches either entrance, it will end in disaster."

"Well, you better come up with something fast. The director is assigning another agent to take over. Find something convincing to hold off this thing. Otherwise, the next guy will order a breach for sure."

"Maybe I can convince them too. Who's coming?"

"You've already met him. It's Agent Terry Mitchell. He was your escort here."

"Shit." Lexi had met very few law enforcement officers who failed to impress her, but Agent Mitchell was one of them. If they had to rely on his judgment on what criteria were needed before approving a breach, every hostage inside was in more danger than five minutes ago.

"Shit is right. When I arrived, I sent Mitchell and his partner to dinner and told him I'd call if I needed him. I'm sure he's gotten the call from the regional office by now, but knowing him, he's at least a half-hour out, so you have that long."

21

Seconds after the shot, Biscuit squirmed underneath Clarence but couldn't free himself. Amanda darted toward them. If she could get the gun, maybe she could convince Biscuit to tell her what was really going on. However, she couldn't locate the pistol, so she shoved Clarence to one side. Zack got up from his seat on the floor and helped roll Clarence over. When Amanda turned to look for the gun again, Biscuit pressed its muzzle against the side of her head.

"Don't move." He picked up the cordless phone by his hip and put it to his ear. "Nolan?" He then grunted and threw it to the floor. "It's dead."

"I only want to help you, Mr. Beckett." Amanda hoped her calm tone would defuse the situation.

Biscuit squirmed several feet backward on his butt, still pointing the gun at Amanda and holding his left arm close to his torso. Blood trickled down his sleeve, but not at an alarming rate. "I'm not buying that for one minute."

Amanda glanced toward Clarence as he writhed on the floor. "How bad is he?"

Zack scanned Clarence's body. "I think he got hit in the lower leg."

"Let me help." Hunter stepped forward. "I flew in the Air Force and know tactical first aid." While Biscuit held the gun at the ready, Hunter located Clarence's knife and sliced his pant leg open, exposing the wound. Blood streamed from Clarence's right calf. "It appears to be a through and through, but I'll need to stop the bleeding. Is there a first aid kit handy?"

"It's by the front door," Bret said, "but we can't get to it without setting off the bomb."

"How about from the store shelves?" Hunter asked.

"You can't get to them either." Biscuit winced. "First aid is on aisle five with one of the bombs, but I don't know how to shut them off."

Two things came to light with Biscuit's statement. First, he confirmed he wasn't holding them hostage willingly. Second, it highlighted the absurdness of their situation. The store had enough first aid supplies to save a small army, but they couldn't get to them to save Clarence's life.

"How about duct tape and some clean cloth?" Hunter asked.

"We have a roll at a register," Bret replied.

"I'll also need some water to flush out the wound and something to clean it with," Hunter added.

"My apron is fresh." Maria removed it from her waist.

"That's perfect." Hunter stretched the apron to its fullest, inspecting its configuration. "The ties will help to bind the wound."

"I have some hand sanitizer," the older woman added. "Would that help?"

"Alcohol is better."

"There's some vodka on the last end cap." Zack rose to his feet. "I'll get a bottle."

They were still one group, no longer strangers. They were working together to save a man each of them had likely walked past every day without acknowledging his existence. Amanda was guilty of it herself but was proud of their teamwork now.

Supplies collected, Hunter poured water on Clarence's gunshot wound, flushing out debris and gunpowder. Next came the painful part. "This is going to hurt, but it has to be done to reduce your chance of infection." Following a confirming nod, Hunter poured vodka liberally over the wound. Screams of pain echoed off the store rafters, but Hunter worked quickly to apply and tighten the makeshift bandage.

Once Clarence was out of immediate danger, all eyes turned to

Biscuit, who still had his weapon trained on the group. The others appeared as if they were ready to tar and feather him in the public square if not for the handgun pointed in their direction. They clearly hadn't picked up on Biscuit's cues and were uniformly focused on their outrage.

When Biscuit winced in pain from his knife wound, Gail, the athletic soccer mom, snatched the knife from the floor several feet away from him. Then Bret lunged toward him. Hurt and scared, Biscuit would likely shoot to protect himself. But if he didn't, Bret, a strong man half his age, would easily overpower him. After that, mob mentality would take over. Something had to be done to prevent the foreseeable mayhem, so Amanda put herself in harm's way, lunging in Bret's path to stop him.

"Wait!" Amanda yelled, putting up both hands chest-high in a stopping motion.

Bret came to a grinding halt. "Are you crazy? That was our one chance of getting out of here." The anger in his eyes was so sharp it could have cut right through steel.

"Have you been listening?" Amanda took in a calming breath. Cooler heads needed to prevail. "Someone forced Biscuit to do this."

"What are you talking about?" Bret snarled.

Amanda spun on her heel, looking Beckett in the eye. He was quivering, half from fear, half from pain. "Tell me I'm wrong."

"They took my family, for God's sake." Beckett held back a sob and dropped the gun in his lap. "They said they'd kill my wife and kids if I didn't do what they wanted."

"Who are *they*?" Amanda asked.

"There are two of them. I met one man who took my family and talked to another man on the phone. Belcher is his name. He's giving the orders and controlling the bombs."

"Why is he doing this?" Amanda pressed.

"All I know is that an agent with the ATF has a history with him, and now he wants his brother out of prison."

"So we're part of a prisoner exchange?" Amanda shook her head, knowing demands like Belcher's were rarely met. "The police are going to stall as long as possible."

"They have two hours to make it happen, or we get blown to pieces." The fear in Beckett's eyes suggested he was telling the truth.

"Then why were you supposed to kill one of us?"

"To teach you all a lesson and show the police that Belcher means business. I tried to ignore him and tell him no, but when someone slipped a note under my door, telling me they'd kill the hostages one by one if I didn't, I realized that one of you is working for Belcher."

An eerie silence enveloped the building. One of them wasn't a hostage after all. They were their captor, but who? Amanda scanned the group, eyeing each one up and down. They were all doing the same. One of them was a mole.

Suddenly, the lights went off inside the store. Even the soda refrigerator stopped working. The police had cut the power, leaving only the battery-powered emergency light near the cash registers to illuminate their area. Amanda turned her head toward the front door, rows of faint light finding their way past the slats of the security screen. But the scary part was the red glow of the proximity device attached to the sliding metal slat door. It was a frightening reminder they were still in grave danger. Amanda then swung around to scan the central part of the store. Her heart nearly stopped, finding a dozen more red glows. They were trapped inside in a veritable minefield.

Amanda snapped her head around at Biscuit. "Please tell me you told the police how many bombs we're dealing with."

"I didn't have time to tell them." Biscuit wiped the sweat dripping from his forehead.

"Then they might not know that one explosion could cascade and bring down the entire building and kill everyone inside. Where are our cell phones?"

"Belcher made me smash them. Wait." Beckett then patted both front pockets with the hand from his uninjured arm. "He gave me a cell phone. It's in my pocket. Can you help me get it out?"

Amanda gingerly slipped her thumb and index finger into his pocket and pulled it out with some effort. She flipped it open, but the broken hinge didn't give her much hope of contacting the outside world. Pressing the green send button, she expected a dial tone but heard nothing. She then tried the power button but got the same results. "It's broken," she sighed. They had one last hope. "What about merchandise? Does the store sell prepaid phones?"

"Yes, but they're on an aisle with one of those damn things. I'm so sorry, Miss." Biscuit groaned loudly, a sign the knife injury was taking its toll. Amanda knelt beside him and pressed a towel Bret had found against his oozing wound. He clutched her sleeve with a bloody hand. "But thank you for believing me. I wanted none of this to happen."

"I do believe you. Now we need to figure out which one of us is working for Belcher before they kill someone." Amanda turned her focus on Hunter as he finished binding Clarence's gunshot wound. Could he be Belcher's mole? She'd paid enough attention to the news and her husband to know he fit the profile—a young white male with a military background. But if he wanted them dead, why would he administer first aid? She put her suspicions aside and ignored the palpable mistrust in the air. "Hunter, can you patch up Mr. Beckett next?"

"I'm on it," Hunter replied, gathering the makeshift bandages and supplies.

Bret snatched the gun from Biscuit and aimed it at his chest. "I still don't trust you."

Amanda watched Hunter tend to Biscuit's wound like a pro. As he wrapped up, a faint banging noise had heads turning left and right, searching for the source. It continued every few seconds. It had to be the police trying to make contact. "I'm going to check out that noise."

"I'm coming with you." Riley caught up even with Amanda and continued, "You're one of the few I trust."

"Who else do you trust?"

"Zack. I met him in high school. He wouldn't harm a fly. But, beyond him, I don't know anyone else well enough to trust them with my life."

"That's good to know, but why do you trust me?" Riley talked a good game, but Amanda couldn't be sure if she'd thrown a fake to make her think she wasn't the mole. Trust would have to be earned.

"Your son. You seem like a good mother. You'd never put him in danger."

"Okay then. Let's find what's causing that noise."

Amanda proceeded with caution, staying clear of every red glow in the building. Each time the banging sounded, she and Riley went in a different direction. This was worse than narrowing down which smoke alarm was beeping from a low battery at three o'clock in the morning.

The noise repeated. This time, Amanda determined its general location —the bathroom hallway. "This way."

After six more bangs, she narrowed it down to the men's room and slowly pushed the door open. The room was dimly lit like the hallway, illuminated by an emergency light. A whirring sound met her next, followed by something hovering five feet off the floor. "What the hell?"

A voice came from the device. "This is the police. What's your situation?"

It took a moment for Amanda to realize she was staring at a police drone. "We're—" she got out before the drone fell to the floor, bouncing once. "No, no, no, no, no." Their only means to contact the outside had crashed.

22

Coby Vasquez glanced at the patrol cruiser speedometer from the backseat. It read ninety-eight miles per hour. *Highway Patrol has all the fun*, he thought. Unlike the movies, the life of an FBI agent was bland, with most investigations happening on computers and most arrests going down peacefully. However, tonight's high-speed escort represented the most excitement he'd experienced during his five years on the job. Unfortunately, tonight, he wasn't looking forward to the task his ASAC had given him and his partner, Lathan Sinclair. When he joined the FBI, he envisioned hauling in the bad guys, not releasing them back into the wild before they served their time. But here he was, doing just that.

He peeked at his watch. They had no time to spare. With the siren whirring and the overhead red and blue lights spinning, the light night traffic on Highway 99 had thankfully pulled to the slow lane along their route from the resident agency location in Fresno to the United States Penitentiary Atwater. If he calculated correctly, they'd arrive ten minutes before the deadline.

A few miles north of central Merced, the officer peeled off the highway onto Franklin Road. She glanced over her shoulder. "We're about six minutes out."

Correction: a twelve-minute cushion. Once they arrived, Coby would have twelve minutes to get Lyle Belcher into the cruiser, on the plane, and dial that satellite phone.

Coby eyed his new partner briefly. Lathan was an unknown. He'd reported to the Fresno office last month, but Coby had yet to see what he was like in the field. Though, his outburst over the jammed copy machine was eye-opening. Kicking a highly sensitive piece of equipment showed himself as a hothead, not a problem solver.

Zipping through the outskirts of town, the officer narrowly avoided a car turning into their traffic lane. The maneuver, coupled with her catlike reflexes, would have earned her a seat behind the wheel with any team in NASCAR. She then zagged her way through potato and tomato fields, past the end of the runway at the regional airport, until making the final sweeping turn onto Federal Way. If memory served, the high-security federal prison and its support buildings were the only structures on this road.

The officer radioed when the prison yard outline, lit by hundreds of fluorescents, came into view. "Approaching via the intake gate." She slowed but cruised through the entrapment area at a decent clip, coming to a stop at the processing building. "Safe and sound, fellas, with time to spare."

"Impressive taxi service, Officer Kimball." Coby leaned forward. "Keep the meter running. We'll be right back with our package."

Coby and Sinclair piled out of the cruiser and jogged the short distance to the entrance with their credentials at the ready. The guard at the door put up a hand in a stopping motion and reached back with his other, resting it on the grip of his holstered service weapon. "Wait. I have to confirm your credentials."

He and Sinclair came to a skidding halt. Sinclair took in a sharp breath. "We don't have time for this crap."

Yep, a hothead, Coby thought. "Just do it," he ordered. Coby had been in the FBI six months longer than Sinclair and thankfully had seniority. His gut told him that keeping this guy in check would be challenging on a night when cool heads were a must.

Coby then flipped his credentials open, displaying his ID and FBI badge. "Agents Vasquez and Sinclair. We're here for prisoner Belcher."

The guard verified their identity in ten seconds and buzzed the exterior door. "Good luck, fellas. He's been brought up and is waiting in a holding cell."

"Thanks." Coby stepped through first. Four people occupied the sterile-looking, brightly lit intake area. Two uniformed, armed prison guards stood beside a thin young man in a cheap suit holding a bulky envelope. In front of them was a woman dressed crisply in a business suit. She was his point of contact. He approached, offering his hand.

"Warden Biggs. I'm Agent Vasquez. This is Agent Sinclair. Thank you for having the prisoner ready for us."

She shook his hand. "When the attorney general calls himself, things happen at breakneck speed."

"Did you locate the sat phone that supposedly was delivered today?"

"We did." Warden Biggs waved up the man standing several steps behind her. He handed the envelope to Coby. "It's fully charged. We worked with your team in Sacramento to get what intel from it we could. Unfortunately, it came back as stolen."

"Very thorough, thank you," Coby said. "Are there any special precautions we should take with the prisoner?"

"He doesn't look threatening, but that's his secret weapon. His small stature and unassuming appearance put our guards at ease when he arrived, but we discovered on the first day that he's stealthy, quick, and very dangerous. He put one guard in a coma and broke both arms of another before we could subdue him."

"What set him off?"

"His soup was cold."

"That's good to know. Can we see him now?"

"Absolutely." Warden Biggs directed the guards to take Agents Vasquez and Sinclair to the holding pen. When Coby turned to follow, she placed a hand on his arm. "Never turn your back on him."

Coby acknowledged with a silent "thank you."

Once inside a secondary secure area, the guard escorted the agents to the middle cell. One man occupied it. He was restrained by a full harness over his khaki prisoner uniform and black work shoes. A belly chain connected leg irons and his cuffed hands in front at the waist. With Belcher's chin pinned to his chest, Coby couldn't see his face. However, based on his posture from his seat on the metal bench, he could tell Belcher was slender.

"Let's get him up." Coby gestured with his hand.

As if his order was a stage cue, Lyle Belcher slowly lifted his chin and stood. The warden's assessment was spot on. He was not more than five foot seven or eight and had the face of an elementary school teacher. If Coby had passed him on the street, he would have never suspected him of masterminding a failed attempt to overthrow the government, putting a bullet into the heads of five people, and ordering the deaths of eighteen more. Amadeus, as he was known to his followers, was a wolf in sheep's clothing.

A guard waved his hand in the air, signaling for someone in the control room to unlock the cell door. When the lock buzzed and clicked, he slid the door open and ordered, "Step forward."

A disquieting grin formed on Amadeus' lips. It was slight, but his silence and steely eyes gave Coby the impression he expected him. That he already knew what his brother was up to, putting Coby and Sinclair at a disadvantage. Other than a general heading of Las Vegas, Coby was in the dark, making the warden's warning more profound. He wouldn't turn his back on this man. Not for one second.

Amadeus stepped out of the cell. Each guard took him by the elbow and led him to the processing area lobby, where the warden was still waiting. She eyed him as he passed, seemingly relieved that Amadeus was no longer her responsibility.

Once outside, the guards ushered him into the back seat of the CHP cruiser. One said, "Good luck," before handing Coby the keys to the shackles and they both retreated into the building.

"I'll take the backseat." Coby heeded the warden's warning. He wanted Amadeus by his side, not at his back. After Sinclair hopped into the front passenger seat, Coby jumped into the back. "Let's go."

Officer Kimball punched it across the yard, out the entrapment area, and onto Federal Way. Lights and sirens weren't necessary. The airfield was already in sight. When she swerved around the end of the runway, Amadeus slid across the backbench and into Coby's side. Sitting next to this evil man was bad enough, but touching him from shoulder to thigh made his skin crawl.

The cruiser came out of the turn, but Amadeus remained pressed against him. He was testing Coby. Squirming or pushing Amadeus away would signal weakness—disgust or fear. Either was a powerful emotion that could be construed as exploitable. Coby refused to take the bait and remained still, testing Amadeus' resolve.

The officer radioed ahead, and the airport gate's rent-a-cop waved her through.

Flying through the access point, the officer gunned it toward the USFD smokejumper plane idling at the end of the runway. She glanced over her shoulder, coming to an abrupt stop near the open passenger hatch. "God-speed, you two."

Sinclair hopped out.

"I'll keep you on speed dial for the return trip." Coby winked before exiting the back and pulling Amadeus by the arm with him.

A pilot wearing an olive-green jumpsuit greeted them and waved them on board. Sinclair ascended the steep, wobbly stairs first and pulled Amadeus up while Coby pushed from the tarmac.

"Anyone else?" he asked.

"No. This is it."

"Buckle in a jump seat. We're cleared for takeoff." The pilot went forward, taking the co-pilot's chair. At the same time, Coby directed Amadeus to a seat near the midpoint of the fuselage and buckled him in. Coby sat directly across while Sinclair sat two seats down from Coby.

The two propeller engines roared within seconds, and they began rolling down the runway. Amadeus leaned his head back as the craft gained speed, letting a broad smile form, acknowledging that he had won. That his freedom was on the horizon.

While still coasting, Coby retrieved the sat phone from his wind-breaker pocket. The instant the wheels lifted off the ground, he showed it to Amadeus. "Your brother is expecting a call. What number should I dial?"

Amadeus said the number, maintaining the slight, evil grin. Coby entered it, pressed send, and activated the speaker. The phone rang three times before the call connected. "Four minutes early. To whom do I have the pleasure of speaking?" the male voice said. Amadeus' smirk meant it had to be his brother.

Coby spoke loudly over the hum of the engines. "My name doesn't matter, Mr. Belcher. It's enough to know that my partner and I are agents with the Federal Bureau of Investigation, and we have your brother. We're in the air and have you on speaker."

"Amadeus?" Belcher asked through the phone.

"Yes, brother. I have waited for you to keep your word."

"You sound well."

"That is because we will be together soon."

"We will celebrate soon, my brother." Belcher sounded annoyingly confident. Coby would like nothing more than to prove him wrong. "Agent in Charge, please pass along my regards to Lexi Mills and Agent Keene for their prompt action. If you do exactly as I say, I will let the hostages go."

"What do you want me to do?"

"In thirty minutes, call me again. I will confirm with my brother that you are still en route and provide the exact coordinates for your destination. Goodbye, brother. We will speak soon."

The call went dead.

Coby returned the phone to his pocket, set his watch timer to go off in thirty minutes, and locked his stare on Amadeus.

During the drive to Atwater, he'd read the files on the Belcher brothers he'd uploaded to his agency phone before leaving the Fresno office. The moment he read the words "the Red Spades," his pulse picked up. The terrorist group's name led every national news for weeks following the failed assassination attempt on the Texas governor. In the aftermath, Agent Lexi Mills had become a legend in federal law enforcement circles. She was an example of how one good agent, simply doing the job they'd trained for, could change the course of history. Now he was in the thick of it with the Belcher brothers, and it was his turn to step up and do his job as well as she had.

23

Amanda darted toward the drone, the door closing behind her. She picked it up. The thing was light, weighing less than a pound. It was hard to make out in the scant light, but she thought plastic shards were on the floor where the drone had fallen. A closer inspection determined a blade had broken and maybe a section of casing. However, the camera lens on the front appeared intact, giving her hope.

She pointed it at her face. "Hello? Can you hear me?" But no response came. She wished she knew what to look for—a light perhaps—for signs the thing still had power. Power? Maybe it was like those dang smoke detectors and needed a fresh battery.

The door crept open. Riley poked her head inside. "Amanda, are you okay?"

"Yes, I'm fine. The police sent in a drone, but it died." Amanda flipped it over, looking for a battery compartment but found a charging port. "This takes a USB cable to charge. Do you have a cable for it? Maybe we can power this thing up."

"No, but we sell them at the checkout stands. I'm sure we can find something."

Energized by a new optimism, Amanda rushed out the door, down the hallway, and toward the registers. She and Riley drew the others' attention while they went from check stand to check stand until they found what they needed. After ripping open the cardboard packages, Riley asked the group, "Does anyone have a charged battery pack?"

"I do. It's at my register." The young cashier stepped to her workstation and fumbled through her pack hidden under the counter.

Amanda plugged the drone in, and the yellow charging light came to life. If this was anything like her son's toys, she'd have to wait a while before it received enough of a charge to use. Her mind jumped ahead to what she should do with it once powered.

"What do you have?" Gail asked. The others who weren't injured gathered around.

"This made the noise. It's a police drone that ran out of power, so I'm trying to charge it."

Gail's eyes lit up for the first time since this ordeal began. "Does that mean we could talk to the police? Could we get a message?"

"I'm not sure. It clearly has a camera, and I know they saw me. I heard a voice before it crashed, so it has a microphone and a speaker. Unfortunately, it cracked when it fell to the ground. It might not work."

Soon, another light turned on near the charging port. This one was green, giving Amanda hope this thing might work. She located and pressed the power button. The thing whirred like it did before, but only one blade spun. "Hello? Hello? Can you hear me?" The speaker garbled static, which was a bad sign. Amanda couldn't be sure if someone on the other end knew the drone had powered up again or if the camera was probably working. It was impossible to know if they could communicate via sign language.

"We're screwed." Riley slumped her shoulders.

"I think you're right." Hopes dashed, Amanda placed the drone on the edge of the register counter, watching the mini spotlight in the front flash on and off several times. *The darn thing must have a short in it*, she thought. She leaned her bottom against the register counter, burying her face in her hands. They were out of options and would have to wait for another sign from the police. It looked like the only way out of here was in a body bag or by some miraculous rescue mission.

Amanda finally let herself cry. She'd held it together until now because she had hoped this event would end peacefully. Getting Dylan out and having the group focus on basic needs had kept her busy. But now, there was nothing more she could do but wait.

"Why so glum, momma?" Clarence asked from his makeshift hospital bed of jackets and cat food bags from the end of an aisle.

Amanda had surmised early on that Clarence suffered from mental illness. His erratic movements and occasional mumbling were common signs of it. She knew he meant well, which required her patience, but she had run out. "Not now, Clarence."

"I don't mean to make you mad, momma."

Amanda took in a calming breath, remembering the lesson she'd taught her children: always be kind even if someone makes you mad. They might be having the worst day of their life. She looked up. "I'm sorry, Clarence. The pressure must be getting to me. I'm upset that this thing doesn't work."

"But it does. It says it sees you."

"What?" Amanda blinked to clear her frustration.

Hunter cocked his head several times. "He's right." His voice ended in an excited uptick. He then turned to Clarence and patted him on the upper arm. "You're a genius. You must have comms training."

Clarence straightened his upper torso the best he could from the floor and gave Hunter a sharp salute. "Staff Sergeant Clarence Weber reporting for duty, sir." Hunter returned the salute.

"What are you two talking about?" Amanda was too tired to decipher Clarence's musings.

"Look at the light." Hunter pointed straight at the drone and paused for several seconds. "It's flashing two letters in Morse code: C-U."

The energy in the room pulsated a growing positive vibe as everyone's attention focused on the tiny spotlight. Amanda studied the flashes, looking for a sign that they weren't caused by an electrical short. In less than a minute, she recognized the pattern of dash-dot-dash-dot, followed by a brief pause and dot-dot-dash, repeating on a loop. It was clear. The police had eyes on them but not ears. It wasn't much, but it was more than they'd had since this ordeal started. "This is great. We can make contact."

"How is this great?" Gail asked. "Other than showing them what's in here, the police can't talk to us."

"But *we* can talk to them."

"How? We don't know if the microphone works," Gail countered.

"It doesn't matter. I can sign and pass along messages."

"What should we tell them?" the older woman asked.

Hunter stood with a perfect posture, finally looking the part of a career military man. Mr. Quiet had found his stride. "We need to show them the locations of the explosive devices first. They need to know what they're up against."

"And us," Riley added. "They need to know who is in here."

"I'll do it." Bret moved toward the checkout stand where Amanda had left the lame drone.

Hunter lurched forward, cutting him off. "We'll do it." He snatched the drone and battery pack from its perch, before stepping toward Amanda and handing them to her. He kept his eye on Bret. "I don't trust you."

"Well, I don't trust *you*. Who in the hell put you in charge?" Bret gave Hunter a forceful shove, sailing him into Amanda. The collision drove Amanda's knee backward too hard and too fast. The pain was instant.

"That's enough!" Amanda barked, grabbing her aching leg. "This is what Belcher and his mole want. For us to distrust each other. To divide us so we'll be at their mercy. If we want to get out of here alive, we need to trust one another." The pain transitioned from sharp to throbbing, signifying that her knee might be sprained or worse. She tested its sturdiness and determined it was painful but usable.

Bret balled his fists, refusing to back down. But then the elderly woman got up from her stool with the look of an angry Sunday school teacher. "Oh, for heaven's sake, young man. Put your peashooter away. This isn't the time for a pissing contest."

A brief round of muffled snickers broke out.

"She's right." Zack stepped forward. "We need to work together like we did to get the little man out. Amanda and Hunter should do it. She's the only one who can use sign language, and if that thing flashes a different message, he needs to decode it."

Amanda inspected the device again. It looked fragile, so she and Hunter would have to be extra careful with it. When she returned it to him, he gave her a firm nod, but she kept her grip on the battery long enough to say, "I trust you."

"Let's get to work, and maybe we'll get out of here alive." Hunter walked several feet toward the front entrance with Amanda, stopping when they had a good view of the rolling security door. They remained a safe distance back while Hunter held the drone, so the camera captured the attached explosive device. "I'll hold it for a twenty count, then turn the camera around so you can sign its location and that it has a motion sensor."

"Got it," Amanda said. After they completed the first device, the drone flashed a different sequence of dots and dashes. "They're sending another message."

Hunter flipped the drone around and observed the flashing light for thirty seconds. "I'm a little rusty with my Morse code, but I think they said 'Received.'"

The exhilaration of hope swelled Amanda's chest. "It's working, every-one! It's working! They got our message!" An optimism-filled chatter started with several asking to get a message to their loved ones. "Hold on, people. Let us finish showing the police the explosives, then we'll be right back."

She and Hunter repeated the documentation process from the end of several aisles until they covered each glowing light in the main store. Amaz-ingly, the path to Beckett's office became clear. Now for the final location: the back door. They cautiously entered the storage area through the double swinging doors, minimizing the motion of the panel Hunter had pushed. Once the rigged door flanked by stacks of produce crates on either side came into view, they stopped and captured the door and its rigged explosive on camera. Amanda then provided context.

"Who do you think is the mole," Hunter asked quietly.

"My money was on you until you patched up Clarence and Beckett. If you wanted us dead, you wouldn't have helped. Now, I'm not sure. How about you?"

Hunter snorted. "I'm not ruling out anyone, even you. As far as I know, you could be signing gibberish. The whole bit with having Dylan in here could have been part of your cover. I find it too convenient that he was the only one to escape."

"That's rather cynical."

"It comes from getting screwed one time too many."

"Then why are you helping if you don't trust me?"

"Because you were right about working together. This is our only chance, so I'm taking it."

"Fair enough." Amanda thought a level of distrust that deep could be useful at a time like this. No one would catch him off guard. "Let's get back to the group."

Hunter held the camera in front of each hostage, with Amanda spelling out their names and passing along brief messages. She started with Clarence, who didn't have a message, but Amanda explained his circumstance and that his gunshot wound was bandaged and the bleeding was under control. Surprisingly, the young cashier was camera shy and took some coaxing. As expected, most choked up when mouthing their messages to their loved ones, even Hunter when he said goodbye to his wife. But Gail remained stoic, saying, "Mommy loves you." Her only emotional tell was nervously dropping her purse and fumbling to pick up its contents. Finally, when she came to Beckett, she explained he was an unwilling participant and that he suspected one hostage was a Belcher plant.

When it was Amanda's turn, she reflected on what she wanted to say to her family, tossing out the idea of creating individual messages to everyone she cared about. That would take too long. Instead, she settled on one. "Mom, Dad, Maxwell, Michael, Tess, Dylan. You have filled my life with joy. No matter what happens, stay strong. I love you all." Amanda signed off with a message to the police. "That's it. Please help us."

24

Squirrelly leaned over the countertop and asked so only Nita could hear, "How much do you need?"

"A quarter," Nita replied. A quarter gram would be enough to give her a taste and keep her mind off the torturous waiting for a few hours.

"I sell by the half."

Double the amount Nita had in mind for a stress reliever, a half gram bordered on excessive. She'd have to exercise restraint to not go overboard and dump the rest before leaving. So far, self-control wasn't a problem. It wasn't like she popped opioids every day. She did it only when she needed them for pain or a temporary escape. Once every week or two wasn't addiction. Was it? *I can do this,* Nita told herself. *I have the discipline to limit myself to just a quarter.*

"Fine."

"That'll be fifty." Squirrelly used a quiet tone. "I'm on break in a few minutes. I'll come by your table."

"That won't work," Nita replied. A disturbing image of Noah slapping the cuffs on her and Squirrelly after wiping French fry grease from his fingers flashed in her head. "Can we go somewhere else?"

"Uptight date?"

"Something like that."

"I can't leave the building." Squirrelly waved to a loud customer when he yelled for another drink. "I'll walk by your table, and we can meet in the bathroom hallway."

Nita grabbed her and Noah's drinks and answered him with a single nod. Then, escaping the patrons crowding the bar, she returned to the table to count the minutes. She placed Noah's beer bottle in front of him.

"Thanks." Noah pointed toward her cell on the table. "Your phone rang while you were gone."

"Thanks." Nita sat and chugged half her drink, debating whether to swipe her screen. If the missed call wasn't from Lexi, it would confirm that she wasn't out of danger yet, and Nita couldn't do anything but wait. But if the call was from her, telling her that the threat was over, Nita would face a decision: was this the life she wanted? She wasn't ready to make that choice with everything going on, especially not in a strange bar halfway across the country after sucking down her first drink she'd had in years. That was something she needed to figure out at home while sober.

Nita placed her cocktail down and ran both hands across her face, rubbing her eyelids. She wasn't sure what was getting to her most, the curiosity or the tension. Whatever the cause, she needed Squirrelly to come sooner than later. Until he showed up with the party favors, Nita would ignore her dilemma and her phone.

"Are you okay?" Noah asked.

"If I was okay, I wouldn't be in a bar having a drink."

"I get how nerve-wracking this is. Would you prefer to go back to the hotel?" Noah's phone dinged to an incoming alert. He picked it up and read the screen. "Great news, Nita. Lexi cleared the devices at the POW site and is back at the grocery store scene." He reached across the table and squeezed her hand. "We can both take a breath now."

Nita massaged her temples in small circles. "This isn't over, Noah. There's still a store full of hostages and bombs. I saw what Dylan drew. There must be a dozen. Lexi might be the best at her job, but can she defeat that?"

"Lexi is smart and calm under pressure. Plus, there's an entire team of SWAT men and women there to help her figure out a way to bring this to a safe end. Trust in that."

Squirrelly approached their table with a dirty bar towel draped over a shoulder. "How are we doing here? Is there anything else I can get you?"

Noah looked at him with a steely eye while sipping his beer. "No, I think we're good."

Squirrelly gave Noah a confirming nod before disappearing into the hallway a few feet away. That was Nita's cue. She downed the rest of her drink and stuffed her phone into her purse without looking at it. Then, she pushed her chair back and stood, slinging the satchel over her uninjured shoulder. "I'll be right back. I need to use the restroom."

"Are you done with your food?" Noah asked. "Should I have it boxed up so you can have the leftovers later?"

"Sure, that would be great." Eating was the last thing on Nita's mind. She would have agreed to have her head shaved if it meant getting out of there before Squirrelly thought she'd changed her mind.

Walking down the narrow, dimly lit corridor surfaced four-month-old flashbacks of the Beebo Club massacre. The eerily similar passageway had her taking shallow breaths as she recalled screams, terrified faces, and the sexy butch dropping dead in her arms. She'd barely escaped with her life, but she was one of the lucky ones. Thirteen took their dying breath in that club. Twenty-seven more were hospitalized with wounds more severe than her single bullet to the shoulder.

"Are you okay, Grey Goose?" Squirrelly's voice snapped Nita out of her recurring nightmare and into her current one. "You look pale."

"What? Yeah. I guess I need the pick-me-up more than I realized." She scanned up and down the hallway before pulling money from her wallet. "Fifty."

"Half a g." He exchanged the money for a small, sealed baggie containing the one white lady who never failed to turn her on. She always gave Nita a euphoria more potent than sex and laid Nita out with one hell of a punch when she left. The climb was as intense as the fall. "This is pretty potent stuff. You should go light on the first taste."

"Thanks." Nita gripped the bag extra tight as if losing it would mean the end of the world. "I appreciate the prompt service. I'll have to give this place five stars."

Squirrelly headed back toward the main dining room, leaving Nita alone. Despite California's progressiveness, an empty public hallway was not the place to gum coke. Slipping into the ladies' room, she quickly determined that only the first of the three stalls was occupied, so she headed for the furthest one.

The first door sprang open when she walked by, revealing a forty-something brunette with a hinged knee brace on her left leg. The woman maneuvered with a considerable limp. If Nita had to guess, she was six weeks post-op from knee surgery, either a replacement or ligament repair. And the hitch in her gait suggested the woman also suffered from hip pain. In Nita's professional opinion, she could benefit from a regimental course of physical therapy to stretch and strengthen her legs and core.

Hearing the woman at the sink, Nita stepped into the last stall. She re-slung her purse and pulled apart the two upper edges of the baggie but froze when she heard a voice. "Excuse me... of course," a woman said.

The main door creaked, making her think the woman had left. She waited a moment, listening to the silence, then confidently reopened her supply of white, powdery bliss. The anticipation born from the experience of several hundred snorts made her mouth water. So did the alcohol, now that it had kicked in fully. But she didn't have the time or tools to chop the coke into fine powder. Her only option was to rub a small amount on her gums. It was a method that worked as quickly as snorting but risked creating lesions with prolonged use. However, two or three times in one night posed only the threat of numbness. And within fifteen minutes, she'd welcome that familiar boost of energy and confidence, two critical attributes she'd lacked for months.

A knock on the stall door startled her. "Nita, I know today has been overwhelming." She recognized Noah's voice. "But this isn't the answer. Let me help you."

Nita brought a shaky hand to her forehead. She'd been slipping for weeks, or was it months? In either case, the woman she'd been living with had been oblivious to her backslide. Tears pooled in her eyes while she weighed the likely explanations. Either she had become too good at hiding her emotions, or Lexi was more attentive to her job than her. Both options spelled doom for their relationship because neither was giving their full measure.

However, in a mere few hours, Noah had diagnosed her predicament and had taken the bold, caring steps of calling her out while offering a life preserver. He'd offered the one thing she'd needed from Lexi since taking that first step downward. If she didn't grab on to the lifeline he was offering, she'd float away.

Nita crept the door open, the hinges squeaking her gratitude. His pained gaze spoke of a genuine worry. "I feel so lost, Noah. I don't know who I am anymore."

"Do you know who you want to be?"

"I want to be the person Lexi fell in love with."

Noah grabbed her left arm and extended it, exposing the bend and the camouflaged reminder of the lowest point in her life—track marks hidden under layers of tattoos. "Then you start by remembering what bottom felt like, flush whatever you bought from the bartender down the toilet, and order a cup of coffee."

"You make it sound so easy."

"Fighting for your life is never easy, but it can be simple if you remember what's waiting for you on the other side."

Nita clutched the cocaine tighter. Noah had said it wasn't the answer, but it was her escape from the truth she refused to face—she and Lexi were pulling apart. "I think it's too late for Lexi and me." She should have listened to her instincts when Lexi left her desk job at the ATF. She should have known that a relationship between a therapist and a former patient would never work. Once Lexi returned to her life before losing her leg, her interest was destined to wane.

"I'm not talking about Lexi." Noah placed his hands on her shoulders, applying light pressure on both to not irritate her injury. "I'm talking about you. Stop finding excuses and fight for the person *you* want to be. Whether you're with Lexi shouldn't matter. You first need to love yourself."

And that was the core of her circumstance. She'd been finding excuses to justify every wrong choice, and he saw right through it. That launched a tsunami of emotion, crumbling her protective seawall and sending her into his arms. He held her tight, stopping her from slipping into the sea. The bottom was in sight, but Noah's strength was infectious. It made her think she could climb her way back up.

"Now, how about you take that leap of faith and give that blow a burial at sea?" Noah released his hold.

Nita laughed through her tears. He'd come up with the perfect metaphor. "Aye, aye, captain." She swayed a bit from the vodka, giving him a two-finger salute. Then, steadying herself, she held the baggie over the toilet and shook its contents into the bowl. The water instantly absorbed the powder, creating a small white cloud before dissipating. If the hurdles she faced could vanish that quickly, she'd be back to her old self in no time.

Nita kicked the handle with the bottom of her sneaker, giving Squirrelly's finest product a salute on the way down. "I feel better already."

"I knew you could do this. You're stronger than you realize, Nita."

"Lexi says the same thing to me when I'm feeling down, but most times, I end up a crying mess when she leaves. And leaving me alone is what she does best these days."

"It's not like she's had a choice. Since saving the governor, her job and the media frenzy have taken away most of her free time. But you, young lady"—Noah spun her around until they faced each other again—"should never doubt yourself. Anyone who can put herself through college and grad school by working two part-time jobs and bounce back from an injury like yours has a deep pool of inner strength."

She wiped the moisture from her eyes, knocking away the top layer of excuses she'd piled up. Flinging her arms around Noah's neck, she squeezed him tight, thankful she had someone in her life who looked below the surface and truly saw her. His embrace came with his full attention, unlike her recent ones with Lexi. Distracted was the best way to describe them. Each time, Lexi's mind was on something else—the job, the next media event, or chasing after Belcher. Anything but her. But this was refreshing, and it felt good.

Nita pulled back a fraction to look Noah in the eyes. Despite her attraction to both sexes, it had been years since she'd been drawn to a man. Women seemed more in tune with her emotions, and Lexi had too until she returned to fieldwork with the ATF. But Noah was an anomaly. He had a rare intuitiveness, which, combined with his gentleness, made him more than a friend. They made him desirable.

The longer he stared into her eyes, the stronger that pull grew. But did he feel it too? A voice in her head said, *how couldn't he?* The energy she felt had sent her heart pounding at a pace she hadn't experienced since her last first kiss. Noah had talked about taking a leap of faith, so she did. Nita leaned in and kissed Noah on the lips, but it felt wrong instantly.

As quickly as she pressed her lips against his, Noah pushed back. "Whoa, Nita. Where did that come from?" He stepped out of the stall and into the central part of the bathroom.

"Out of stupidity." Nita brought her hands to her face. Guilt didn't merely creep up. It burst on the scene with an ear-splitting explosion. "I'm so sorry, Noah. I'm not excusing what I did, but the alcohol has clearly clouded my judgment."

"When was the last time you had a drink?"

"Six years ago, when I kicked the meth." Nita rubbed bumpy scars at the bend of her left arm, regretting everything about this night.

"You're right. It doesn't excuse it, but you're probably drunk."

The main door swung open. A blond woman walked in, but she came to a sudden stop, jerking her head back. "Excuse me, but I think you're in the wrong bathroom."

"I was just leaving." Noah turned on his heel and shimmied past the shocked woman, leaving without a word. This entire day had been a disaster since stepping foot off the plane with Nita making one poor decision after another. And moments ago, she'd jettisoned what was left of her self-respect with that stupid, stupid kiss. Unfortunately, her friendship with Noah likely went with it.

The woman stared at Nita with curiosity etched on her face, but explanations would not be forthcoming. Instead, Nita marched down the hallway to their table, where Noah pulled cash from his wallet.

"Please tell me we're okay, Noah."

He plopped in his chair, rubbing a hand down his face. "I'm not sure yet."

"I feel horrible." She fell to her seat with equal force. "I ruin everything good in my life when I'm not sober."

"You put me in an awful position, Nita. How can I face Lexi and not tell her what just happened?"

"I don't know, but please let me be the one to tell her first." Nita imagined Lexi's reaction if she learned about this from Noah. She wasn't the type to fly off the handle, but she was the type to walk away. Considering their growing distance for the last few months, Nita had predicted an inevitable breakup, but not over this. The last thing she wanted was to break Lexi's heart. But deep down, Nita was sure she already had, and there was no going back.

Her cell phone vibrated in her purse. The distinct muffled ringtone meant her girlfriend had a sixth sense. At least the incoming call told Nita that Lexi was still alive. Opening her bag, Nita pushed aside her gut-wrenching guilt, located her phone, and thumbed the screen.

"Lexi." Nita broke down into quiet sobs.

"It's all right, Nita. I'm all right." Lexi's calm voice cut like a knife through Nita's heart. Of course, Lexi would think her outburst was for the relief she felt, but she couldn't be more wrong. It was one hundred percent guilt. Lexi was risking her life for people she didn't know, yet Nita repaid her by nearly cheating on her. She was scum. No. She was lower than scum. She was the muck that floated up when city workers dredged the pond near their apartment.

"Noah told me." Nita pulled herself together bit by bit. "When can you leave?"

"Not yet. Things are coming to a head, but we need your help again. The official interpreter has been delayed, and we don't have time to find another one. Can you come back and help us translate some sign language? Dylan's dad is here, but he can't sign. Can you believe that?" The urgency in Lexi's voice was unmistakable. Something big was about to happen.

"Of course, I'll help again. We're just a few blocks away. I can be there in a few minutes."

"Thank you, Nita. I knew I could count on you. I love you. See you soon."

"See you soon." Nita tried to say the three most important words back to Lexi, but she couldn't without feeling like the world's biggest ass. Before she repeated them, she'd have to come clean with the truth.

She disconnected the call and turned her attention to Noah. "We have to go. They need my help again."

"You're not going to translate half-drunk, are you?"

9157

"I don't have a choice. Lexi said they're out of options." Nita owed her this. She needed to do whatever it took to get herself alert enough to get Lexi whatever she needed.

"Then let's get some coffee down you." Noah scanned the room for their server.

"There's no time to wait for her. I'll go up to the bar. You pay the bill."

Nita weaved her way through the crowd, targeting where Squirrelly was working. She waved him down, and he popped over. Nita leaned in. "A black coffee to go and another half."

25

The last few minutes had the command post occupants on an emotional roller coaster. First, a shocked silence had enveloped the van with the news that Amadeus had boarded the plane. He was still in federal custody, but anything could happen outside the confines of the penitentiary walls. It was like watching the Twin Towers fall. Everyone felt helpless and had a keen awareness that life had changed.

But when the drone feed came back to life the next minute, the space buzzed with excitement. Lexi had to hand it to Sergeant Carver for coming up with the Morse code idea. It was pure genius. Learning the layout of the store and devices was a treasure trove of tactical information for SWAT and the bomb squad, whose primary driver for action remained the wounded. They worked on a breach plan, including where to stage the hostages safely for extraction. At the same time, Lexi pored through the recorded video from the downed drone, focusing on the make-up of the explosives.

The device attached to the front door had the best video vantage point, and thankfully the drone pilot zoomed in on the device's face. It differed from the ones guarding the entrance of the POW building. It was home-made with a magnetic base. But the perplexing elements were the light source and sensor face. They were two separate parts. She began to think the light was a red herring designed to instill fear.

Lexi focused on the sensor. It was small, only a half-inch square. She racked her brain to recall where she'd seen a similar device. She instinctively remembered she'd seen one recently, but where? She then ran through everywhere she'd been in the last few weeks—home, the Dallas office, Nita's office, her prosthetist, her parents.

Wait.

That was it. Her parents had added a cheap driveway monitor system to their access road. Those things had a sensor range of thirty to fifty feet but had a limited receiver range of less than two football fields. Belcher's team could have easily cannibalized one to daisy chain a dozen devices into a single receiver.

Lexi got the attention of Detective Nolan Hughes and waved him over from his conference with Carver and Agent Maxwell Keene. "Make it quick, Mills. Carver is wearing down Agent Mitchell for a quick breach."

Lexi glared first at Agent Keene. He definitely wasn't Father of the Year material. How could a man parent a deaf son for seven years and not learn sign language? If not for his adamant stance on taking every precaution before charging into the grocery store, she'd recommend a profound alignment of his priorities. But that was for another day. He was losing his argument with Agent Mitchell, who had arrived five minutes ago.

Lexi shifted her stare to him. Mitchell's puffed chest and extra-straight posture were a full one-eighty from his earlier interaction with Lexi. He'd taken on the look of the man in charge, relishing his newfound responsibility. The possibility of this situation ending without more bloodshed was becoming unlikely.

Lexi then directed Hughes' attention to the screen with a still image of the explosive at the front door. "I wanted to run this past you first. We might have better luck if we present a united front."

"I'm listening."

"I've studied the video and believe each device is packed with stolen nitro and connected wirelessly to a central receiver somewhere in the store. Each device would work independently if we could instruct Beckett to locate and turn off the receiver. That would eliminate the danger of a catastrophic, simultaneous explosion. If that were the case, I could get behind a breach through either entrance if planned correctly."

"Could? Not would." Hughes was an expert at dissecting each word. It was a talent born from years of hostage negotiations where a single word could tip the scales to a resolution.

"I'd be more comfortable once we translate Amanda Keene's commentary. I have a nagging feeling we're missing something."

"I can support that. The entry control point radioed me a minute ago. Nita passed through on foot. She should be here in a few minutes."

"If you don't mind, considering her state when she left, I'd like a few moments alone with her."

"Take a few, but based on the look on Mitchell's face, we don't have much time."

Lexi descended the command van stairs into the warm Gladding evening air. Emergency vehicles had gone dark, but mobile lights illuminated the secured area, creating a stadium-like atmosphere with artificial light below the dark sky. Several SWAT, fire, and EMT personnel dotted the glowing scene, but the excitement that had energized the vicinity when Lexi first arrived had settled into an uneasy lull. She couldn't blame them. They'd been waiting for hours for the on-scene commander to call them into action.

Lexi cast her stare toward the ECP, searching for Nita and Noah. She knew what needed doing. Until today, Nita had only a notion of what Lexi's job entailed. But today, she'd gotten the full taste by listening to the play-by-play action of her rescue attempt. Nita needed reassurance that Lexi was in one piece, unhurt, and had taken no unnecessary risk. Though it wasn't as if anyone could call going into the kill zone without body armor low risk, Lexi needed to present it as such.

She first recognized Noah's unique wide-brimmed fedora coming in her direction. Then to the left of him, Lexi zeroed on Nita. Her gait, while rushed, appeared tight, not like her relaxed running form, confirming she was still out of sorts.

Lexi took several steps to intercept them at a respectable distance from the nearby officers and paramedics. Expecting their emotional connection to reel her in, Lexi never felt it. Even toe to toe, the distance between them was jarring.

Nita's eyes were swollen, a sign she'd been crying. Then, following several unnerving silent moments, she wrapped her arms around Lexi and pressed their bodies together. "I'm so sorry," she said between sobs.

Lexi squeezed her tight and whispered, "I understand why you left. I'm okay."

Nita shook in her arms, repeating, "I'm sorry. I'm so sorry." Several silent moments passed with both in each other's arms. Then she loosened her hold but remained entwined. "I don't deserve you."

Lexi pulled back until they were face to face. The faint smell of alcohol filled the air between them. Under any other circumstance, she wouldn't broach the subject until they were alone, in the privacy of their home, but people were waiting for Nita to translate.

"Have you been drinking?" Her trembling lips answered the question, driving Lexi to pull her into a second embrace. "You can get through this, Nita. I'll be with you every step of the way." Lexi pulled back again. "But I need to know if you're sober to translate some video."

"Yes." Nita gave a decisive nod. "I had coffee and walked it off. I'm fine to look at a screen."

Lexi searched her eyes. They spoke of regret, but nothing in them suggested Nita was underselling her condition. "Okay." Lexi cupped both sides of her jaw and pulled her in for what she intended to be a brief kiss. But Nita's trembling response encouraged her to make it last longer. When she broke it, more regret filled Nita's eyes. "You're stronger than you realize, Nita."

Lexi glanced past her. "Thank you for taking care of her, Noah. I couldn't have gotten through today without knowing she was with you." He tipped his hat but remained quiet. Clearly, their conversation had made him uncomfortable. "The van is pretty full right now. Would you mind waiting out here?"

"I could use the fresh air," he replied before walking away. His brusqueness was out of character and perplexing, but Lexi didn't have time to explore his reason.

"Let's get you inside, Nita. Your translation could save a dozen lives." Lexi held Nita's hand and led her to the bottom of the stairs. Her posture was stiffer than expected. Perhaps she shouldn't have said the part about saving lives. More pressure wasn't what Nita needed right now. She stopped and kissed the back of her hand. "You'll do fine. We need to know what Dylan's mother is signing in some video we acquired from inside the store."

Nita gave a reluctant nod. "Okay."

Once inside, Hughes sat Nita at his workstation with the cued-up video. He explained its contents and how they got it. "Amanda signed commentary after showing us the explosives and each of the hostages. We need you to translate."

"Sure," Nita said.

Lexi watched from a distance without hovering over Nita's shoulder. Nita worked quickly, using the remote to control the video, jotting down notes after every pause. In fact, her speed was almost too fast, giving Lexi the impression that she might miss something if she didn't slow down.

Stepping forward, Lexi whispered into her ear, "Are you okay? Do you need to slow down?"

Nita glowered out of the corner of her eye. "Do I tell you how to do your job?" Her voice traveled farther than Lexi's, drawing the officer's attention from the next workstation.

Lexi leaned in closer and kept her voice low. "This translation is critical, Nita. We need to make sure it's accurate."

"If you don't trust me, maybe I should leave." Nita gritted her teeth. Lexi hadn't seen her this mad since the unexpected phone call with her mother last month. The gall of that woman, asking Nita for money after cutting her out of her life for years. Nita would be the first to admit that she'd burned every bridge with nearly every friend and family member when she hit rock bottom with meth. Nothing could convince her mother that she'd changed until she needed money. The anger Nita displayed that day rivaled the look on her face now.

Getting into an argument wouldn't help get the hostages out safely, so Lexi tabled her concern that something deeper was bothering Nita. She bent at the knees, positioning herself closer. "I'm sorry, Nita. I do trust you. Please stay. Anything you can tell us about the video will help." She gave Nita's hand a brief squeeze and stepped back.

Nita continued her work, rolling her neck periodically in apparent frustration. Lexi's pep talk may have kept her here, but it failed to douse her resentment.

Nita called Detective Hughes over when she finished and turned over her notes. "Amanda was signing really fast. I think I got most of it, but you should have a professional interpreter study the tape."

"Of course. This is very helpful, thank you." Hughes glanced at the papers before directing his attention to Lexi. "We need to brief Keene and Carver and decide on a course of action."

Lexi raised an index finger, asking him for one minute. He then stepped away. She knelt beside Nita again. "I love you. Why don't you ask Noah to take you back to the hotel? You could use some sleep."

Nita dipped her chin. "I... I'd rather stay and go back with you."

Those few words gave Lexi hope that she and Nita would be all right and that Nita would claw her way back to sobriety. "I'll be right back." Lexi gave her hand another squeeze before striding away.

Lexi pushed back her worries about Nita and joined Hughes, who was stepping the others through Nita's notes. He detailed Amanda's narration as she walked through the store, documenting the explosives and the hostages. He then acknowledged Lexi. "Agent Mills has some information about the devices."

Lexi outlined her theory about the driveway monitor system and how to disable the daisy chain effect. "We should send a message, asking Beckett where the receiver is and have him turn it off."

"Were we looking at the same tape?" Carver asked. "Beckett was stabbed. Your translator said the bleeding was not under control. We have two hostages who could bleed out before we track down this receiver, assuming it exists." Lexi glanced at Nita, wondering if she'd gotten that part wrong. The bandages on the two injured hostages made her believe otherwise. "We've studied the video and are confident we can extract the hostages by breaking through the bathroom window wall."

"I agree with the plan, but I still think it's premature." Lexi focused on Keene and Mitchell. "We still have time before your agent on the plane gets the final coordinates on where to land. We should use that time to minimize the risk to the hostages." When Agent Mitchell exhaled deeply and set his jaw, Lexi knew she'd lost him.

Mitchell looked to Carver. "How long will it take you to set up?"

"Ten minutes," he replied.

"Don't do this, Terry." Keene's jaw muscles contracted one, two, and three times. "Amanda is in there, for God's sake." The desperation in his voice was heartbreaking.

"While I appreciate your and Agent Mills' abundance of caution," Mitchell said, "I can't put your wife's life above the other hostages. We have two injured who can't wait for medical assistance. Nor can I risk letting Lyle Belcher out of custody. He poses an extreme danger. We don't know what surprises Tony Belcher might have in store for us or how much longer we'll be in communications with the plane. We have to act while we still have strings to pull." He then shifted his attention to Sergeant Carver. "Send a message to the hostages. The extraction is a go."

Keene stormed out of the van.

"This is a huge mistake, Agent Mitchell." Lexi felt the doom in her bones. They were moving too fast for no reasons other than a SWAT commander's bravado and an FBI agent's reluctance to take a risk. This was all too much, and Lexi needed air, too. She followed Keene out, slamming the door behind her.

26

Trust was at a premium inside the store. Since learning that one of them wasn't a hostage but a plant by the mastermind of this horrifying ordeal, people divided again, this time into three small groups. But with everyone aware that someone wasn't who they appeared to be, no one wandered off to the bathroom or for food alone, opting to stay in place. It was interesting to see where loyalties fell.

After filming the explosives and hostages, Amanda stayed with Hunter and the wounded, offering Biscuit and Clarence water and food while Hunter tended to their injuries. The five employees stayed in a loose group, with Zack and Riley sitting at the periphery. Meanwhile, the elderly couple sat on their stools while Gail comforted the young high school girl near their feet.

Everyone had drawn their lines, clearly assuming the mole was among one of the other groups. Even Amanda had her suspicions. She racked her brain, recalling who had wandered off for food or the bathroom before Biscuit had come out. Unfortunately, she could only rule out the elderly woman and Maria, the baker. That left everyone else, including Clarence and Hunter in her own group, as suspects.

Amanda then focused on each alliance and its advantages. The employees had Bret, the tallest and strongest, and Biscuit's gun. The customers had Clarence's knife. And Amanda, among the outcasts, had the drone. This division was precisely what Amanda had been trying to avoid. Without working together, their chances of getting out alive were greatly diminished.

The thick tension was stifling. Then Zack tapped his empty Coke bottle against the floor three times. He did it again. And again. Then Riley joined in, pounding her hand against the side of the checkout counter twice and clapping once. The other clerk joined in. Then Maria. Then the high schooler. Then Clarence. Even the elderly couple. Riley sang, "We Will Rock You." Soon Bret joined in. Then Gail. And finally, Hunter and Biscuit. The three groups pounded, clapped, and sang in unison. Each round was louder and more intense. The resulting sea change shifted the mood from mistrust to unity. It reminded them they weren't three islands of suspicion but were in this together.

Then in the middle of the fourth round, Riley stood and pointed in Amanda's direction. "It's flashing again." The pounding and singing came to a slow, rippling stop. All heads turned. Unity morphed into anticipation. Optimism.

Amanda shifted her stare at the drone. "What is it saying, Hunter?"

"It's too much to remember." Hunter raised his hand, asking everyone for silence. "I need to write it down."

The young cashier scrambled for pen and paper from the register. "Call out. I'll write."

Hunter waited for the message to repeat before he started reciting the letters. Amanda, like the others, followed along. A hum of excitement filled the air when it became clear the police intended a rescue attempt by breaching the bathroom wall in ten minutes. They were to take cover in the hallway outside the men's room and be ready for immediate extraction.

"We're finally getting out of here," one said.

"We get to go home," another said thickly.

Emotions were running high at the prospect of a rescue attempt. Amanda was tempted to let herself get swept away by the groundswell, but she tempered her reaction. She remembered seeing stacks of produce crates on either side of the back door. One violent shake could send them tumbling and trigger the explosive there. She had the impression that if one device went off, they all would. But this wasn't the moment for stark realism. For the first time, fear had left everyone inside the store, replaced by excitement. She supposed they might be far enough away from the door and the group of explosives on the main floor to avoid a major blast, so she said nothing.

"Is that it?" Amanda asked.

"They want you to acknowledge the plan." Hunter flipped the drone around so the camera faced Amanda.

She signed, "Acknowledged. Breach in ten minutes. Will be ready."

Hunter studied several more flashes. "They will signal again one minute out. We better start moving the wounded."

Zack was the first to stand. Surprisingly, he walked to Biscuit and offered him a hand off the floor. "Come on, Uncle Del. Let's get rescued."

Biscuit accepted his assistance and his gesture. "I'm so sorry about picking you as the one I was supposed to shoot, but I couldn't make another family suffer."

"I get it, Uncle Del. But when this is over, I expect a big, fat raise." Zack pulled him up. He and Riley then guided him toward the bathrooms.

Amanda shifted her stare to Hunter. "I guess that leaves you and me with Clarence."

"I'll help." Bret shoved the pistol into his waistband at the small of his back and helped Hunter raise Clarence. Each put an arm over their shoulder, helping Clarence hobble toward the corridor.

"I'll be damned," Amanda mumbled quietly. Zack's impromptu concert couldn't have come at a better time. It pulled everyone together right when they were the most divided. They were a team again. She remained in the back row with Gail and the young cashier with the ladies' room door at their backs. The wounded and the elderly should go out first.

"If anyone has to pee, this is the time to do it," Hunter announced.

No one took the opportunity. Instead, the thirteen hostages assembled in the hallway and remained in place. Shoulder to shoulder. Silent. Everyone's breathing shallowed as tension grew again. Amanda eyed each one for the final time before she had to watch the drone for the police signal. She still couldn't figure out which of them was working for Belcher. But it didn't matter at this point. In a few minutes, they'd all be dead or in the hands of the police. Then they'd let the authorities sort out who was who.

Zack tapped his foot again in rhythm to "We Will Rock You." Everyone able to stand on their own joined in, pounding their shoes on the linoleum. The resulting sound was reminiscent of warriors priming themselves for battle to the beat of a drum. But they weren't soldiers. They were victims, preparing for the worst while hoping for the best. And the absence of singing highlighted their collective nerves.

Then, the drone flashed several times. The tapping stopped.

"This is it, people." Amanda swallowed past the grapefruit-size lump in her throat. The next few seconds would determine their fates.

27

Lexi stomped down the command van stairs. She located and approached Agent Keene, who had his hands on his hips and was kicking parking lot gravel in the near darkness with his shoe. Frustrated didn't come close to describing his state. He was at the end of his rope. The hope of saving his wife was evaporating, and she felt the same.

"I'm sorry, Agent Keene. I don't know what else I can do to make them listen."

"It's not your fault, Mills." He rolled his neck, eyes closed, clearly pushing back the volcano brewing inside.

"I can't help but feel that I've missed something. If I only had more time."

"That's not the Lexi Mills I know," a male voice said from behind. Lexi didn't have to turn to know it belonged to Noah Black. His voice had become as familiar as any partner she'd had in her nearly eleven years as an ATF agent. He stepped forward.

"Noah, this is Special Agent Maxwell Keene of the FBI. His wife is a hostage in the store. Agent Keene, this is Detective—"

Keene extended his hand to Noah. "It's a pleasure, Detective Black. I'm scheduled to introduce you and Agent Mills at tomorrow's banquet, but I doubt that will happen after tonight's events."

"It's a pleasure." Noah returned his attention to Lexi. He had a look of confidence in his eyes. "If you think you missed something, you better get your butt back in there and find it."

Before Lexi could give Noah a proper hug for encouraging her and taking care of Nita tonight, a hand fell on her shoulder. She turned toward it, discovering Kathy, Beckett's busty wife. "Please tell me I got here in time, Lexi."

Lexi placed both hands on her upper arms. "Yes, Kathy. You're in time. The police are about to attempt a rescue through the bathroom wall."

Kathy rolled her eyes. "We just remodeled."

Lexi ignored the unfeeling comment. "We think someone involved with the hostage situation and your kidnapping may be inside. Would you be willing to look at some video and see if anyone looks familiar?"

"If it will help my Pookie, of course."

"We have about seven minutes to find it."

Lexi rushed Kathy up the stairs, flew the van door open, and marched her to Hughes' workstation. Not surprisingly, Nita was there, reviewing the same videotape Lexi had returned to scour. Lexi knew Nita was relapsing, but seeing her tonight, she was sure her downward journey had just begun and was salvageable.

Nita looked up, narrowing her eyes briefly before returning her focus to the screen. "You came back to make sure I didn't miss something. I'm way ahead of you." Her accusatory tone was concerning, but Lexi didn't have time to address it. Nita was advancing the recording of the wounded hostages at three-quarter speed, observing every nuance of Amanda's sign language. She then pressed pause and pointed. "There. Does she look like she's scratching her chin or giving a sign?"

Lexi squinted at the screen as Nita played it back. "I can't tell."

"Well, it could mean the difference between their bleeding is under or out of control. If I got it wrong, the wounded are doing fine, and there's no urgency." Nita's concern that she might have made a mistake meant she doubted whether she was in the right condition to help in an active investigation. But that was a subtlety they'd have to address later.

"I wish it mattered at this point, but I'll let them know," Lexi said. "We don't have much time. I need you to fast forward through the hostages' faces for this woman to see if she recognizes any of them."

Nita craned her neck, giving Lexi the narrow eyes of irritation. "Sure."

"Thank you." Lexi kissed her on the cheek before pulling a second chair for Kathy. "Let me know if one of them was your kidnapper."

When Lexi stepped back, Detective Hughes waved her over to the wall of monitors. According to the digital countdown clock above the screens, they had less than four minutes before SWAT would be ready to breach.

She raised an index finger, asking for one moment, when she saw the SWAT commander stepping toward the exit. "Sergeant Carver, wait. I have new information from the interpreter." She waited for him to rejoin Agent Mitchell, whose sweaty brow was a troubling sign he might be in way over his head. "She's reviewed the tapes and thinks Amanda had conveyed the hostages' conditions are more stable than we first thought."

"I hope you're right about their conditions, but it doesn't change my decision. We're going in." Agent Mitchell glanced at Sergeant Carver, who gave him a confirming nod. She was up against not one but two brick walls, and there was no going around them.

"My proposal will only take a few minutes," Lexi argued.

Carver lasered his stare at her. "Did you consider that asking the entire room of hostages to unplug a driveway receiver might push Belcher's mole over the edge before we're in place? This way, we're delaying the risk until the last possible moment."

"Did you consider that the vibration from ripping out the wall might teeter the stacks of produce crates next to the back door enough to set off a chain reaction? Both options are risky, but I like the hostages' chances better with my plan."

"Look, Agent Mills, there's nothing better to go on. We have to breach." To say Mitchell was stubbornly by the book was an understatement.

"I have Beckett's wife here right now, looking at the hostage images. If she picks out her kidnapper, the others could subdue them. Would that be enough for you to delay the breach?"

"It would buy us a little more time," Mitchell said, "but I'm still concerned about losing control over Amadeus."

Carver glanced at the wall of monitors. "The hostages appear in place.

We need to go outside." He ushered Mitchell out of the van before giving her a definitive answer. She rubbed her temples, staving off a mounting headache. She'd worked with stubborn commanders before, but these two topped the list.

Lexi returned to Hughes near the screens and gestured her thumb toward Nita and Kathy. "We're out of options unless the wife over there IDs the mole."

She watched the images on the screens as precious time counted down. The clock above them now read under two minutes. SWAT had launched a larger drone and had it hovering above the parking lot. It followed the activity of the two tow trucks backing up and officers preparing grappling hooks to attach to the interior sides of the bathroom window frame. The other feed showed the hostages huddled in the corridor. The feed vibrated at regular intervals in a distinct pattern. Then it stopped. Amanda pointed the drone camera at herself, giving a thumbs up.

"We have something!" Nita yelled.

Lexi shot her stare at the countdown clock again. One minute. Their window of opportunity would expire in seconds. Her pulse increased two-fold at the possibility of stopping this ill-fated mission. She dashed to the workstation. "What do you have?"

Kathy pointed to the frozen image on the screen. "This person was in my house and took us to the POW site."

Lexi's mind went into overdrive, remembering this section of the tape. Something about it had caught her attention before. "Fast forward several frames. There. Stop." She'd seen what she needed. Several objects lay at the person's feet, including a garage door opener. She'd found the mole. Now, she had seconds to get Mitchell to stop this lunacy.

She darted out the door and down the stairs but landed awkwardly on her prosthetic. Her residual limb slipped deeper into the socket, pinching her skin. The pain was sharp, but she didn't have time to adjust it. Instead, she located Agent Keene but didn't see Mitchell or Carver. She then fixed her sights on the grouping of SWAT officers standing near the perimeter of the inner cordon. The dark made them hard to make out, but the tall one in the center looked like he was wearing a suit, not a tactical uniform. That had to be Mitchell.

The seconds counted down in her head while she ran. The pain considerably altered her gait, but she refused to let it slow her. "Mitchell, wait!" she called out. Lexi heard thundering footsteps behind her, realizing Noah and Agent Keene had followed her. "We can stop this!" Mitchell and Carver glanced back. Their confused expressions meant she'd failed to get her message across. "I know who the mole is, and they have a remote detonator."

Mitchell shifted his attention to Carver, who had lifted his tactical radio to his mouth. "Breach. Breach. Breach."

28

"You idiot," Lexi roared. Noah and Agent Keene came to an abrupt stop behind her.

"Belay that order, Carver," Mitchell yelled, but it was too late. The two truck drivers had screamed their engines. The next second, a loud crumbling noise followed.

Lexi cringed, waiting for the secondary vibration to settle. She counted in her head. One. Two. Three. Four. Five. If the crates hadn't fallen yet, they were likely stable and posed no immediate threat. She snapped her head around to look Carver in the eye. "Have your officers isolate Gail Jones. She's the mole. She has a trigger that can take down the entire building with a single press of a button."

Maxwell Keene took off toward the store, gun drawn, using solid strides.

Damn ATF rules, Lexi mumbled to herself. Since her travel to Sacramento wasn't official duty for an investigation, she didn't have her firearm. Neither did Noah. They were unarmed, with only their credentials around their neck, running into a chaotic hostage scene orchestrated by her greatest nemesis. If there was ever a time she needed her service weapon, it was now.

The pain below Lexi's left knee slowed her, but Noah kept even, proving he'd always have her back. He'd be by her side when facing danger without being asked, and Lexi wouldn't have it any other way.

Keene was pulling away with his long legs. By the time Lexi and Noah reached the building corner, Keene was waiting impatiently several feet from the hole, bouncing on the balls of his feet. The tow trucks had only done a partial job, so two SWAT officers were pounding a lower section of the cinder block wall with sledgehammers. Each strike posed another opportunity for the crates to wobble, making Lexi think they were too close. They might not be impacted by the cascading rubble, but the blast shock wave would knock them off their feet and force air from their lungs.

The final blows took out the toilet, clearing a path for entry. Two officers entered, setting off flash-bang grenades five seconds apart. Anyone with their eyes open and not shielded by protective goggles would be momentarily blind. The result would create several minutes of confusion, enough time for the officers to extract the first of the hostages safely.

Radios squawked Carver's commands to escort the hostages to the main parking lot outside the inner cordon and separate them. "Take the wounded to the EMTs. Search everyone. Look for a remote trigger."

Moments later, the first dazed hostage emerged. It was Clarence with the gunshot wound. He grimaced as an officer inside the confining bathroom stall space helped him into the waiting arms of another SWAT officer on the outside. While the first officer returned inside, the second lifted Clarence's arm over his shoulder. He guided him slowly over the rubble before ushering him away.

Then Beckett, the other wounded hostage, emerged, blinking rapidly and appearing equally dazed from the flashbang. The elderly couple was next. Though appearing less dazed, they looked visibly shaken from their ordeal. Each was handed off to an officer and fast-walked to the safe zone.

Keene was a nervous wreck as the hostages funneled through the hole one by one. Each time a head popped through the rough open, his twitching and hand-wringing increased speed. Meanwhile, Lexi kept count in her head and with her fingers, tracking the sex of those coming out. The next man through was hostage number ten and meant all six men were out. That left three inside, all women, including Amanda and the mole. The eleventh came out, and so did an officer from the inside. Then the second officer who had gone inside emerged immediately behind him. Lexi was confused.

"Where's Amanda?" Keene yelled.

"That's it!" the last officer out yelled.

"No!" Lexi yelled, running toward the last woman out and the officer escorting her. If memory served, she was a cashier. "Where are Amanda and Gail? Were they behind you?"

The woman was hunched over and quivering beneath the officer's arm. She looked Lexi in the eye. "Aren't they out here? They were waiting with me toward the back before all hell broke loose. Then there were loud bangs and flashes, and everyone screamed and shifted. I couldn't see anything for several minutes. I thought they got out before me."

Lexi approached the last officer out and spun him around by the arm. The force slid the weapon he'd swung over his shoulder down to his elbow. "There are two more women in there. One is the plant with the trigger."

The officer re-slung his weapon. "No one is in the corridor, but the bomb squad has to go in and clear the explosives before we can conduct a search."

"Amanda!" Keene yelled before sprinting toward the opening.

Lexi and the officer reached out but couldn't stop him. "I'm an ATF explosives expert. I'll go after him." She glanced over her shoulder to Noah while Keene wobbled through the rubble. "Stay here. Don't let anyone inside."

Lexi dashed through the crumbled wall debris when Keene had one leg inside the opening. Each step pinched the skin around her residual limb harder and harder, but she pushed through the pain. The faint smell of gunpowder from the flash grenades assaulted her nose. Finally, she caught up to him before he left the confines of the men's room. "Keene, wait! You'll set off the bombs if you're not careful."

He yanked the door open leading to the hallway but remained inside, calling out desperately, "Amanda! Amanda!"

Lexi stepped through the stall, crunching the ceramic toilet bowl pieces lying on the floor. Before positioning herself directly behind Keene, she paused to shift her prosthetic socket slightly, relieving the unbearable pressure. "Let me take the lead. I know what I'm looking for."

He bent at the waist, lifted his right pant leg, and retrieved a snub-nosed .38 Special revolver. "You'll need this."

"Thanks." Palm around the hand grip, Lexi instantly felt less exposed. "Where do you think they are?"

"They likely didn't get far in the chaos. They may be hiding in the ladies' room across the hall."

"That area is clear, right?" He paused at Lexi's affirmative nod. "Then I'm going first this time. She's my wife." He re-gripped his service weapon. The distinctive click of the safety being flipped sounded. He then darted across the hallway and barreled through the restroom door, leading with his shoulder. The metal handle clanked and echoed off the ceramic wall.

Lexi followed, remaining at the doorway, gun drawn, to provide backup.

Keene kicked open the first stall door and moved on quickly to the second. The final one belonged to the handicapped stall, an ideal hiding place. He paused, drew in a deep breath, and pushed through the door with a shoulder. His posture slumped instantly when he lowered his weapon. "They're not in here. What next?"

"My guess is that Gail not only controls the detonator but can turn each infrared sensor on and off. Unless she's on a suicide mission, she's looking for a way out. She likely took Amanda to the back exit in the storage area because the rescue team isn't working that side of the building."

"Let's go." Keene stepped past Lexi toward the double swinging door.

"This is where I take the lead. I know how close we can get." He replied with a firm nod.

Lexi pulled out her cell phone, activated the flashlight, and held it over her hand with the revolver. Unfamiliar with the complete layout of the storage area, she eased the door open with a shoulder, cringing when the squeaky hinges announced their incursion.

The corridor, lit by one dim emergency light, continued for ten feet. The end opened in all three directions to a larger area awash in a red glow that was more prominent on the right side. Lexi replayed Amanda's video in her head, trying to recall if she turned left or right when she filmed the back door. Right. She definitely went right.

Lexi turned off her flashlight, activated her camera, swiped it to video, and pressed record. She then inched the top of her phone around the corner and held it there for five seconds before pulling it back. She played her recording, letting Keene see it as well. Gail and Amanda were standing fifteen feet from the back door, Amanda with her hands zip-tied behind her back. Gail held a gun to her head while rummaging through the contents of her purse with her free hand. The video also confirmed the explosive device attached to the door was the source of the red glow.

Keene clenched his free hand into a fist while pressing his lips into a straight line. Despite his obvious instinct, going in hot was not an option. Gail and Amanda were dangerously close to the infrared range. They'd all go up if Keene or Lexi rushed in before Gail disarmed the sensor.

Lexi returned her phone to her pocket and wagged her hand up and down, asking Keene to remain calm and follow her lead. She spoke loudly. "Gail, I know you're desperate to get out of here alive." She paused when something banged on the polished concrete floor. "We all are. I know you're working for Tony Belcher, but we can protect you if you give yourself up."

"I'm not doing this for Tony," Gail shouted. "I'm doing this for Lyle."

Lexi racked her brain, recalling the file she'd assembled on Amadeus. She remembered seeing an intel report that a woman attended every day of his trial and sat directly behind him. The supposition was that she was his girlfriend, but facial recognition didn't flag her as Gail Jones.

"You must be Taryn. I know you and Lyle were close before he went to prison."

"We still are."

"Then more killing will only make things worse for him. If you kill us, Tony loses his leverage. Is that what you want, to end this by making sure Lyle never gets paroled?"

"It won't come to that." Taryn's certainty meant Lexi had an uphill battle of convincing her to stop this craziness. Then the red glow from the back area disappeared, telling Lexi that she'd turned off the explosive, maybe all of them, if they were daisy-chained together wirelessly. This was their chance.

Lexi turned the corner, training Keene's .38 on Taryn, or where she should have been in the video, but she'd moved. Taryn pushed Amanda closer to the door, poking her in the back with the pistol. "Taryn, stop!"

Keene rolled out from behind Lexi. She glanced back, seeing he'd aimed his weapon at Taryn. The crazed, desperate look in his eye convinced her he was about to fire. "Keene, don't!" She lunged toward him, pushing his firing arm higher as he pulled the trigger. The shot went off target toward the ceiling. "You could have hit the bomb."

"Maxwell!" Amanda shouted.

The back door flew open. Taryn pushed Amanda out first, with her following close behind. The moment they cleared the door frame, the hairs on the back of Lexi's neck stood on end. They were in the kill zone, but the person with the trigger was now in the clear. Her gut told her she and Keene had only seconds to get out.

She grabbed him by the arm, pulling him toward the exit. "We have to leave! Now!"

Stretching his stride, Keene picked up speed, passing Lexi in two steps. He clutched her jacket sleeve on his way by, pulling her outside. She slammed the door closed, hoping the shaped charge would direct most of the force inside the building. Five feet past the frame, Lexi heard the explosion a split second before she felt the shock wave. It knocked her from her feet and ripped the air from her lungs. She gasped and struggled to make her diaphragm work while multiple explosions sounded rapidly.

Lexi finally took in a dust-filled, choking breath. Cement particles coated her throat, causing a coughing attack that made her dry heave. The darkness made it impossible to see through the smoke and dust cloud enveloping them.

She called out, "Keene. Where are you?" Then she heard a moan and pushed herself to her knees. She didn't have to inspect her left leg to know her prosthetic had been knocked cockeyed. The socket biting at her skin the entire length of her thigh proved it.

Lexi dragged herself toward the repeating groans, crawling over chunks of cinderblock and sharp lengths of twisted metal. Coughing out the remaining dust in her throat, Lexi reached Keene, who was pushing himself to his bottom. He coughed and called out, "Amanda!" But he was too late. She and Taryn had disappeared into the darkness.

29

Heart pounding. Hands tied behind her back. Amanda ran down the dark street moments after the massive explosion rocked the quaint town of Gladding. Her knee was still tender from the fracas between Hunter and Bret. Tears clouded her vision, making it impossible to see the curb until her foot caught the edge, and she went tumbling. She couldn't stop sobbing even as her knee hit the sidewalk, hurting it more and likely scraping it into a bloody mess. She'd heard her husband's name called out right before the gunshot, so Maxwell must have been inside the grocery store when the bombs went off.

"You killed my husband, you bitch," she cried at the madwoman with the gun who was right on her tail. Belcher's mole picked her up by the collar and pushed her along.

"Keep moving," Gail ordered. Or was it Taryn? The person who had passed herself off as another hostage for the last ten hours called herself Gail Jones. But according to the voice in the store, her name was Taryn, and she was close to someone named Lyle. He must have been Belcher's brother, the subject of this insane hostage exchange.

"He's alive, you idiot." Taryn pulled Amanda between two buildings while the chaos of responding firefighters built at their backs. "We need him that way for now."

"Which means you need me alive, too." Amanda stopped and stood her ground. She had leverage, but it would only do her some good if Taryn was rational. The crazed look in her eyes suggested that wasn't the case, and now wasn't the time to test her theory.

Taryn pushed the muzzle into Amanda's kidney. "Alive doesn't mean unhurt, so get a move on unless you want a bullet in the arm."

The important thing was that her husband was alive and knew she'd been taken. *Stay alive*, she told herself. *Maxwell can get you out of this.* Cooperating seemed much better than the alternative, so Amanda continued down the dark alley.

Streetlights illuminated the other end, allowing her to navigate a dumpster and several stacks of crates safely even with her limp. Exiting onto the sidewalk, Taryn pushed her across the vacant street and into a second alley. Despite this one being longer and not as well lit, Amanda navigated her way past several obstacles of trash, blankets, and a lean-to made of cardboard boxes. She shuddered to think that this was Clarence's home.

Once on the next street, two blocks from what used to be McBean's, the flashers on a sedan parked two storefronts down flickered on and off. Taryn pushed her in that direction. Amanda scanned the street up and down, but it was void of people like the previous one. Unfortunately, there was no sign of a police blockade, so yelling for help wouldn't do her any good.

Taryn yanked the front passenger door open and pushed Amanda into the seat before buckling her in and closing the door. Amanda shifted and frantically felt behind her and around the door, hoping to locate something sharp that could cut or weaken the plastic strap binding her wrists. She found nothing.

The driver's door opened, and Taryn slid into the seat. She buckled, pressed the ignition, and pulled away slowly from the curb. The fevered look that had painted her face minutes earlier was replaced by determination. Amanda expected Taryn to appear rattled after narrowly escaping an exploding building, but this woman had nerves of steel. She'd barely broken a sweat and was uncannily focused. Clearly, she'd had military-type training, or worse, had experience doing this type of thing.

"Was any of that about having children true? Or was it all a lie, Gail? Or Taryn? Or whatever your name is?"

"It's Taryn, and does it really matter?" She kept her speed down and turned north on the drag that led toward the rural, unincorporated parts of Gladding with large rolling properties of mandarin orchards, horse ranches dotted with oak and manzanita, and gated compounds with small vineyards.

"I'll take that as a no, which explains how you remained so calm when sending a message to your quote-unquote kids."

"You seem offended." Taryn smirked.

"Wouldn't you be? You masquerade for hours, getting us to trust you. I hope this Lyle character is worth it."

"He is."

"No man is worth risking a life sentence. My husband can cut you a deal and make sure you never set foot in prison. If you stop this now, he can get you into witness protection and set you up with a new life."

"You don't get it." Taryn glanced at Amanda, steady and unemotional. "This isn't about the man. It's about the mission."

"And what mission is that? Some 'take over the government' thing? I finally remembered where I'd heard the name Belcher. His band of nuts was associated with the other band of nuts that failed miserably to assassinate the governor and take over the Texas government."

"That was a temporary setback. You have no idea what the endgame is."

"Enlighten me."

"You're an unbeliever." Taryn curled her lip as if being an unbeliever was more disgusting than stepping in dog crap. "You'll never understand."

"Try me. If I can understand two teenage kids, I can understand just about anything."

"The Rapture is coming. We need to cull the unbelievers so God will know who to take with him."

"And Lyle is supposed to help with that."

"He composed the plan. That's why we call him Amadeus."

"And who gave him the idea that the Rapture is coming."

"The hand of God."

"And who is that?"

"His brother."

Oh boy, Amanda thought. She could reason with this woman if her motivation was for money or drugs or power or to right a wrong. But this was some cult thing. She'd been brainwashed into thinking death and destruction were justified to guarantee her a seat in the eternal afterlife.

"Nope. You were right," Amanda said.

"About what?"

"That I wouldn't understand. Violence is never okay. Believe what you want about God, the Rapture, and the afterlife, but don't involve the rest of us. Jim Jones had it right. When the authorities came knocking at the front gate, he ordered a mass suicide, not a mass killing of innocent people."

Taryn dug her fingers deeper into the vinyl of the steering wheel. She gave Amanda the same look her teenagers did when they tried to explain the nuances of hashtagging, only more intense.

"Most of us just want to be left alone to live our own lives. Why can't you let us roll the dice and be unprepared when the Rapture comes and let God sort it out when he gets here?"

"Because that's not the way it works."

"Then tell me. How does it work?"

"The population has gotten too big. Too many false believers will shout their lie that God won't hear the true believers. A revolution will pit the unbelievers against one another and lessen their cry."

If reasoning with Taryn wouldn't work, perhaps a little psychology reserved for her kids might. "Oh, you mean liars like someone posing as a hostage to keep an eye on the rest of us who were being held there against our will."

"That was a necessary lie."

"So lying is okay as long as it supports the mission. I'd think that God would frown upon that."

"It's like a cop going undercover. I had to do it." Taryn's head jerking meant Amanda had chipped away at her foundational beliefs. If she could keep this up, maybe Taryn would see that Amadeus and Belcher had been leading her astray.

"So now you're comparing yourself to a cop who puts their life on the line by infiltrating a gang selling drugs to children. Are you saying that by lying, you were saving lives?"

Taryn glanced at Amanda again with a look of pure confusion. "I was lying because Belcher said we need Amadeus to come up with a new plan to save our eternal souls."

"So you weren't saving lives. You lied for your own benefit. Doesn't the Ninth Commandment say that you shall not give false witness against your neighbor? If I remember my Sunday school teachings, some take it to mean not to lie when testifying in court. But the more broadly held interpretation is to not lie. Period. What will God think when he learns you lied to us all day about something this important just to benefit yourself?"

Taryn shook her head. "Your teenagers don't like you very much, do they? You twist everything until you get them to say or do what you want."

"It's called parenting. My job isn't to make my children like me. It's to teach them. I brought them into this world, so I have to make sure they are good stewards of it. And that means getting through their thick teenage skulls that history didn't begin the day they were born. That sometimes, parents know better because we've already lived it. That some things are tried and true for a reason. But mostly, my job is to teach them to treat others with respect and kindness. If your mother had done her job correctly, we wouldn't be in this car today."

"You know nothing about my mother."

Damn it, Amanda. You went too far. She needed to soft-pedal it back and get Taryn thinking about doing what was right. "No, I don't. But I know there's not a mother in the world who would want this for their child. You're risking your life and freedom for an assumption. Remember the rule about history. How many people believe in what the Hand of God Belcher has been telling you? Not many, I'm betting. History has shown us that every prophet who claimed to have a direct line to God and know when the Rapture and the Second Coming would happen was a fake. Does that sound familiar?"

"And Jesus was crucified because the powerful were afraid of him and his message."

"That's a good point, but are you willing to risk everything on the hope that you've backed the next Jesus when history tells us he's not?"

"It's a little late for second-guessing." Taryn turned the steering wheel, making a tight right turn. Gravel crunched beneath the tires, signaling they were now off the beaten path.

Amanda popped her head around. Their headlights outlined the crude single-lane road with two ruts of dirt and pebbles separated by a strip of weeds. The sides were strewn with wild brush. The area didn't look familiar in the dark, but if Amanda's internal radar was working, they were five or six miles north of town. She'd explored this part of Gladding after moving to town, but the only things of interest were a small reservoir a few miles up and two stops on the local winery trail.

Taryn made another turn, pulling onto a broken asphalt road laden with more weeds bisecting an expansive field of live oak trees. Then, a thirty-foot-wide stretch of ground in their path dropped for no reason. They continued down the slope. Their low beams illuminated a fifty-foot-deep quarry with a white van parked at the far end with the windshield facing them.

Each foot further down the path felt like they were descending into a subterranean abyss. Amanda glanced upward out the windshield, confirming the stars were still above. "What is this place?"

"A trap, and you're the bait." Taryn's cold, steely tone signaled that Amanda had failed. That nothing could detour this woman from her path.

Near the bottom, Taryn executed a three-point turn, parking the car so it faced the mouth of the pit and gave the van a clear exit. She then circled the car, pulled Amanda out the passenger door, and led her to the side-panel van by the arm with a firm grip.

The back door slammed shut as they neared the tail end. A clean-cut, trim, muscular man in his late thirties or early forties stepped into view. "You're all set." He handed her a funny-looking phone and a small remote device. A second man appeared behind him. This one was younger and larger with the shape of a bar bouncer. "He's your early warning system. Give him your car keys. Once Mills arrives, activate the bomb and wait for Belcher's call that Amadeus has landed. Then, let the woman go and reset the bomb."

"And Mills?" Taryn handed the large man her key fob.

"Leave her. Whatever you do, don't kill her. Belcher wants her to die in an explosion. With any luck, she'll play hero and blow herself up before the timer goes off. But just in case"—he handed her a second remote, this one looking like a garage door opener—"blow the tunnels once you're topside.

That will seal her in. Belcher is expecting you at the compound by tomorrow night."

Taryn pulled Amanda to the end of the pit and a semicircular rusted metal wall about fifteen feet in diameter. When she pulled open a vertical hatch door, the old hinges squeaked, sounding eerily reminiscent of a coffin lid in horror movies. The interior was dimly lit, making it impossible to determine what lay inside.

Once Amanda was through the hatch, the temperature dropped by twenty or thirty degrees. Another step in, a string of shop lights came to life. She gulped when she realized where she was. She'd heard stories from her teenagers about an abandoned Cold War missile complex that was up this way. They'd explained that it was privately owned and that an independent movie company had recently filmed there. Also, according to their friends, the venturesome high schoolers took pride in breaking into the hatched entrance, tagging the walls with graffiti, and memorializing their exploits with selfies. She laughed silently. She'd given her kids a stern warning to steer clear of this place, but here she was, going deep inside it.

Taryn crawled through and pushed and pulled Amanda along barely lit tunnels and down two levels of corroded metal stairs. The words "This Way" and an arrow had been spray painted onto the wall at every turn as a roadmap. They reached a domed room about one hundred feet in diameter. It had only one entry point—the one they'd come through. Amanda noted that the same type of device on each grocery store door was attached to the doorframe.

Taryn pointed to the center, where a pipe jutted up a foot above the concrete floor and ran horizontally for five feet. Attached to it were six pipe bombs and two short chains, each with a set of heavy metal wrist shackles. She ordered, "Sit." Amanda sat on the cold floor, and Taryn cuffed her to a chain, so both hands were tied tightly around the pipe. "Don't move." Taryn sat several feet away. "Or we'll both be buried down here."

The air was musty, chilling Amanda to the bone. She felt her throat thicken, realizing that she was sitting in her own tomb. "Now what?"

"We wait."

30

A firefighter rushed to Lexi's side as the dust cleared and lifted her from the rubble by the elbow. "Can you walk?" he asked.

"I'm not injured, but my prosthetic leg needs setting." Lexi coughed several times and leaned into him after slinging an arm over his shoulder. The smell of smoke filled her nose. Considering the abundance of combustibles in the grocery store, the cascading explosions likely ignited a fire.

"Was there anyone else inside?" the firefighter asked.

"No. All the hostages got out." Lexi coughed more, watching a second firefighter help Agent Keene to his feet. "Can you take us to the command post?"

"Let me help." Keene shrugged off the assistance and lifted Lexi's other arm over his shoulder. Then the two men supported Lexi toward the corner of the crumbling building. Red emergency lights flashed atop fire trucks, and portable spotlights had the parking lot as bright as a baseball stadium. Firefighters were pulling hoses through the lot. Supervisors were barking orders.

The scene was total chaos.

"Lexi!" Noah came running with a look of dread on his face. Seeing how frightened he was punctuated just how close she'd come to dying. Her first thought went to Nita. She'd witnessed another close call of hers and was likely a nervous wreck.

"I'm fine. I need to see Nita." Lexi turned her attention to the firefighter. "We got it from here."

"Let an EMT check out your lungs. You likely inhaled too much dust." The firefighter then joined his partner and circled around to the front.

Lexi accepted Noah's arm as support and limped toward the inner cordon. When they passed the flow of responders moving in and out, Nita came into view. Noah steered Lexi directly toward her. She was rocking on her heels, and when they locked eyes, she flew a hand over her mouth.

Three steps away, Lexi mouthed, "I'm fine," withdrew her arms, and enveloped them around Nita. She trembled. They both did.

"I love you," Lexi whispered. Escaping the explosion and knowing the hostages were safe was a relief, but Lexi was also afraid for Nita. This day had been one perilous event after another, and Lexi had been at the center of each one, with Nita witnessing every terrifying minute.

"I love you, too." Nita squeezed her tighter before breaking the embrace. "Do you need help with your prosthetic?"

"Yes, please." Lexi smiled.

Nita and Noah guided Lexi to the EMT rig, where a paramedic gave her oxygen for several minutes. When he finished, Nita carefully raised the inner zipper of Lexi's left pant leg and moved the fabric out of the way to expose the length of the socket covering her thigh.

Nita winced when she saw how twisted the socket had become. "Ouch. That must hurt like hell."

"It does." Lexi wasn't overselling it. She'd been walking and running on her off-kilter leg since stepping oddly out of the van, and now her residual limb was throbbing, feeling like she'd hit it with a hammer.

Nita rolled the neoprene sleeve over the socket, releasing the suction holding it in place. She then eased the leg off, taking care to not aggravate Lexi's sore limb. The relief was instant, but now Lexi faced putting the darn thing back on without letting the skin and flesh properly air. "Do you have your tool handy?"

"Of course." Lexi fished her Allen wrench from her cargo pocket and began adjusting the set screws to align the foot and ankle with the socket.

Meanwhile, Nita lightly massaged Lexi's limb through her four layers of cotton socks and nylon liner. The touch was more clinical than loving, a departure from Nita's typical technique with her. But, considering their surroundings, that was the most Lexi expected.

"I won't ask about a fresh liner," Nita commented without looking up.

Lexi snorted. "I have a few in my backpack, but I haven't seen that for hours." She touched Nita's hand. "Have you eaten? You look tired."

Nita smiled. "I had a burger, but I should ask you the same thing."

"Somebody brought subs into the SWAT van."

While Nita cared for Lexi's leg, their back and forth felt unforced, providing a brief respite of calm and normality. But tonight wasn't over. Keene's wife had been taken, and the FBI agent on the plane carrying Amadeus was close to getting the final coordinates for landing. Both situations had disastrous implications.

Noah approached and whispered into Lexi's ear, "Keene needs you right now."

She scanned the area, finding Agent Keene standing with Agent Mitchell. They were arguing. "Tell him I'll be right there after fixing my leg."

Once Noah retreated, Lexi focused on Nita's face. Tears had pooled at the lower rims of her eyes. Reality had sunk in with her too. "I have to go."

Nita's lips trembled, expressing the fear Lexi felt from her. "Come back to me, Lexi."

She lifted Nita's chin and pulled it close, kissing her lips. "I will." After donning her prosthesis and zipping her pant leg, Lexi stood from the back of the EMT rig, testing her repair job. "It's nearly perfect."

Nita forced a smile. "Go. They're waiting. I'll stay in the van with Dylan." That brave front deserved one more kiss. Lexi pulled Nita close, pressing their lips and bodies together for longer than she should have given the urgency on Keene's face. But she couldn't help herself. Nita deserved her attention as much as he did. When they pulled apart, the fear in Nita's eyes looked less prominent, giving Lexi the assurance that she'd be all right. At least for now.

By the time she set off to talk to Keene, his animated gestures and jerky movements had escalated. She picked up her pace when he wound up to give Mitchell a right cross on the jaw. Noah stepped between them and held Keene back. Detective Hughes had also joined the group, helping to keep Keene from giving Mitchell a fat lip. Whatever was going on didn't bode well for Amanda.

"What the hell, people?" Lexi asked, bouncing her focus between Keene and Mitchell. "What's the word on Amanda?"

Keene gripped his cell phone so hard Lexi swore she heard the protective case crack. "Belcher called. He's willing to exchange Amanda's life for his brother's release, but stick up the ass here is calling off the exchange."

Lexi cocked her head back, taking in the sudden turn of events. "But why?"

"I have my orders from the AG. Under no circumstance are we to lose custody of Lyle Belcher. He agreed to this ruse to buy us time to get the hostages out. We did that."

"All but one," Lexi barked.

"If we give in to Belcher for threatening one of our family members, every nut job with a brother or cousin in prison will come out of the woodwork and try to leverage for their release. We can't set the precedence."

"You're condemning her to die, you son of a bitch." Keene lurched toward Mitchell, but Noah held him back again.

"Look, sir. I'm sorry, but my hands are tied." Mitchell didn't look sorry. He looked like he was doing a job that was way over his head. "This came from the AG himself." He pulled out his cell phone and dialed. "Patch me through to the plane... This is ASAC Mitchell. Abort mission. Repeat. Abort mission."

Keene buried his face in his hands as Mitchell walked away. He was a victim of policy and politicians and against an uncaring, immovable wall. Then as quickly as he fell apart, Keene steeled himself, acquiring a look of determination. "Then I go around him." He checked his watch. "I don't have much time to put this together, Agent Mills, but I can't do this without you."

"What do you have in mind?" she asked.

"Belcher had one catch to sparing Amanda's life." He took a weighty breath, foretelling the demand involved something he had no control over, but Lexi did.

"He wants me."

"I offered to take her place, but he said he'd only let Amanda go in exchange for you and his brother. You've already risked your life multiple times today to save people you don't know. I don't have the right to ask you to do it again."

Lexi placed her hands on her hips and lowered her chin, taking in the situation's enormity. Belcher would not have taken this path if she hadn't stopped the Red Spades from assassinating the governor and lighting the fuze of revolution. She was responsible for his desperation. "Yes, you do. He's holding your wife because of me, so I need to do what I can."

"But I can't ask you to sacrifice your life."

"If we do this right, Amanda and I can both walk away. But we have one problem. Mitchell has recalled the plane carrying Amadeus."

"I know the agent on that plane. I trained him. He'll listen to reason." Keene removed his phone from his blazer pocket and dialed. "This is Assistant Deputy Director Keene. Put me through to Agent Vasquez of the Sacramento Field Office on his sat phone."

Keene straightened his posture, rubbing the back of his neck while waiting for the call to connect. When Lexi first met him in the SWAT van, he appeared worried but collected. But now, his sweaty brow and pale skin suggested he was grasping at straws. Finally, he slumped his shoulders when someone answered. "Coby, it's Maxwell. I'm putting you on speaker. I'm here with Agent Lexi Mills of the ATF and Detective Noah Black of the Nogales Police Department. I have a big ask."

After Keene explained Belcher had taken Amanda again and demanded the exchange continue, Coby asked, "What do you need from me?"

"I can't ask you to let Amadeus go, but can you buy me time?"

"We're already returning to Castle," Coby said.

"That's going to get Amanda killed. Belcher can track the satellite phone location in real-time." The desperation in Keene's voice flowed like a whitewater river. It was relentless. "I need you to turn the plane around and make that call as scheduled. Give us time to get to her."

The silence on the phone was unsettling. Amanda's life rested on the trust Keene had built with the man on the other end. Then Coby said, "You owe me, Maxwell. I'll take this as far as possible, but I can't lose Amadeus."

Keene wobbled. "Thank you, Coby. I won't forget this. We'll call your direct line the second Amanda is safe."

When Keene disconnected the call, Lexi asked, "What were Belcher's instructions?"

"You are to drive north out of town. Only you. Unarmed. I'm to send him a text that you've left. Then ten minutes later, he'll text you the coordinates of her location. If there's a hint that law enforcement is following you or are close by, I'll never see Amanda again."

Lexi searched the hectic parking lot for Nita, first looking near the EMT rig, but she wasn't there. She then followed the path to the SWAT van with her eyes and glimpsed Nita at the top of the stairs. She looked back, locked eyes with her, and offered a small, tentative wave. Lexi waved back in the same manner, struck by the feeling that this might have been their final goodbye.

Noah gripped her sleeve and waited to speak until she shifted her gaze to him. His stare was unblinking and immovable. "I'm not letting you go alone, Lexi."

"This is between Belcher and me. I can't ask you to go."

"You're not the only one who gets to play hero. I'm going with you." Even if Lexi said no, Noah would find a way to follow and protect her.

Lexi's grateful smile answered him first. "Okay."

Keene dialed the last incoming number. The call connected. "Belcher, we have a deal."

31

Standing steps outside the cockpit area, Coby Vasquez returned the agency-issued satellite phone to his windbreaker front pocket. He realized his career was over unless everything went right on both ends. Next month he would cross the five-year mark with the FBI, but now he wasn't sure if he wanted a sixth. He'd taken an oath to keep the world free of assholes like the Belcher brothers, but at what cost? If helping the mentor he idolized came with consequences, he wanted nothing to do with it. He'd prefer to quit rather than be forced to play everything by the book.

He dipped his head inside the cockpit, taking a deep breath before saying the words that would likely seal his fate as an agent. "Change of plans, fellas. I need you to resume a heading toward Las Vegas but slow it down as much as possible."

"You got it." The pilot radioed whatever control tower was tracking their flight and entered into a slow turn.

Coby returned to his seat and focused on the prisoner, refusing to close his eyes except to blink. The smug look on Amadeus said he knew circumstances were changing rapidly and that the pendulum had just swung in his favor.

Coby checked the timer on his watch. Thirty seconds. The plane was heading in the right direction again, so the stage was set to give Keene the time he needed. Pulling out Belcher's sat phone, he had to put on the performance of his life. He pressed the last number dialed and put the call on speaker. It connected on the third ring.

"You deviated from the flight path and slowed your speed." Anger fueled Belcher's tone.

"It's your own damn fault," Coby barked. "You people blew up the store and spooked the agents on the ground. But Keene is back in control and will meet your demands. Once we turned around, the FAA had us slow to accommodate other traffic."

"Brother?" Belcher said.

Amadeus sat taller in his seat. "Yes?"

"Have they mistreated you in any way?"

"No, they've been excellent hosts."

"Then we will toast your freedom tonight." Belcher then passed the coordinates to Coby. "If you haven't landed within thirty minutes, Amanda Keene will die."

Coby disconnected the call, set the timer on his watch for thirty minutes, and relayed the landing location and timing requirement to the pilot. "Can you tell me where it is?"

The pilot entered the information into the inflight computer. "It's a landing strip on the north rim of the Grand Canyon. It's about one hundred eighty miles east of Las Vegas."

"What's close by?"

The pilot typed more on the keyboard and scrolled through several screens. "It's on a working cattle ranch and tourist destination. The nearest town looks to be about seventy miles north."

Wow, Coby thought. Belcher had picked the perfect remote location. Even if Keene dispatched someone to the area, they couldn't get there before their plane landed. "It looks like I won't have any backup on the ground."

"Don't worry, Agent Vasquez, I'll drain every possible second and be wheels down right on time."

Coby thanked him and got Keene on his agency phone. He told him their destination and described its remoteness. "I'll stall as long as I can, Max, but know this. I'll shoot Amadeus before losing him."

"I hope it won't come to that, Coby. Agent Mills is getting set to leave. With any luck, we'll both be heading home in less than an hour with Amanda and Amadeus in hand."

Once Coby completed the call, he returned to his seat, focusing on his prisoner.

"This is a game you'll never win." Amadeus' grin was cocky and annoying.

Against his better judgment and with nothing more to lose, Coby engaged. "Why is that?"

"Because people like you don't think strategically."

"And what kind of people is that?" Coby had read Lyle's file and knew the answer, but he wanted to hear his bigoted rationale firsthand.

"People who wear badges."

"So, because I enforce the law, I'm incapable of employing a rational thought process that focuses on analyzing critical factors and variables?"

"The badge makes it an impossibility. It makes you a puppet of the government, which means you are limited by a convoluted construct of rules and regulations. By its very nature, the government stifles thinking that does not conform to that construct."

"I won't disagree with the general assumption, but your limited thinking doesn't account for individualism, nor does it explain why governments evolve. Instead, it supposes a static environment where the human need for betterment doesn't exist."

Amadeus harrumphed. "I wouldn't have expected such critical thinking from you."

"Why is that?"

"Because of your heritage."

"So, because my skin isn't as white as yours, that automatically makes me incapable of critical thought?"

"You brought up skin color, not me."

"That's a copout. You judged me based on what you see, not on who I am."

"That's because biology is immutable. You must have white blood running through your veins."

"So only the white part of me is the reason for my logic and abstract thinking."

"Your people rarely think in those terms."

Coby crossed his arms in front of his chest and leaned back in his jump seat. He was going to enjoy this. "Enlighten me. How do Latinos think?"

"They think they can come into this country without waiting their turn in line. That despite having no legal right to be here, they can take up limited resources. They expect handouts in the form of food stamps and welfare. And they expect others to pay for their healthcare and education without lifting a finger for it."

His partner snorted. "You just described half of the Democrat Party."

"Oh boy," Coby mumbled, thinking about the hours he might be stuck in a car with Sinclair for future stakeouts.

"So you understand why they must die as an unbeliever." Lyle's eyes lit at the possibility of sitting across from a compatriot.

"Not on your life," Sinclair said. "A difference of opinion or political or religious belief is never cause for violence. Mocking maybe, but never brutality as you have done. You're an animal who needs to be caged for the rest of your life." He pointed at the chains around Amadeus' wrists and ankles. "This hostage exchange proves those are well deserved."

Coby formed a wry grin. The jury was still out on Lathan, but other than being a hothead, he seemed to be precisely the type of agent he'd want to have his back when shit hit the fan.

Amadeus raised his bound hands as far as they would reach. "These are proof that I will never bend a knee to a corrupt government of unbelievers, especially to this one." He sneered at Coby before narrowing his eyes, taking on the look of pure evil. "The Gatekeepers will unleash a hell you have never seen if you interfere with the revolution again."

Lathan dropped his smile. "We'll see about that."

A chill washed through Coby, prompting him to check the timer on his watch. They had twenty minutes before they would have wheels on the ground. At that point, he'd have to decide how far he was willing to let this go to save Amanda's life. He was sure of one thing: Amadeus could not be let loose on the world again.

Coby's mind drifted to what his mother, the optimist, used to say to him as a child. *"Hope for the best but prepare for the worst."* The way this day was going, he expected the worst and was prepared for it. The best he could hope for was to stay alive.

32

Lexi sat on the back bumper of Hughes' personal truck he had brought over earlier. She inventoried the carefully selected items he'd rummaged up for her—a mini pocketknife with a sharp blade, a six-foot strip of rolled-up duct tape, a small makeup mirror, and the teeniest flashlight he could find. During her ten-year career with the ATF, she'd used a combination of these tools to render safe ninety percent of the explosives she'd run across. The only difference with these was that she needed to sneak them past whatever guard might be waiting for her. But she had a solution.

Lexi removed her prosthetic and loosened the shoelaces, exposing the lip of the shell covering her high-tech foot. Feeling inside with two fingers, she estimated the gap between the plastic shell and the metal strut provided enough space to stow the tools. Stuffing them into a baggie, Lexi crammed everything into the foot and relaced her shoe. She wasn't sure if she'd have to disarm any device, but it sure as hell made her feel better knowing she had the right tools.

While re-donning her leg, Lexi considered giving Nita one more kiss but couldn't bring herself to walk inside the SWAT van. An emotional goodbye wouldn't provide her the clear head she needed. So once finished, she joined Noah, Keene, and Hughes a few feet away.

Hughes handed her a key fob to his personal truck he had an officer drive over a few hours ago. "I still have thirty-two payments to go, so please try to bring it back in one piece." He then flipped down the tailgate and climbed into the bed. Noah followed, slinging a Gladding PD sniper's rifle with a night vision scope over his back.

Hughes lifted the lid of the built-in toolbox at the far end. "I'd never fit, but you should be fine in here."

Lexi was too short to see over the side of the truck, so she circled to the back. The corrugated metal box ran the width of the bed and reached the lip of the sides. She compared its volume to Noah's size. It would be a tight fit with his rifle. "You're not claustrophobic, are you?"

"I'm about to find out." Noah double-checked his radio earpiece and borrowed Glock before stepping inside. He then laid down with the rifle flat against his chest. Once Hughes showed him how to release the latch from the inside, he closed the lid.

Lexi pressed the mic on the tactical radio Keene gave her. "Can you hear me, Noah?"

"Loud and clear."

"How is it in there?"

"Not bad, but don't dawdle."

Lexi hopped into the driver's seat and closed the door. She then plugged her phone into the charging cable in Hughes' truck, leaving it in the cupholder in the center console next to the tactical radio. Adjusting the seat and mirrors, she started the engine and leaned her head out the window, focusing on Keene. "Text Belcher my number. I'll be back soon with Amanda."

Lexi pulled forward. Before passing through the entry control point, she looked in the rearview, catching one more glance of the SWAT van. The door opened, and Nita appeared at the top of the stairs, holding Dylan's hand and walking him down. God, she was beautiful inside and out. She had a sense of grace that made Lexi's heart full every time she entered her orbit. A year with this woman wasn't nearly enough time.

"I'll come back, Nita."

Lexi pressed the gas and started on the route north out of town. Traffic was light. The sky was dark. The cab was silent. And Lexi's heart was pounding nervously. She was heading into Belcher's trap, one he intended to bury her in.

Her phone rang. The unique ringtone made her smile. Swiping the screen, she put the call on speaker. "Is it bumpy back there, Noah?"

"If I didn't know you better, I'd swear you're hitting every pothole on purpose."

"It's that or swerve. Pick your poison."

"I'll take the potholes."

"Noah." Several moments of silence passed while Lexi put thought into her next words. They needed to convey her gratitude while keeping a cork on her emotions. "Besides my parents and Nita, I've trusted only two people well enough to walk through fire for—Trent Darby and you. I'm honored that you trust me enough to do the same."

"I didn't take that shot in Bowie just to let you do this without backup." Noah was rightly proud of taking out her only lead to Belcher back then. If he didn't, David Lindsey would have taken out his trailer and Lexi along with it. But that seemed like a lifetime ago, especially now that Belcher had Lexi exactly where he wanted her.

"If something happens to me, I need you to watch over Nita and get her home. She's very fragile right now."

"She's at a crossroads, Lexi. When this is over, you two need to have a long talk." Noah's allusion to Nita's emotional state suggested he'd pieced together her struggle with addiction.

"I'm guessing you know more than you're letting on, Noah." His silence confirmed her suspicion. "And you know why she'll need a familiar face if I don't make it back. Please, keep her from slipping to the bottom."

"Let's focus on getting you and Amanda home tonight." Noah sighed.

Lexi's phone dinged to an incoming text. A glance at the screen confirmed it was from a blocked number and that the message contained geo-coordinates. "This is it. I'm pulling over so I can enter the destination into my GPS. I'm hanging up and switching to the tactical radio."

"Hey, Lexi."

"Yeah?"

"I got your back."

"I know you do." Lexi disconnected their call and pressed the mic on her radio. "I have the location." She repeated the numbers as she entered them into the GPS app. Once finished, she continued on the designated route.

Hughes came on the air. "You're heading to an abandoned Cold War Titan missile silo complex. If they take you deep inside, cell phones won't work. Neither will our radios. I remember some kids were trapped in there years ago, and the only signals that reached that deep were satellite phones. You'll need to get topside to radio us that you're free."

"Wonderful," Lexi replied. As if swapping herself as a hostage in Belcher's deadly game wasn't bad enough, she was about to go deep inside a dark, subterranean tomb. When she was a child, she hid in the cellar once when a tornado threatened to rip through her home. Each time, the thought of being buried alive far below the surface had creeped her out. Tonight, she would have to go deeper with the certainty that Belcher intended her to die there.

"It's all farmland out there," Hughes continued. "The nearest house is about a mile away. If we send any backup, Belcher's people will see them coming for miles."

"It looks like we're on our own, Noah," Lexi said.

"What else is new?" Noah added through the radio.

"We'll start some units in that direction, but they'll lay back at the next farm."

Lexi followed the GPS directions, turning from the country road onto a weed-laden gravel path that was bumpier than a rollercoaster. "Sorry, Noah. I'll try to miss the big rocks."

"Don't worry about me," he said. "Just drive."

After nearly a mile, Lexi turned onto another trail littered with broken chunks of asphalt and more weeds from years of neglect. This appeared to be the original road built by the Air Force but was now home to lizards and wild rabbits.

When she neared a grouping of oak trees, the outline of a compact sedan appeared in her headlights. A moment later, a large man with an automatic rifle sprang from the trees. He positioned himself in Lexi's path and aimed his military weapon at the windshield. "This is it. I'm being stopped by a white male. Thirties. Geez. He's as big as a house."

"Good luck, Mills," Keene said.

"Yes, good luck," Hughes added.

"See you in a few, Lexi." Noah's confident tone gave her the boost she needed. If they both stayed focused, she might survive this.

Lexi slowed the truck, coming to a stop five feet from Bruiser. He yelled, "Get out of the truck." The muzzle aimed at her face gave no wriggle room.

"Lexi, before walking away from the truck," Noah said, "knock twice if I'll be seen getting out of here. Otherwise, knock once. That will tell me whether to come out hot."

"Will do, Noah. And if this goes south, tell Nita that all I want for her is to be happy. Tell her to find love again."

Lexi turned off the engine, took a deep breath, threw her earpiece on the passenger seat, and opened the door. Slipping out, she tossed the fob underneath the truck, making it inoperable, and eased herself to the ground, using the sidestep. She raised her hands shoulder high. "I'm unarmed."

"Let me be the judge of that." He wagged the rifle toward the hood. "Hands on the car. Don't give me any trouble if you want that woman to live."

He looked inside the cab before peeking his head over the sides of the bed. He tried lifting the toolbox lid where Noah was hiding, but it didn't budge. Then, seemingly satisfied that no one else was in the truck, he slung the rifle over his shoulder and returned to Lexi. He patted her down, starting with her arms. Moving to the front, he groped her breasts unnecessarily long and hard and pressed his body against her back and bottom. If he'd tried this in any other setting, he'd walk away with two broken arms.

Lexi kept her hands on the smooth fender but raised her good leg six inches and stomped on his right foot. "You can move on."

"Watch it, bitch, or I'll have a little more fun with you before heading down."

"And that would be the last thing you do on Earth."

He continued searching her waist and beltline, making her skin crawl. Finally, he moved on to her right leg, then her left. "What the hell is that."

"It's my prosthetic leg. If you want me to walk anywhere, you better leave it on. Otherwise, I'll be crawling."

He harrumphed and stepped back, un-shouldering his weapon. He poked the muzzle in her back like a cattle prod. "Start walking. We're going to the bottom of the pit."

"Then what?"

"You go inside and follow the signs painted on the walls."

Lexi knocked her knuckles once on the fender before stepping away, giving Noah the signal that he could climb safely from his hiding place without being seen. She walked down the path, partially lit by the truck's headlights. Twenty steps in, the ground sloped downward, and the dirt walls grew taller on either side. It felt like she was descending a forty-foot-wide ramp into an underground parking garage. At the bottom, about two hundred yards away, a dim light illuminated a small section of a wall.

Her prosthetic foot slipped on a rock, making her wobble. Steadying herself before she face-planted, Lexi glanced over her shoulder, confirming Bruiser was five steps behind her. "Do you have a flashlight?"

"Just walk."

Before Lexi pivoted to continue her march, Noah called out, "Hey, asshole." Two steps behind Bruiser, he wielded the rifle butt square into Bruiser's forehead, creating a loud thud. The man tumbled unconscious to the rocky ground.

"I thought you'd never come." Lexi gave Bruiser a firm kick in the gut, wishing he was awake to feel it. "That's for groping me, asshole."

Noah furrowed his brow and gave the man a second belly kick. "Asshole."

He handed Lexi her cell phone and tactical radio. She checked the timer. They had eight minutes before Amadeus should be on the ground. That didn't leave them with much time to spare. "We better keep moving."

She and Noah continued down the rocky slope toward the light. After another hundred feet, they reached the pit bottom. A rusty metal wall rounded at the top guarded the end. It had a three-foot-wide hatch door, looking like a portal into a piece of history where Amanda Keene was being held. But Lexi knew what really lay inside: her fate.

33

Lexi looked up from the bottom of the pit. She had to be at least sixty or seventy feet below the surface. The thought of going into a deep underground hole made her shiver. Memories of hearing the twister roar like a freight train overhead from the basement of her childhood home came flooding back. Her mother had huddled with her in the corner while her father held the rattling cellar doors in place. It was the only time she'd witnessed genuine fear in his eyes. Since that day, she'd equated bad things with cold, dark, underground places.

Without time to waste, she shook off the bad feeling and pulled the hatch open. Raising her leg over the lower lip, she stepped through, awakening a string of shop lights hanging from the ceiling. The warm night air instantly chilled, like she'd walked into a refrigerator. Even the smell reminded her of moldy fruits and vegetables from her produce drawer.

"At least we won't be in the dark," she mumbled.

The rusty, dank, graffiti-laden room was void of equipment or signage, but its large dimensions suggested it once had an industrial purpose, not administrative. She followed the lights to a doorway that led to a murky corridor. Maybe she'd spoken too soon about the dark. But once she stepped through, another set of lights turned on, extending to the left. Apparently, the lights were Belcher's automated breadcrumbs.

Following the lights and arrows painted on the walls down another corridor and two flights of stairs, Lexi stopped at an intersection of tunnels. IEDs made of pipe bombs were wired into the string of lights above her head. They could be connected to a master trigger, and if they went off, every tunnel would be sealed.

She checked her phone, confirming her fear that she wasn't getting a signal this deep inside. She then pressed the mic on the tactical radio. "Keene, can you hear me?" She tried again but received no response. "We're too short on time for both of us to go down and radio Keene that we have Amanda. You need to stay topside. Otherwise, Amadeus will get away."

"I don't like this, Lexi."

Neither did she. The idea that her backup would be minutes away on foot was unsettling, but she couldn't chance unleashing the madman on the world again. "It's the only way. Once Amanda is safe, radio it in. Then come back."

"These lights will take away the element of surprise when I do."

"It's a chance we'll have to take."

"If we lose Amadeus and you're still not out, I'm coming in." Noah's stern expression meant there was no talking him out of it.

"Fine." After a brief hug, Lexi left, following the lighted path at a sharp pace.

Anger was fueling her resolve to get this over with, not courage. She was mad as hell at Belcher for concocting this elaborate scheme to reconstitute the Gatekeepers' leadership while exacting his revenge on her. She was mad about the things Nita had seen today and how they'd brought her to the tipping point. But mostly, she was mad at herself for resting on her laurels. She'd done nothing the last four months to look for leads on Belcher. Maybe if she had, none of this would have happened today.

Lexi went down another long tunnel. More sections of lights turned on the farther she went, like the frozen food compartments in her grocery store. When she reached the end, her only option was to make a left. She stepped on the grated metal platform, the clanking echoing down the tunnel. Finally, a doorway came into view. It was lit by a similar red glow as the bombs at the POW site and grocery store. *Great*, she thought. A proximity bomb was impossible to get around in these cramped conditions.

A woman called out, "Stop right there."

"Taryn, it's Lexi Mills. I'm alone. Your man topside sent me down."

"I'm surprised you came," Taryn said.

"Well, I'm here. Let's get this over with."

The red glow disappeared. "All right, come in."

Lexi's pulse quickened. Once she stepped over the threshold, she would be trapped. No going back. But she was responsible for Amanda being here, and she couldn't be the reason Dylan would be without his mother. Being resolved, however, didn't come without fear of dying. Her only disappointment was not proposing to Nita earlier. Now, Nita would never hear Lexi say that she wanted to go through life as her wife, not merely as a partner. That construct might not hold meaning to some, but for Nita and Lexi, it represented a commitment beyond faithfulness. It meant their journeys started and ended with each other.

Lexi swallowed her regret and entered. The large dome room took her by surprise. She'd expected Belcher to have chosen a smaller space for Lexi's demise so she'd feel caged, precisely what she wanted for him. But looking up at the concrete walls forming a smooth, continuous surface to the ceiling, she understood his choice. This appeared to be the control room, where officers once sat, ready to unleash unholy nuclear hell on the world. The room meant that Belcher was in control and was about to do the same to Lexi.

She focused her attention on Amanda, chained to a pipe on the floor in the center of the room. Her slumped posture and tight expression suggested she was exhausted and scared. A collection of pipe bombs of the same configuration she encountered at the POW site was beside her hands. It had one addition—a small metal box with a digital screen. It was likely a timer. Unfortunately, the wires running from the bomb to the timer were encased in metal.

There was enough explosive material there to collapse this entire dome. Then Lexi considered its genius location. It was isolated from the rest of the complex, which meant other sections would survive when this one was destroyed. That would give Taryn time to get out safely if Lexi detonated the explosives prematurely. It was a nearly perfect trap. Their only weakness was not having enough security topside.

Directly behind Amanda, Taryn was pressing the muzzle of a gun to her head. Taryn's stiff posture and straight face hinted she was anxious but not overwrought. That was the first positive thing Lexi had seen tonight. Her captor was calm, not emotional or strung out on drugs. At the very least, the likelihood of her accidentally triggering an explosion was low.

Taryn lifted her left hand and pointed it toward the entrance. She was holding a remote device similar to the one Lexi had seen in the drone video among Taryn's belongings when she'd dropped her purse. Lexi glanced over her shoulder. The reappearance of the red glow on the door explosive confirmed Taryn was holding the trigger. They were locked in here together.

"Chain yourself to the pipe," Taryn ordered. "If you try anything, she dies."

Lexi sat next to Amanda. "Are you okay? Did they hurt you?"

"No, I'm fine. But what are you doing here?"

"They would only let you go if I came."

"What about Belcher's brother?"

"Him too. It's a two-for-one," Lexi explained.

"I don't know how you fit into this, Lexi"—Amanda's eyes expressed her gratitude—"but you're a hero for doing this."

"You can get to know one another in a minute." Taryn waggled the pistol at Lexi.

Lexi laced one hand under and the other over the pipe before placing the three-inch-wide metal shackles around her wrists. They looked like a prop from the *Fifty Shades of Grey* set, and Lexi didn't want to know where Taryn had gotten them. Taryn then attached a heavy-duty padlock, securing them in place.

"Now what?" Lexi asked.

"We wait for Belcher's call. That will tell me whether she dies with you."

Five minutes earlier, the pilot announced they had begun their descent into Hells Hollow, the valley where they were to land at a remote strip north of the Grand Canyon. The hum of two prop engines changed, signaling they were close to their destination.

Coby lifted his stare to Lyle—or Amadeus, as he called himself. He'd sat smugly following his earlier rant without another word. Thank God. Coby wasn't sure if he could stomach another lesson in racism and bigotry. Though, he was surprised that Lyle's blathering didn't include more of a religious tone. The report he'd read about the Gatekeepers said that his brother was considered the hand of God by his followers. Piousness must run only so deep in their family. Lyle's bent was more earthly, based on hatred rather than devotion.

The pilot poked his head around the partial wall separating the flight deck from the passenger area. "Buckle up, fellas. We land in two minutes." Coby and Lathan acknowledged with their thumbs.

Coby tossed Lathan Belcher's sat phone and pulled out his agency-issued one. He dialed Keene. The call connected on the first ring. "We land in a minute. I'll stay on the line with you."

"Thank you, Coby. Mills made it to where Amanda is being held, but she hasn't been released yet. Once Amadeus calls his brother and says he is on the ground, I'm confident he'll let her go. Then it's a race against the clock. I'll let you know the second she's in the clear."

"We'll be ready."

A jolt rocked the plane as the wheels skidded along the tarmac. Then a second. The brakes engaged, slowing their momentum. As instructed, the pilot taxied to the end of the runway and turned into the wind, readying for a quick takeoff. When they came to a stop, the engines continued to idle.

Coby entered the flight deck and looked out the windshield. The area was dark, with only the moon, stars, and a collection of lights in the distance a mile or two away illuminating the sky. He searched for people or a waiting car. Despite seeing nothing but brush and gullies surrounding the airstrip, he sensed they were being watched. "Keep the engines running. Things might get a little dicey." He returned to the passenger area, still holding the phone with the open line to Keene. He looked at his partner. "Make the call."

Lathan called the last number on Belcher's sat phone, putting it on speaker and holding it close to Lyle's face. The call connected, and Lyle smiled. "I've landed, brother."

"Yes, I know. Our people have eyes on you."

"He's here," Coby said. "Now let Amanda Keene go."

"Not until you release him and he's walking across the tarmac," Belcher replied. "You can start by opening the hatch."

"No deal." Coby hoped to draw this out to the last possible second. "I want proof that Amanda is safe."

"Then she and Lexi Mills both die, and we do this all over again with another agent's wife. Perhaps yours, Agent Vasquez. Or yours, Agent Sinclair."

How in the hell did Belcher know their names? That meant their families were at risk as much as Keene's. Rage for the threat against their wives fueled him. He opened the passenger door, letting in the cool desert night air. He looked outside but still saw no one. He then dragged Lyle to the open hatch and held the muzzle of his service weapon to the back of his head. Lathan held the phone close. "I know you can see me. Let me talk to Lexi Mills to confirm Amanda is released, or I'll put a bullet in your brother's head."

"You are brave when it's not your wife whose life is at stake."

"I'm holding you to your word."

"Fine, we'll do it your way." A moment of silence passed. Then Belcher returned. "I have Lexi Mills conferenced in."

"Mills? This is Agent Vasquez. I have Amadeus. Are you with Amanda?"

"Yes, I'm here alone with her and Taryn, Belcher's operative," Mills said. "We're being held underground in an abandoned missile complex."

He recognized her voice from his earlier call with Keene. He deciphered her comment that "alone" meant Noah Black wasn't close. "Let me know when she lets Amanda go."

"I will, but she won't be safe until she gets outside," she said. "The entire place is wired to blow, including the tunnels."

"Feeling like you're out of options, Agent Vasquez?" Belcher laughed. "I'm keeping my word, but you can't be sure she's out of harm's way until Amadeus disappears into the night."

Coby gritted his teeth. Belcher was right. He'd boxed him into a corner. They had one secret weapon left. His last hope was good timing with Noah. "Fine. I'll let Amadeus go once Lexi gives me the word."

34

"Let the woman go." Belcher's order was music to Lexi's ears. Now it was a matter of timing.

Bending to unchain Amanda from the bar, Taryn had the emotionless expression of a brainwashed disciple, not that of a stone-cold killer. Though, killing was much easier when it didn't require looking the victim in the face when they took their last breath. Lexi imagined she was a devotee whose life wouldn't have purpose without the Belcher brothers and the Gatekeepers. In her experience with followers like David Lindsey, there was no reasoning with them, only catching them off guard.

Lexi noted Taryn's every move after she laid the phone on the floor. She shoved the gun in the waistband at the small of her back and returned the keys to her front righthand jeans pocket after unlocking Amanda's padlock. Taryn stepped back, retrieving the gun and aiming it at Amanda with her right hand. Reaching into her lefthand jacket breast pocket, she inspected the remote before returning it. She then retrieved a second remote from the right pocket. The two units appeared different. The first one resembled a garage door opener, leaving open the possibility that the devices in the tunnel were hardwired into a base unit. But where? It wasn't in the room, and Lexi didn't see it coming in. However, it had to be within fifty feet for the remote to work. She must have missed it right outside the door. Merely unplugging it or disabling the remote would sever Taryn's ability to blow up the tunnels.

Taryn pressed the second remote, turning off the proximity device guarding the entrance. She then returned it to her pocket. When she reached down to lift Amanda by the elbow, that was Lexi's chance. She might not get another opportunity to have her within striking distance.

Lexi gripped the bar for leverage, shifted her weight to her right side, and kicked out her left leg, hitting Taryn in the knee and sending her tumbling to the ground. The gun fell from her hand, and the remotes spilled from her pockets. One was within reach of Lexi's foot, so she kicked it, sending it hurtling toward the wall. When it reached the concave concrete, it disappeared into a gap between the wall and the floor.

When Taryn scrambled for her gun, Lexi yelled, "Run, Amanda. Run."

Amanda dashed out the doorway. The lights in the corridor turned on. When Lexi heard the clatter of feet hitting the grated metal platform, she knew Amanda was in the long tunnel. If she kept running, she should be out the hatch two levels up within two or three minutes, and Noah could radio Keene in time to snatch Amadeus before he got away.

Taryn rushed to her feet, gun in hand, and located the last remaining remote unit. Lexi couldn't see which one it was—the one that controlled the proximity device or the one that would detonate the tunnel bombs. She pressed it.

Lexi slammed her eyes shut, waiting for the blast in the tunnels. But it never came. She then looked up and saw the red glow had reappeared, and Taryn had fury in her eyes that made Lexi think she had but seconds to live.

"That was a stupid try, you bitch." Taryn picked up the sat phone. "She's gone. Let Amadeus go." She then stuck the phone in Lexi's face. "Tell them."

"Amanda's free but the—" Before Lexi could finish the sentence that Amanda was in no danger, Taryn slugged her in the jaw with her pistol. A sharp, searing pain ripped through her face, momentarily dazing her. When her vision cleared, Taryn was standing over the stack of pipe bombs chained to the bar, pressing buttons on the digital box attached to it.

"You're lucky I have orders not to kill you. Otherwise, I'd shoot you between the eyes." Taryn pressed the remote, turning off the doorway device.

"You think you've won," Lexi spat. "You haven't, and neither has Belcher. After getting out of here, I won't rest until I track him down."

"I'll be sure to tell him that tomorrow." Taryn reactivated the proximity bomb and turned on her heel down the corridor.

"You won't have a chance to!" Lexi yelled moments before hearing the clomping of feet on the metal grate.

She tugged at her hands, but they were still bound closely around the metal bar. She then shifted to see what Taryn had done to the pipe bombs and discovered she had set a timer. It was at nine minutes and forty-six seconds and counting down. She had to hurry.

Lexi slung her prosthetic leg close to her hands, gripping a shoelace with her fingertips. Once she'd loosened the shoe, she strained to pull out the baggie from her foot shell. She twisted and pulled, but it wouldn't come out. She was stuck, and Noah had no way in without Taryn's remote.

Lexi slumped, resolved to her fate. She'd never get a chance to see the love in Nita's eyes after proposing. She'd never get to fall asleep in Nita's arms again, smelling the fresh scent of orange blossoms after her shower. She was certain Noah would watch over her until he got her home, but what would happen to her after he left? Nita had no family other than her cousin to help her through her grief. Lexi wished she'd called her mother and asked her to stay with Nita. To take her in to make sure she didn't slip into the clutches of addiction again.

"I'm sorry I couldn't keep my word, Nita. I love you."

Noah emerged from the hatch door. Once he secured it and the creaking hinges quieted, he heard moaning. The big brute he'd clocked with his rifle had apparently woken. Unfortunately for the man, Noah didn't have duct tape to quiet him, so he did the next best thing and clobbered him again with his rifle butt. This time he dragged him to the pit's edge to make him less visible. Then, remembering he'd passed a low cropping of rocks about three-quarters down the slope, he jogged in that direction. It was the perfect location. The rocks hid him from below, and the short fifty-yard distance made it an easy shot with his night-vision scope.

He first pulled out the tactical radio Hughes had given him and pressed the mic. "Mills is inside. I had to stay topside to signal you when Amanda is in the clear."

"Copy," Hughes said. "We're standing by."

Noah wished he'd had time to take a practice shot like he did in Bowie before taking the precise one that saved Lexi's life. But he couldn't chance the loud noise echoing and scaring off Amanda or their captor before he could take the kill shot. He'd have to rely on his training and luck.

Noah placed the radio on a nearby rock and positioned himself for his shot. He turned on the scope, wiped the sweat from his brow, and aimed at the hatch. His surroundings turned from darkness to a mix of bright and brighter neon green. He adjusted the focus until he clearly saw the curved metal handle. He was set. Now he had to wait.

The pit was silent. Cold and dark. Even the birds knew enough to stay away.

Then.

The door opened. The longer hair and slender body told Noah it was Amanda. He took another second, waiting for her to turn her head so he could see her face. And there it was. Just like the photograph Keene had shown him. It was her. He lifted his radio without taking his eyes off her and pressed the mic. "Amanda is clear. Repeat. Amanda is clear."

"Copy," he heard.

Half of his job was done. Hopefully, it was in time to retake Amadeus. He called out, "Amanda, this is the police." She froze. "Keep coming." He saw through his scope that she was scared or confused, so he called out again. "I'm with Lexi Mills. Keep coming quickly."

Amanda resumed jogging up the slope, and Noah followed with his scope. Her sneakers crunched the gravel every second. She had exceptional form and seemed in excellent shape, but the steepness slowed her progress. She was forty yards away. Thirty. Twenty.

Then.

The door hinges at the bottom creaked, drawing Noah's attention instantly. He swung his aim in the door's direction. Even through the green neon filter, he could tell the person coming through the hatch was a woman. She appeared to be four or five inches taller than Lexi and had longer hair. She finally turned uphill and started running. It definitely wasn't Lexi. She had a pistol in her right hand.

Noah called out, "Police! Hands up!" His command prompted the woman to stop and aim her weapon in his general direction. That was sufficient provocation. He took a regular breath, exhaled halfway, held it, and focused his sights on center mass. He then eased his index finger back in one smooth motion, increasing the pressure until the shot fired. In one second, the bullet found its target. The woman lurched backward, falling to the ground. He kept focus on her for two seconds to ensure she wasn't moving.

She was motionless.

Noah scanned the slope for Amanda and finally found her. She'd dropped, covering her head with her arms. Noah stood, slinging his rifle and drawing the borrowed Glock. He went straight for Amanda. "Are you hurt?" he asked, helping her up by the elbow.

"No, I'm fine. Just a nervous wreck."

"How was Lexi when you left?"

"She tried fighting off that woman but was chained up. She can't get out."

The hairs on the back of Noah's neck tingled, warning him that Lexi was in imminent danger. "I have to help her. There's a black pickup at the top. Get in and stay there. I'll be back."

Noah ran down the slope, not stopping when Amanda yelled, "Wait!" When he neared the woman he'd shot, she twitched once, so he snatched up her weapon and shot her in the leg on the way by. He didn't have the time to secure her.

He ran to the bottom, ripped the hatch open, and dashed through the first room. The lights came on, section by section. He followed the same route as before, down tunnels and two flights of stairs to the intersection. He then followed the signage down a tunnel and then another long one. At the end, he turned left, the only available direction, pounding his feet on a metal grate walkway. Finally, he entered a corridor that ended at a doorway.

"Noah, stop!" Lexi yelled.

He came to a skidding stop ten feet short of the door. His heart was hammering in his chest like pistons in a V8. "Lexi?" He was mildly out of breath. "Are you okay? I can help you get out."

"You can't. There's a motion sensor on the doorframe. If you get close, you'll set off a bomb."

"What can I do to disarm it?"

The several seconds of silence meant Lexi's prospects weren't good. "We need the remote to turn it off. Taryn has it."

"I'll get it. I shot her in the pit." Then, as he readied to turn around and retrace his steps, Lexi called out.

"There's not enough time. She set a time bomb in here. I have less than four minutes left. You need to get out of here, Noah. Save yourself."

"I won't leave you."

"Please, Noah. Go. Someone needs to be there for Nita. If it can't be me, it needs to be you." The pain in Lexi's voice told him she'd resolved herself to dying in there.

He was ten feet from Lexi, but it felt more like ten miles. They'd done everything according to the plan, but Belcher had outsmarted them. He'd laid just enough traps to make it impossible to get Lexi out.

His frustration erupted with a violent boom. He clenched his fists and pounded them against the metal wall. He screamed so loudly that his voice echoed down the tunnel. "Damn it, Lexi! Damn this to hell. I can't lose you."

Tears released from his lower lids, moistening his cheeks. He couldn't remember the last time he'd cried. Maybe it was when his uncle died, but he couldn't be sure. But he recalled the pain he felt when he came home and learned that the man who'd raised him since he was in grade school had passed away from a heart attack. It was like getting a knife in the gut and having the wind knocked out of him at the same time. Having Lexi tell him to go made him feel the same way. Her dying would cut his soul in half.

"Please, Noah. Go," she repeated.

"I love you, Lexi Mills." And with those five words, Noah did the most gut-wrenching thing he'd ever done. He turned and left.

35

The prop engines were still revving in the darkness, swirling the desert air around the open passenger hatchway. Amadeus' feet were hanging on its edge, with only his toes delighting in the cool taste of freedom. It was a grim moment for Special Agent Coby Vasquez. His grip on a flimsy collar and the chains around Amadeus' wrists and feet were the only restraints keeping him in captivity. If he let go, Coby feared no one would be safe from the evil he'd unleash on the world, but he was out of options. If he didn't give Belcher what he wanted, his mentor's wife would be dead within the hour.

Lathan held Belcher's sat phone up for Coby to hear while Coby kept his agency phone pressed against his ear. The race was about to start.

"Run, Amanda. Run," Lexi yelled through the phone.

"She's gone. Let Amadeus go," the captor growled. "Tell them."

"Amanda's free, but the—" Lexi stopped.

Belcher cut in. "Release Amadeus, or I'll order the tunnels blown."

"This isn't over." Coby gritted his teeth, rippling his jaw muscles, but he finally let go. Releasing Amadeus sucked every ounce of self-respect from his soul, forging the harsh truth that he'd never wear the badge with pride again. Being manipulated into doing a criminal's bidding was more than he could take.

Amadeus hobbled down the stairs with his legs still chained. Coby wasn't about to unlock them and make his escape easier. He couldn't consider the possibility that his wife might be the next victim. Instead, he had to buy Noah Black the minutes needed to report that Amanda was safe.

The moment Amadeus stepped clear of the wing and faced the open runway, a set of headlights appeared in the distance on the other side of the fence. Belcher's eyes on the ground and Amadeus' ride had finally exposed themselves. The car moved. Its headlights bobbed up and down, revealing the rocky terrain surrounding the airstrip. Limited access points thankfully made the distance between the plane and Belcher's people greater than he'd expected, giving him a few extra precious seconds.

Coby's stomach knotted at the thought of Amadeus disappearing in the vast night desert, so he needed to better the odds. Holding the sat phone to his ear, he descended the stairs, moving his feet at lightning speed until he cleared the wing. Then he stopped.

Lathan caught up to him. "Whatever you have in mind, I'm backing you up."

Coby continued walking toward Amadeus without responding. He matched his slow speed, drew his service weapon, and clenched it against his moving hip to avoid presenting an obvious threat. Lathan did the same.

Keene's heavy breathing on the other end of the satellite phone confirmed the line was still open. Unfortunately, it also established that Amanda had yet to appear. And time was running out. The vehicle was picking up speed, and the chances of losing Amadeus were growing exponentially.

The car came close enough to make out the distinctive front grill of the Jeep brand. It stopped several feet from Amadeus. The front passenger door opened.

Then.

Coby heard in his ear, "Amanda is clear. Repeat. Amanda is clear."

He dropped the phone into his pocket and sprinted toward Amadeus at full speed. The pinging footsteps behind him said that Lathan had too. When a man stepped from the car and opened the rear door, Coby raised his weapon. Then he saw a gun in his hand. He didn't hesitate. He fired in three double-tap bursts on the fly, striking the man at least once and sending him limping back toward the Jeep.

Amadeus sped up his waddle, the clanking of the chains now outstripping the low rumble of the airplane engines. He was five feet from the vehicle and reached for the door with his bound hands, giving Coby no other choice. He aimed low, hoping to hit his target in the leg, but Amadeus tripped on his foot chains before he pulled the trigger and rolled onto the rough tarmac.

Lathan opened fire, striking the Jeep multiple times and shattering the side windows. The driver gunned the engine, burning rubber against the asphalt. The Jeep spun sideways before lurching forward. Its tires screeched until the driver straightened the car and sped down the strip.

Coby and Lathan rushed to Amadeus, each grabbing him by the arm. They brought him to his feet and pushed him toward the plane. Coby didn't know if the Jeep would be back or if Belcher had a larger force waiting. They had to get into the plane and in the air.

The harder Coby and Lathan pushed, the more Amadeus fought, giving them no other choice. They holstered their weapons, lifted him by the belly chain around the waist, and dragged him to the plane. At the foot of the steps, they heaved Amadeus through the hatch. He landed with a loud thud that would likely leave bruises for weeks. Lathan climbed the stairs first, and Coby followed, closing the hatch after himself.

"Go! Go! Go!" Coby yelled to the pilot.

The twin-prop engines whined. The plane moved forward, increasing in speed with every second. Coby raised Amadeus by the elbow, bringing him to his knees. "Look who's bending a knee now."

Lathan helped drag and secure the prisoner into a seat before buckling himself in.

Coby buckled in moments before the wheels left the ground. He let a grin of satisfaction form for a brief second before saying into his sat phone, "We have Amadeus." He'd beat Belcher in this round, but what about the next? He had a sinking feeling he or his wife would be in Tony Belcher's crosshairs soon.

"I love you, Lexi Mills." Noah's footsteps meant that was it. Those would be the last words she'd hear.

Lexi slumped into her last three minutes on earth. She'd reserved saying "I love you" for those who had shaped her life, leaving an indelible imprint on her heart—her parents, Nita, and a few select friends. Only three other people had warranted those words from her. The first was her father's crew chief, Gavin. He'd known her since she was tall enough to reach over the fender and tug on a torque wrench. And when her father shunned her after she'd come out as gay, he was there to pick up the pieces. She'd loved her partner Trent Darby, too, but she never told him so. Noah had made that same mark on her life, and she wouldn't make that same mistake with him.

"I love you, too, Noah Black."

The sound of feet stomping on the metal grate was the sign that she was alone, but then she heard a voice. "I thought you might need this."

Then, the red glow of the proximity device disappeared, and Noah and Amanda stepped through the door. She was never so happy to see his unique face. The only thing that could have made this moment better was his smile. It had a way of putting Lexi at ease when everything around her was falling apart.

"Do you have the padlock key?" Lexi asked Amanda.

The sadness in her eyes told her the answer. "I couldn't find it." The optimism she felt a moment ago faded instantly into the pores of the concrete. The chains and wrist bindings were too thick to break through by hand.

"Let me try shooting the chain or lock."

The proximity of the chain and padlock to the bomb made Noah's option too risky. "They're too close. The shrapnel would set it off," Lexi explained. "Help me get the tools from my foot."

"Your what?" Amanda asked.

"Her prosthetic." Noah loosened the laces on Lexi's left shoe, exposing the lip of the foot shell. He quickly slipped out the baggie and emptied its contents onto the concrete floor. "Tell me what to do."

"My only chance is to disable or disconnect the timer. If that doesn't work, you need to get the hell out of here and past the first tunnel." Lexi glanced at the timer. "Two minutes left. You both leave when it gets down to one."

Noah looked up. "What first?"

"Swipe the screen." She doubted it would be that easy, but sometimes the easiest solution was the right one. But when he did, a lock screen appeared, asking for a four-digit code. "That's out. Open the pocketknife to the screwdriver. I didn't see any obvious casing screws, but we need to pop off the top of the timer to get to the power source."

"Got it." Noah inspected the timer casing sides and top. "I'm seeing only two small holes, one on either side, but the knife and screwdriver are too big."

"Those should give access to the locking pins. Does the pocketknife have a toothpick or something narrow?"

"Toothpick." He inserted it into one hole. "I can feel the pin going in."

"Now the other side."

He shifted, tried the other hole, and pulled on the cover. "It's not coming off. Let me try again." He repeated the steps but got the same result. "It's not working. What else can I try."

"The pins must be retractable and need to be pushed in simultaneously. Break the toothpick in half."

"I can't, Lexi. The ends would be too short." Noah ran his hands through his stringy, dark hair. They were running out of time and options. "I don't know what else to do, Lexi."

She glanced at the timer—one minute and twenty seconds. "You two need to leave." Noah's eyes filled with moisture and emotion. The pain he was feeling was contagious and stabbed Lexi in the heart. She didn't want to die, and seeing how devastating this was on her friend worsened the inevitability. "It's all right, Noah. We did our best."

"I promise. I'll get the son of a bitch who did this." His voice cracked on his last word.

Lexi turned her head toward Amanda, but her stare settled on her long hair. She remembered Amanda had it up earlier, but it was down now. "Your hair. Do you have a bobby pin?"

Amanda patted the pockets of her hoodie. "Yes, one." She handed it to

Noah, eliciting a smile from him and Lexi. That uniquely beautiful smile gave her a boost of certainty.

Noah turned to Amanda. "Go. I'll be right behind you."

Without argument, Amanda nodded her concurrence. She kissed Lexi on the forehead, whispered, "Thank you," and ran out the doorway. By the time her feet clomped on the metal grate, Lexi knew she would be safe, and Noah had the bobby pin and toothpick inserted into both holes.

"Got it." He lifted the cover. "Is this going to be a 'cut the red or blue wire' thing?"

"I doubt it. We just need to locate the battery." The Gatekeepers' bomb makers weren't sophisticated. Their triggers had been effective but rudimentary. She glanced at the timer—twenty-five seconds.

"I see it." He blinked and cocked his head, which wasn't a good sign. "A screw is holding it in." He extended the screwdriver again and twisted.

Twenty seconds.

His hand slipped. Twice. This was not the time to learn that Noah's skills only extended to sharpshooting and cooking. Her life depended on whether he was as handy with a screwdriver as a high-powered rifle.

"You just have to loosen it and slide the securing arm over."

Fifteen seconds.

"This damn thing is so tiny." He tried again.

The sweat forming on his brow wasn't reassuring, but she still had faith in Noah. He had to save her. Lexi wasn't ready to die without putting a ring on Nita's finger. Nita deserved to know how deep of an imprint she'd made on Lexi's heart and soul.

He twisted the screw one, two, and three revolutions.

Ten seconds.

"Any time, Noah." Every muscle from neck to toe tensed. This couldn't be the end.

"I got this, Lexi. Don't be pushy." He slid the arm over, crammed the flat screwdriver under the battery, and pried.

Pop.

The timer screen turned dark.

The most beautiful combination of sight and sound relaxed every muscle and tendon like a deflating balloon. Her body went limp, feeling the enormity of how close she and Noah had come to being Belcher's next victims. Her anger for him gave way to the relief that she would make her way back to Nita tonight.

Noah plopped his butt next to her on the floor, knees up and arms resting atop them. He scooted, so their upper thighs touched. "That was too damn close."

"You're telling me." She tugged on her wrist bindings. "Do you mind getting someone down here with some bolt cutters?"

"There you go, being pushy again."

"And that's why I love you, my friend." Lexi finally let a smile form.

Noah nudged her with his shoulder. "Ditto, but let's not do this again."

36

Stepping through the hatch, Lexi was hit with the bright floodlights the SWAT bomb squad had erected in the pit to help in their disposal mission. They signaled this nightmare had finally ended. Carver's team would have their hands full for hours with the devices wired along the tunnels and inside the dome room. And that was a job Lexi happily handed over to the team leader after touring him around the complex and explaining her observations. She'd had enough tension for one day and wanted a hot shower, a decent meal, and to curl up in Nita's arms.

Lexi shielded her eyes from the glare and scanned the area for Noah and Amanda. The only people she saw were two officers dressed in black tactical uniforms, preparing the disposal chamber for the IED extraction. When she walked past them, each gave her a welcoming thumbs up and a congratulatory pat on the back for surviving another of Belcher's traps. But this last encounter was different. When Noah had first arrived, those minutes with him marked the only instance Lexi had time to consider her death, knowing she couldn't stop it. And it had shaken her to her core.

Her ability to walk headfirst into danger was rooted in confidence. She'd committed to memory details of every known explosive. She knew every trick in the book. Those alone had helped her out of every dicey situation. But tonight had her wondering if she still had what it took to do this job well enough to not lose another limb or worse. Or had becoming an amputee forever shaken that bedrock of certainty? Belcher had outsmarted her, and if not for Noah's and Amanda's quick thinking and steadfastness, she'd be buried under several hundred tons of concrete and earth.

Lexi trudged up the pit's steep slope. The pressure on her residual limb accompanying each step with her prosthetic made it impossible to push her doubts aside. Instead, the upward trek magnified them. The consequences of her job, starting with her leg loss, had morphed into a monster she couldn't control. And that monster had a name—Tony Belcher. Her obsession had entangled so many innocent people today and had cost the Becketts' housekeeper her life. Maybe it was time to examine her choices.

She reached the top, discovering more lights and a collection of emergency vehicles. An unmarked sedan and Nolan Hughes' big black pickup were among them and parked side by side. Agent Keene was doting over his wife at the sedan, adjusting a blanket over her shoulders and unscrewing the top of a plastic water bottle for her. Noah had leaned against the pickup's grill with his legs comfortably crossed at the ankles, sipping on some water. He'd dug his wide-brimmed fedora out of the toolbox and had it tipped back on his head like a tired cowhand fresh off the roundup. She knew the feeling.

Ready to return to town, Lexi walked toward them. Noah was the first to lock eyes with her from twenty yards away. Despite the low lighting, his bright smile would have been recognizable from the moon. If she hadn't felt like she'd been through the spin cycle today, she would have returned it. Instead, she forced a closed-mouth grin.

Amanda shed her blanket, handed Keene the half-empty bottle, and closed the distance between her and Lexi. She let her eyes express her gratitude while stroking Lexi's upper arms. She then pulled Lexi into a tight embrace without shaking. Her heavy sighs were the only signs that her emotions threatened to mar her image of strength and courage. It was a beautiful, silent moment of mutual respect and appreciation.

When Amanda pulled back, she smiled. "You're family now, Lexi Mills. You'll always have a seat at our table."

They'd met only briefly inside the dome room while chained together and when the prized bobby pin saved Lexi's life, but after the long day and watching her on the drone tapes, she felt like they were old friends. "That goes both ways."

Keene approached. "I'm not much of a hugger—"

"I can vouch for that." Amanda smirked.

Her husband narrowed his eyes in playful annoyance. "But I could use one." He wrapped one arm around Lexi in a brief awkward hug. "I can't thank you enough for putting yourself in harm's way to save my wife. You've made a friend for life, Lexi Mills. If you ever need a favor, just ask."

"You're welcome, Agent Keene. What's the word on Amadeus? Has he made it back to Atwater?"

"Yes, and the warden has placed him in isolation until further notice. We want to keep him in the dark about the extent of Belcher's attempt to get him out."

"That's probably for the best. I'm just relieved that your team didn't lose him."

"Thanks to you and Noah." Keene glanced in Noah's direction.

"I need to get back to my life partner. I've kept her waiting far too long."

"Hughes sent the perfect escort." He waved over two uniformed police officers who had been standing in the shadows of their cruiser. When they approached, Lexi recognized them instantly. "We'll follow behind you."

Lexi shook their hands. "Sergeant Thompson. Officer Powell. Considering your close call today, I would have thought you'd been off shift hours ago."

Thompson rested her forearms on the gear of her equipment belt. "We were about to sign out when word broke about your involvement here. We couldn't pass up the opportunity to escort you back to town again."

"Well then, let's roll." Lexi felt like a Hollywood star being offered a stroll down the red carpet as she stepped toward Noah.

He pushed himself from the front bumper and tossed her an unopened water bottle. "I'm driving. I've had enough of your pothole avoidance for one night." After climbing inside and buckling up, he started the engine but paused with his hand on the gear shifter. "We need to talk soon, Lexi, but not tonight. Maybe tomorrow after you've spent some time with Nita."

"Should I be worried?" No matter his response, she was concerned.

"Just talk to her." He put the truck in drive and followed Sergeant

Thompson through the bumpy field, onto the main road, and back to the once sleepy town of Gladding.

Lexi's mind bounced between the day's events during the return trip. One theme colored every memory—its impact on Nita. Each escalation of danger had chipped away her resolve to remain sober. And Noah's cryptic allusion made her think Nita had a more arduous road ahead than she'd first thought.

Upon arriving at the grocery store site, Lexi noted the scene had lost its chaotic feel. The fire department was mopping up, dousing the smoldering sections of the burnt-out building skeleton with water. Meanwhile, others picked through the debris with pokers to quicken the cooling process. The EMTs had cleared out, and only a handful of SWAT personnel was still there securing their equipment. Local police and sheriff's deputies guarded the collapsed perimeter at the edges of the parking lot.

Noah parked beside the SWAT command van with Keene pulling up beside him. The headlights shined on Nita sitting on a folding chair with Dylan on her lap. She was holding her phone, the screen was glowing, and they appeared engrossed in a video. She looked up, patted Dylan on the shoulder, and pointed at their cars.

Dylan ran toward Keene's sedan when the passenger door opened, and Amanda stepped out. Lexi waited in the truck to watch the emotional reunion. So did Noah.

Amanda scooped Dylan up, pressing him tight against her chest. Dylan responded with a death grip around her neck, making Lexi's throat swell. Amanda was clearly the center of this young boy's life, and the love glowing between them gave meaning to the danger Lexi faced at the missile silo. But this thing with Tony Belcher was far from over.

"If we don't stop Belcher, there will be more Amandas and Dylans." Noah handed her the truck's key fob.

"I know." Those words were like a knife to Lexi's heart, but chasing Belcher would have to wait until she was certain Nita was on sure footing. She shifted her stare to the woman who owned her heart. It pained her to think that her job had caused Nita to slip, but Noah made her wonder if something more troubling was in the works.

What secrets are you hiding, Nita? she thought before opening the passenger door. Nita stood from the chair, waiting patiently for Lexi to exit. She led carefully with her natural foot and followed with her prosthetic. The skin on her residual limb pinched when she put her weight on that side, making her wince.

Nita rushed to her, offering support with an arm around her back. "Let me help."

"Thank you." Lexi leaned into Nita's loving touch. If it were anyone else, she would have brushed them off, saying that her pain was commonplace and nothing of concern. But Nita wasn't just anyone. She was the woman who would, hopefully, be wearing her ring tomorrow night.

"Let's get you inside. I rummaged through your luggage and found a fresh liner and some socks. We'll wait until we get you to bed to apply your lotion."

"Bed sounds wonderful, but after a shower and some hot food." Lexi let Nita guide her to the SWAT van, enjoying the extra attention while it lasted. "I've got it from here, Nita." She kissed Nita on the forehead, walked up the stairs, and opened the door. Hughes and Carver were at their workstations, typing away at their laptops, likely completing their incident reports.

Nita and Noah stepped in behind her.

Carver was the first to look up. She expected a lukewarm reception for running around him and Mitchell, but instead, he offered her a respectful nod. "Glad you made it, Mills. That took guts."

"Thanks, Carver." Lexi turned to Hughes when he stood from his chair. She tossed him the fob. "It needs a bath, but we didn't put a scratch on it as far as I can tell."

"My insurance carrier thanks you." Hughes cocked a grin that said he'd offer to buy a round of drinks before it was time for them to leave. But Lexi was too tired for the gesture and would settle for a genuine hug and the promise to keep in touch.

"Let's get that leg cleaned up." Nita shimmied past Lexi and entered the onboard bathroom.

Lexi sat in a chair and focused on Hughes. "We need to leave after this."

"I figured as much."

Nita returned with a wet towel and the fresh items for her prosthetic.

Lexi then unzipped her pant leg and doffed her prosthesis. After the day she'd had, she didn't care about privacy. Instead, she cared about cleaning her leg quickly and getting out of there.

After Nita stowed Lexi's dirty items in her luggage, she and Noah shook hands with Carver and Hughes. They offered to take Lexi's things to his rental car while she donned her leg again.

"You impress the hell out of me, Mills." Lexi got the feeling Hughes didn't say that to too many people.

"Thanks, but I don't feel impressive." Lexi put on her fresh liner and socks. "It's my fault all of this happened today."

Hughes sat beside her, his expression turning serious. "Don't beat yourself up, Lexi. Belcher is a wildcard. You're not responsible for his craziness."

"That might be true, but you and I know he won't stop. I'll be on his radar until one of us is dead, and I intend to be the last one standing."

"My dad once said that one of his college professors said something during a lecture that changed his life. I didn't really understand it until last year when I went through my divorce. It's too late to save my marriage, but not my relationship with my adult children. I'd hate to see you make the same mistakes I did."

"What did that professor say?" Lexi finished putting on her leg and stood.

Hughes stood too. "He said to never give up what you want most for what you want now." He gave Lexi a hug and walked her to the door. "I hope you figure it out before it's too late."

37

Nita Flores stared out the side window, watching cars pass on the freeway and thinking, *six years, five months, and four days*. She'd walked into rehab that long ago, swearing to never find rock bottom again. To never make seeing it a possibility. Those numbers now sounded more like a countdown to a cold, hard truth than a remembrance of her rebirth. Tonight, she was standing at the top of the cliff with the bottom dangerously in sight. Peeking over the edge should have terrified her, but it drew her in. Anything was better than remembering she'd failed the woman curled up in her arms.

Lexi had fallen asleep five minutes after hopping into the backseat of Noah's rental. She'd laid her head against Nita's chest, letting it rise and fall with Nita's breathing until they'd cleared the city limits. Then, Lexi had whispered, "There's no sweeter sound than hearing you breathe." Those loving, undeserved words had streaked Nita's cheeks with tears. They left her thinking that the bottom was a better option than hurting Lexi more than she already had.

A half hour later, when Noah took the downtown offramp to their hotel, she glimpsed his eyes in the rearview mirror after checking that Lexi was sound asleep. She had to know. "What did you tell her?"

"Only that you two need to talk."

She swallowed past the thick emotion in her throat. "Thank you."

"Don't thank me yet." Noah took in a frustrated, deep breath. "I'm talking to her tomorrow."

Nita expected nothing less. Noah had become more than Lexi's friend following the events in Bowie and Spicewood. He'd become her protector. Living with a secret of this magnitude between them was a burden Nita would never ask of him. The whole truth needed to come from her. "Tomorrow," she whispered.

Noah pulled through the hotel breezeway, stopping short of the valet stand. Nita then nudged Lexi awake with a rub on the arm. "We're at the hotel, Lex."

"I know," she said, tingling the hairs on Nita's arms. Her voice was clear, not groggy from being pulled awake. It was a disturbing sign that she'd been conscious and heard Nita and Noah talking.

"You said food, shower, and sleep." Nita unbuckled her seatbelt and grabbed the bagged sandwich at her feet. Thankfully, Noah had found an all-night grocery store a few miles outside of Gladding. "Let's get inside so you can eat your sub."

Before she opened the door, Lexi pulled her face close and pressed their lips together in a sweet kiss. When Nita tried to pull away, Lexi deepened it. Whatever Lexi might have heard, it clearly didn't matter. Finally, the kiss ended, and Lexi smiled in the darkness. "Now we can go."

Once inside and wheeling their luggage against the tiled lobby, they stopped at the main desk. Lexi righted her suitcase and addressed the night clerk. "Lexi Mills and Noah Black checking in."

"Yes, ma'am. We've been expecting you. Maxwell Keene called ahead. We've upgraded your rooms to our best spa suites with his compliments."

"That's very nice of him. Is one handicapped accessible?" Lexi thumped her knuckles against her hard polymer socket. "Prosthetic."

"I'm sorry, ma'am. We have two accessible suites, but those are occupied tonight."

Nita understood Lexi's weighty sigh. The day had been overly taxing, and she likely didn't have the strength to stand long enough to shower without assistance. She rubbed the small of Lexi's back. "Let's just take your original room."

"Thank you." Lexi turned her attention to the clerk. "Is it available?"

"Yes, it is."

"We'll take that one."

"Very well, ma'am." The clerk punched in something on his computer keyboard. "An accessible suite will be available tomorrow. After checkout, I can have housekeeping move you for your last night with us."

"That would be great." Lexi earned a playful hip thrust from Nita. She acknowledged with one of her own.

"Well, I'll take a suite tonight." Noah stepped up to the counter. "I could use a long bath." After checking in, he said goodnight at the elevator with the promise to meet for lunch.

Nita and Lexi continued to their first-floor room.

Lexi dropped her suitcase near the door and flopped spreadeagle onto the mattress. Completely spent, she didn't have the energy to unpack and eat, maybe one but not both. Then, soft, pillowy lips pressed against her forehead briefly.

"After I set up your dinner," Nita said, "I'll unpack and prepare for your shower."

"Thank you."

Nita stacked the pillows at the head of the bed, forming a fluffy backrest, before laying out Lexi's sub sandwich, chips, and water bottle. She then patted the covers. "Come on, Wonder Woman. Eat. I'll be right back."

This was why Lexi loved this woman. Thoughtful, attentive, and playful. Nita had a plateful, yet she put Lexi's needs first. It had become abundantly apparent in the car that Nita *had* slipped further. Noah had said little, but their back and forth in the car convinced Lexi of it.

Putting her feet up and taking the first mouthful was better than an hour-long massage. Maybe it was the food or perhaps the thought that Lexi didn't have another bomb to face, but when she swallowed, the weakness in her arms and shoulders ebbed. Bite by bite, her strength returned, making her rethink her decision to turn down the spa suite for the night. Nita's doting deserved a better reward, but it was too late now. Nita had tried to hide it, but her creased brow in the lobby when Lexi asked if the suite was accessible suggested she was disappointed. Without a doubt, Lexi would have to make it up tomorrow night with a romantic proposal.

Nita returned from the bathroom, took out their nightclothes, and placed them at the foot of the bed. Her stare went to the empty wrappers on the covers. "Someone was hungry."

"I didn't realize how much until I took the first bite." Lexi crumpled and gathered everything in the plastic bag and tossed it toward the wastebasket near the desk in the corner. She missed but didn't care enough to pick it up.

"Ready for your shower?" Nita asked.

"God, yes." Washing off the day's grime would be refreshing, but it would also help Lexi put the day behind her. The tension. The harried memory of her razor-thin brush with death. It would all swirl down the drain.

Though Lexi didn't need the assistance, she let Nita help her from the bed and support her weight to the bathroom. She then sat on the toilet lid and unzipped her light jacket. Once it was off, she moved to take off her T-shirt, but Nita whispered, "Let me."

Nita first gently grazed her left cheek where Taryn had hit her. The area was still tender, but the throbbing had stopped. She then cupped her right hand under Lexi's chin, angled it upward, and leaned in for a soft kiss. It was brief, but it set the tone for how this shower was about to unfold. And tenderness was exactly what Lexi needed tonight.

Lexi raised her arms, allowing Nita to lift her top over her head. She avoided looking in the brightly lit mirror, dreading what her short hair might look like. Instead, she smoothed it with her hands when Nita tossed her shirt to the floor.

"You look fine." Nita eyed her with a smile. "You're still my handsome butch."

Lexi snorted. "Yeah, sure."

"Let me be the judge of that." Nita raised the lower seam of her sports bra, carefully exposing each breast before lifting it over her head and tossing it onto her shirt. "Yep, very handsome."

Nita kneeled, gliding her hands slowly down Lexi's outer thighs until she settled into position. Tenderness was transforming into a sensual touch. She removed the shoe and sock on Lexi's natural foot and raised the zipper on the inner thigh of her left pant leg. Next, she reached high on her left thigh and rolled down the neoprene sleeve, inverting it over the socket until she reached its top. She then gently rocked the prosthetic off and leaned it against the nearby wall. The outer layer of socks covering her residual limb was replete with sweat lines from the leftover moisture in her socket, reminding her of tonight's harrowing events in the missile silo.

Nita's brow furrowed. "You look swollen."

"I feel swollen." The edema in her limb had traveled to her knee, making the joint stiff.

"We'll work that out later." Nita winked, foretelling her plans for other things first.

She fumbled with Lexi's waistband, loosening the button and lowering the zipper. When she gripped the band at her flanks, that was Lexi's cue to raise her bottom and let her remove her cargo pants. Nita eased them off quickly, tossing them atop her shirt. She then removed the thigh socks and liner, adding them to the pile. Having her skin exposed gave Lexi the feeling of normalcy. Her flesh was no longer encased in layers and layers of fabric and plastic to help her walk. She never took the hours without them for granted.

Nita's fingers slid up Lexi's inner thighs, starting at her knees and ending at her apex. The erotic touch awakened Lexi's core with a fierce roar. She rocked her head back and spread her legs wider, welcoming the opportunity to feel more than anxiety and fear.

"Not yet." Nita used a low rasp, drawing a knowing grin from Lexi. A quick release was not in the cards tonight. Instead, this would be a desperately needed protracted expression of love and passion.

38

Lexi and Nita lay naked in bed with their hair and skin still moist from the cascading water. Their bodies entwined. Lexi's heart pounded with the realization that she was damn lucky to be holding this woman in her arms tonight. She was lucky to be breathing. *Proposing can't wait another day*, she thought. She lifted her arm and shifted to hop from the bed, but Nita kept her in place. "What do you need? I'll get it."

"My backpack." Lexi watched Nita step to the desk, appreciating the extra sway she added for her benefit. If she was this alluring on the return trip, the proposal might have to wait until after the next round.

Nita grabbed her bag and another water bottle, turned, and cocked a hip with a mischievous grin. "Enjoying the show?"

"What do you think?" Lexi pushed herself up to lean against the headboard and fluffed the pillows to keep her mind off the familiar ache that roared during Nita's walk back. *Focus, Lexi. Focus*, she told herself as she pulled the covers over her breasts. *More sex can wait until she's wearing your ring.*

Nita slid into bed, mirroring Lexi's reclined position. She rested the backpack between Lexi's upper legs and cracked open the water. "Thirsty?"

"Parched." Lexi took a long, slow sip, struggling to recall the words she'd practiced in the mirror a dozen times in the weeks leading up to their trip. The recitation of how they'd met and how Nita had pulled her from her depths after becoming an amputee now paled to the clarity Lexi experienced tonight. A prepared speech wouldn't do. Her proposal had to come from the heart.

She returned the bottle to Nita before digging through her pack and locating the tiny red velvet box she'd carried for months. She cupped it in her hand, palm down, lowered her bag to the floor, and waited for Nita to finish drinking. Nita tightened the cap, took aim, and launched the bottle toward the waste can. It clanked against the lip and rattled the sides until landing squarely at the bottom.

"Nice shot." Lexi chuckled. Of course, she'd make it. Nita had hit the mark with her since their first kiss. "I thought I'd do this tomorrow night in my tux, but after the day I've had, it can't wait." She took a deep breath. "Today confirmed one thing for me: we make each other stronger. We struggle a little less every day because we face it together. It's an unshakable bond that goes beyond faithfulness. It goes to our souls. I want to walk through life with you, always." Lexi opened the box, exposing a single diamond mounted on a thin gold band. "Will you accept my grandmother's engagement ring and do me the honor of becoming my wife?"

Nita took a pronounced swallow and turned her head away. The unexpected response had Lexi confused and worried. Was her proposal too soon? Had she misread their level of commitment? Or was her struggle with sobriety at play?

Lexi waited for an answer, but when Nita's shoulders quaked to silent sobs, she closed the box, placed it on the mattress, and said, "Talk to me, Nita. What's wrong?"

Nita looked up with tears welling in her eyes. The pain behind them was more palpable than the passion they shared in this very bed minutes earlier. "I don't deserve you."

She raised Nita's chin a fraction. "Don't say that. We're both flawed. We've both made mistakes. I should have never involved you in this case. It's hard enough knowing the dangers I face, but it was cruel having you witness it."

"I won't lie. Hearing what you were going through as it was happening was too much, but it doesn't excuse what I did next."

Lexi shifted on the sheets and caressed Nita's cheek. "I know you're slipping, but we can get you through this together."

"I did more than slip." Nita closed her eyes to a disturbing grimace. "I hurt you."

Lexi dropped her hand and sat straight, waiting for Nita to explain. However, she remained silent with quivering lips, foreshadowing devastating news. The delay was agonizing and tested Lexi's patience. She then scooted to the edge of the bed and dressed hastily in her nightclothes. Nita did too. Lexi donned her prosthetic with only the liner and sleeve and stepped toward the door.

Nita circled the bed, grabbing Lexi by the arm before she passed the bathroom. "Where are you going?" Her tone was drowning in fear.

Lexi spun around. For the first time since becoming a couple, she doubted Nita would tell her the truth. "I heard you in the car. If you won't give me an answer, Noah will."

"He's a good man, Lexi. Please come back, and I'll tell you everything."

All Lexi wanted was an explanation. She needed to know what had unsettled Nita that she couldn't respond to a heartfelt, albeit impromptu, marriage proposal. "All I want to hear is the truth." She hit the rocker switch on the way by, bringing up more of the room's lights.

Nita guided them to the foot of the bed. They sat. She started by brushing back several strands of hair behind both ears. It was her way of showing vulnerability by exposing more of herself. "I won't try to excuse my actions but will explain them. Yes, I was upset hearing you go after those bombs. And yes, I slipped. I drank. Too much. I wanted to feel alive, not worried about your death, but the booze wasn't doing the trick. I knew from experience that cocaine is the safest, fastest rush, so I bought some." Nita rolled her neck, signaling that she was coming to the hurtful part. "Noah figured it out and convinced me to flush it. I could blame it on the alcohol, but it was more than that. He gave me his full attention when I needed it the most."

Lexi tried to rein in her imagination, but she jumped ahead. She conjured up the crushing picture of them pawing each other while her life hung in the balance inside that POW hut filled to the roof with nitro. Digging her nails into her palms, she ordered, "Spit it out, Nita."

"I kissed him, but I knew it was wrong and regretted it the instant I did."

Nita was right. Despite not rising to the level of a worst-case scenario, it still hurt. It broke the trust between them. The last person this close to her to break Lexi's faith in them was her father, and she still felt the impact. That same stifling pain of betrayal hit her like a Gatling gun. It fired relentlessly, unmercifully, stripping down her love for Nita, bullet by bullet. Everything she felt for Nita would be laid to waste if she didn't leave now.

Lexi stood, numb from the barrage. She rummaged through her suitcase, put on a clean hoodie, grabbed a room key, and stepped to the door. Nita rushed behind, enveloping her arms around her waist and pressing their bodies together. Nita wept against her back. Gripping the handle, Lexi felt her sorrow, but her pain outstripped it. "I need to go while I still love you."

"If you come back to me, I swear to live up to your trust."

"Even if it means rehab?"

"Even if it means walking through fire." Nita gave her one last squeeze and let her go.

Lexi's legs felt like lead weights. Each step down the corridor required more effort than the previous, and by the time she reached Noah's door, she was running on fumes. Her stomach churned, threatening to bring up her food. She considered turning around to save housekeeping an unpleasant cleanup, but she needed answers tonight, not tomorrow. She knocked.

The door opened. Noah was dressed similarly in shorts and a tank top. His expression drew long. "She told you."

"Tell me what happened." Noah opened the door wider, inviting her in. Stepping inside, Lexi was struck by the elegant living room and whistled her appreciation. "Nice digs."

"You should have said yes." He tossed her a complimentary can of Coke from the mini-fridge and grabbed one for himself. He then gestured to the couch. Once seated side by side, he asked, "Short or long version?"

"Whichever one will take away the pain." With the feeling this might be a long night, she popped open her soda and took several gulps.

"That would be neither, but I'll tell you what I think you need to know. Nita screwed up, but I'm certain she loves you. The kiss wasn't about attraction. It was about fear. She doesn't know how to be a cop's partner. Most can tuck away the dangers of the job because ninety percent of a cop's job is boredom. But your job is different. Every call you go on is imminent danger. Today, she got more than a taste of it. She got a mouthful, and it terrified her. Add on her struggle with addiction, and she was a powder keg. She had to blow."

"But kissing you?"

"I know. It surprised me too, but then I considered the circumstance. I'd noticed her track marks the first time we met at your apartment."

"With her job, it's not something she readily talks about. That's why I never told you."

"I get that. I wasn't sure how far along she was in her sobriety, but—"

"Six years."

"That explains why the alcohol hit her hard and why she wasn't in control of her emotions."

"She said she bought some coke."

"I'm glad I got to her in time and talked her out of it."

"Thank you for that." She leaned back. Her eyes searched the ceiling for forgiveness. "I proposed to her tonight."

"I thought that was supposed to be tomorrow."

"It was, but after today, I couldn't wait."

"Of course you did. I would have, too."

"Even knowing she'd kissed someone else?"

"Yes. I'm not saying sweep what Nita did under the rug, but that wasn't her tonight. That was unbearable chaos."

"I think it's my fault." Lexi placed her soda can on the coffee table and rested her elbows on her knees. "I've suspected for weeks that she's been using opioids more frequently than necessary, but I haven't had the time to talk to her about it." Lexi punched herself on her right thigh, trying to absorb her guilt. "I've been too damn busy with these media events."

"Don't beat yourself up, Lexi. Our lives haven't been our own for months. That's the price of heroism splashed over every channel and paper for five news cycles."

"I'll be glad when this dies down."

"That makes two of us." Noah patted her between the shoulder blades before leaning forward with her. "What do you plan to do about Nita?"

"Forgive her."

"Then you better get going. No offense, but I'd like to get back to my Egyptian cotton sheets."

"You're cruel, you know that?"

Minutes later, Lexi inserted the key card into the lock leading to her and Nita's hotel room and pushed the door open. The lights were still on when she walked inside. She locked gazes with Nita, sitting at the desk. Regret, sorrow, and love etched her face. Lexi closed the distance, stopping a foot away. A small baggie filled with white powder resting on the desk's corner caught her attention. Lexi was afraid to ask, but she had to know. "What's this?"

"Cocaine."

"Are you on it now?"

"No. And I'll take a blood test if you need me to prove it."

"Were you on it earlier tonight?"

"Yes. I gummed some to sober up from the shots at the bar so I could translate for you. It was a horrible decision, one I won't make again. I was going to flush it after you left, but I wanted you to see how committed I am to do whatever it takes to prove myself worthy of your trust again."

"I appreciate the gesture, but—"

"But it's not enough." Nita turned her head, visibly swallowing again. But this time, her lips didn't quiver. Instead, she stiffened her spine and turned toward her. "I'm not giving up on us, Lexi Mills."

She stepped forward, lifting Nita's chin with a hand. This woman had a long, tough road ahead, but Lexi was sure she was meant to travel it with her. "Neither am I."

39

Standing in front of the entryway mirror of her hotel room, Lexi slipped on her black single-button, wide peak lapel jacket. She then inspected the bruise on her left cheek where Taryn had clocked her with a pistol. The bruise was less tender and had turned a gruesome mix of dark red and purple, but Lexi was proud of it. While it reminded her how close she'd come to death, it was also a badge of honor. She'd beaten Belcher... until the next time.

Lexi adjusted her matching bowtie but failed miserably to straighten it. Never in a million years would she have predicted she'd own a tux, let alone wear one to anything other than her wedding. But after the first formal event in the wake of her and Noah's whirlwind stardom, it had become abundantly clear owning was cheaper than renting. But owning a tuxedo didn't mean she'd mastered dressing in it.

"I hate this damn thing." Lexi fumbled with the tie again, achieving the same lackluster result. "I should have gone with the clip-on."

"And deny me the pleasure of untying it later tonight?" Nita settled behind her, angling her head to the right to see in the mirror. She snaked her arms underneath Lexi's and tightened the bowtie on both sides. "Are you sure you don't want some concealer for your bruise?"

"I've survived thirty-four years without using makeup. I'm not about to start now." Lexi settled her gaze on the ring on Nita's finger, recalling the moment she'd slipped it there. It was a renewal of their commitment to one another after being tested. Giving it was Lexi's promise to walk her arduous journey with her, and accepting it was Nita's promise to let her.

Nita released her hands. "There."

"How do you do that?" Lexi inspected the perfectly straight tie.

"I had a patient recovering from hand surgery who wore one as his trademark, so I adapted his therapy sessions to include doing this."

"Of course you did." When Nita shifted to walk away, Lexi glimpsed her A-line V-neck sleeveless black dress. It highlighted her trim waist and showed just enough leg to be distracting. She grabbed Nita's wrist before she stepped out of reach. "You look beautiful."

"And you look positively handsome." Nita inspected Lexi up and down before turning her expression serious. "Are you sure you're okay with me coming with you and Noah?"

Lexi placed her hands on Nita's hips, pulled their bodies together with a seductive force, and let her lips provide the answer. She kissed Nita's neck, taking care to not smudge her makeup. Intoxicated by the fresh citrus scent of her shampoo, she let the kiss linger but kept her hunger in check. If her internal clock was working, Noah—*Knock. Knock. Knock.*

Lexi pulled back. "I'm sure."

Lexi walked into the ballroom filled with law enforcement professionals representing every state and federal agency in the nation. Tuxedos and formal gowns mixed among uniforms accented with polished gold, silver, and brass. She was amid family, a brethren with one thing in common—their oath. But not one compared to the people she walked in with. She had Nita on her arm and Noah by her side. Not much could have made this night better. She was alive and engaged to her best friend. Then she felt a hand press against her back. She turned.

"Mom? Dad? I thought you weren't coming to this one." Whatever the reason, having them here was the perfect addition and just what Lexi needed. The call she'd made to them this morning had drained her emotionally, but she wanted them to hear the story of what she'd gone through from her, not some talking head on the news.

Her mother pulled her into a welcome bone-crushing hug. It spoke of worry and relief. "Of course we'd come after what you went through. I'm so glad you're safe, Peanut."

When her mother finally loosened her hold, Lexi got a good look at her. She was beautiful in her black three-piece georgette pantsuit. It blended well with her dark mahogany skin. Her father was handsome in his handlebar mustache and rarely worn dark suit but appeared paler than usual.

He extended his arms and gave her a giant bear hug reminiscent of her childhood. It was like she was ten years old again and had run into her father's garage after school. He'd then scoop her up into his arms and squeeze her until she screamed, "Uncle." His hug was once the best part of her day, and it was becoming so again. Fifteen years of estrangement would soon be a distant memory.

Following more hugs and handshakes for Nita and Noah, Lexi thanked her parents for coming, adding, "Let me see if I can get you a seat for dinner."

"Already done." Maxwell Keene joined the group with Amanda on his arm. He was dressed nicely yesterday in a business suit, but tonight his tux and salt-and-pepper hair gave him a polished look. Amanda was gorgeous in a strapless, calf-length black sheath dress. Following hugs, he continued, "The event organizer nearly had a stroke when I had her put them at our table."

Lexi looked between her parents and the Keenes. "So you've met already?"

"Oh yes," Amanda replied. "And your mother and I have already exchanged apple pie recipes."

"Of course she has." Lexi laughed. The sconce wall lights flashed three times, signaling dinner was about to be served. "Shall we?"

An hour later, servers cleared the tables and brought out dessert. That was the emcee's and Maxwell Keene's cue to start the official part of the night. They ascended the stage and stepped up to the podium at the left. Behind them was a colorful display of every state and territorial flag.

The United States flag was positioned several feet ahead in a place of honor.

Following a brief welcome and explanation of the purpose of tonight's festivities by the emcee, a large screen lowered from the ceiling, covering nearly the entire width of the stage. After that, the room lights went dark. Then, a documentary played. The Hollywood-quality production started with a short exposé on the Red Spades and General Calhoun. It segued into a recreation of the attack on the governor's mansion in Spicewood. It included interview snippets with Lexi, Noah, Simon Winslow, the governor's security chief, and Lieutenant Sarah Briscoe of the Texas Rangers. Closing out the fifteen-minute film was Governor Ken Macalister.

"If not for my very own MacGyver and Rambo in Lexi Mills and Noah Black, I wouldn't be alive today. Their actions that day were a master class in courage, ingenuity, and dedication. The National Peace Officers Association couldn't have made a better choice as law enforcement officers of the year. Lexi and Noah are true national heroes."

The crowd erupted in roaring applause when the credits rolled. While the screen rose, the emcee returned to the microphone. "Ladies and gentlemen, please welcome the vice president of the National Law Enforcement Association, Assistant Deputy Director of the Federal Bureau of Investigation, Maxwell Keene."

The emcee retreated during the applause, and Keene stepped up to the microphone. He cleared his throat. "Governor Macalister and I are members of a very exclusive club. We both had the privilege of having Lexi Mills and Noah Black in our corners when faced with overwhelming odds. Moments ago, you just saw the story of how these two heroes came onto the national scene. Let me tell you about the sequel. It started yesterday morning in the sleepy town of Gladding..." By the time Keene finished detailing yesterday's events, culminating in the safe return of his wife and son, every person in the room was on the edge of their seat. "Fellow officers, it gives me great pleasure to present this year's Peace Officers of the Year, Special Agent Lexi Mills and Detective Noah Black."

Everyone rose to their feet in a deafening ovation with whistles and shouts. Several officials reached out to shake Lexi's and Noah's hands as they made their way to the stage. After passing the podium and reaching center stage, Keene greeted them with a thankful embrace, presented each with a commemorative plaque, and posed for pictures to more applause.

Lexi and Noah left the stage without speeches. Neither was good at them, and neither felt like a hero. They had agreed before walking in tonight that anyone in that room would have done the same.

When the fanfare had ended, and the photo ops were over, Lexi, Noah, and Keene returned to their table. Lexi's father was the first to greet her. The gleam in his eyes was pure joy. "I'm so proud of you, Peanut." Those six words meant more to her than every speech and word of praise she'd heard in the last four months combined. Knowing she had her father back swelled her heart.

The group sat, sipped on wine and coffee, and chatted about what was next in their lives. Maxwell and Amanda planned to take the family on a long vacation to Hawaii. Noah would return to Nogales tomorrow and start his new position as the Chief of Detectives. Lexi squeezed Nita's hand, kissed its back, and announced, "Nita and I will start planning our wedding."

Lexi's mother flew a hand to her chest, her face glowing with excitement. "It's about time, you two."

The rest of the table sang their congratulations. When the conversation slowed, Lexi's mother yawned. Her father slung an arm over the back of her chair. "I think it's time we call it a night."

"Us too." Amanda yawned.

Everyone pushed out of their chairs. Keene checked his cell phone, scrolling through several notifications. "Lexi. Noah. I almost forgot. Delmar Beckett's wife sat down with a sketch artist today. She gave us a decent facsimile of the other kidnapper who came to her house." He showed them the image on his phone.

"Was this one of the people who tried to pick up Amadeus?" Noah asked.

"Agent Vasquez only saw one, but he said this guy looked nothing like the one he shot," Keene replied.

"Let me see that again." Lexi studied the drawing. Something about the image seemed familiar, but she couldn't quite place it. However, one word stuck in her head: hero. She'd heard that word so many times in the last four months, but she tried to remember where she was when someone first called her that. Then it came to her. It was on the plane when she flew to Nogales for the tunnel bombing. She'd never forget his square jaw and cleft chin. His hair was a little longer in the drawing, but Lexi was sure it was him.

"I know this man. He called himself Rick Ferrario. He said he was a former Army combat engineer who now teaches demolition techniques at Fort Leonard Wood." Lexi's jaw muscles tensed. If she was correct, she'd sat next to one of Belcher's thugs for hours. "I met him on the plane the day of the tunnel bombing."

A look of determination formed on Keene's face. "If you're right, we now have a name and face." He concentrated on the drawing. "This bastard nearly killed my wife and son. He made it personal. I'm forming a task force to go after Belcher and the Gatekeepers." He looked up at Lexi. "I want you to head it up. What do you say?"

Lexi briefly considered what Nolan Hughes told her last night about never giving up what she wanted most for what she wanted now, but she knew Belcher. This was far from over. He wouldn't give up until one of them was dead. The only way she could find peace with Nita was to kill him first. But she'd only help Keene under one condition. She turned to Noah and asked, "Are you in?"

A half-cocked smile grew on his face. "I always have your back."

EPILOGUE

Stepping off the plane in Lubbock, Rick hated to admit it. He'd likely made a colossal mistake hooking up with the Gatekeepers. They were in complete disarray. Frankly, he couldn't give one shit about believers and nonbelievers. It was all Kool-Aid to him. But when Amadeus approached him three years ago about a job to scout locations for their militant operations and report back on the results, he jumped at the chance. He believed in one thing, money, and Amadeus had offered him the biggest payday he'd seen. However, after Amadeus' arrest and the Red Spades debacle, Belcher had become desperate to get his brother back. Against his better judgment, Rick had agreed to become an active participant in their operations for double his salary. But even that failed. Now, he had a decision: cut bait or continue upping the price tag.

Wheeling his carry-on across the busy terminal, he debated whether to buy a ticket home or meet Belcher as planned. His primary concern centered on Belcher's obsession with Lexi Mills. He was up for any job if the pay was good, but obsession often invited unnecessary risk. No amount of money was worth dying for a cause he didn't believe in. Or at least no one had yet to offer him an amount worth the risk.

Reaching the bottom of the escalator, he made his choice and turned left toward the ticket counter. With any luck, he'd be back in his one-room apartment by dinner time, with his feet propped up on his recliner and a beer in his hand. But before he could queue in the four-person line, two large men dressed casually in golf attire flanked him. They'd positioned themselves too close to him to mistake their intentions as anything but an attention-getter. It worked. His antennae went up. Had Belcher considered him a loose end? Or did he send a greeting party? Either case, Rick was sure the encounter wouldn't be friendly and continued walking.

His defensive training kicked in when one of the men touched his shoulder. He swiped the hand away and had the goon in an armbar in two seconds. "Never put a hand on me."

The burly man groaned in pain while his partner stood by, clearly debating whether to intercede. "He wants a word with you now, not tonight," the debater said.

"Then he should call." Rick gave the man's arm a fraction more pressure to emphasize his point.

"He said he'd make it worth your while." The debater maintained his ground. He was pretty brave for being the one not in Rick's armlock.

"Tell him I'll see him tonight as scheduled." Rick had no intention of keeping the meeting, but he needed the head start. He'd never used his real last name with either Belcher brother and never provided it while scouting, so he could simply disappear into the woodwork.

"Now," Debater said. "He'd hate to let Ty know that you've gone back on your word."

Rick became edgy, sensing his rage pound in his ears. He thought he'd been careful and covered his identity, but the mention of his son's name told him otherwise. Now, he was trapped. The only way out was death—his or Belcher's. Trapped, he released his hold, resigning himself to one more job with the Gatekeepers. "Fine. Take me to him."

Burly rubbed his arm and rolled his shoulder, testing its range of motion. He then turned around, looking as if he wanted to use Rick's face as a punching bag. Rick wagged an index finger at him. "Uh-uh. That was just the appetizer." Once the man relented, he turned to his partner. "Lead the way."

The two bruisers led Rick out of the main terminal, where a large black SUV was parked curbside near the entrance. One opened the back passenger door, inviting him inside. Rick poked his head inside, discovering a man in the backseat who had to be Belcher. *He must be one hell of a speaker*, he thought. Neither Belcher's stature nor his looks were overpowering. His trimmed blond hair and closely cropped beard were professional, but his pudginess screamed a lack of discipline to those with Rick's background. Belcher would never survive Ranger School, let alone boot camp.

Rick handed off his suitcase to the debater and slid onto the backbench. "What couldn't wait until tonight?"

"You let her slip away."

"I didn't pick the team. You did. If you'd given me reliable people, Lexi Mills would be dead, and Amadeus would be chest-deep in a hot tub."

"That unreliable person was Amadeus' woman. He won't be happy to learn that she's dead." Belcher shifted on his hip to look Rick squarely in the eyes. "You need to make amends."

His threat didn't need further explanation. The mention of his son's name earlier outlined the consequences if he didn't do as Belcher said. "What do you have in mind?"

"Time is running out. The end days are coming. We need to raise the stakes to free Amadeus."

"And how do we do that?"

"We break out my brother's ultimate plan." Belcher's eyes turned cold and dark as the deepest ocean. "It's time to leverage our inside connection."

IMPACT
Lexi Mills Book 3

A religious zealot has plans to bring the country to its knees. Lexi Mills is hellbent on taking him down.

ATF Agent and resident bomb expert Lexi Mills is on a mission. Commanding a task force of hand-picked specialists, she sets her sights on a terrorist organization known as The Gatekeepers. A religious sect with a violent plan to cull the nonbelievers before the coming Rapture, the group is headed by its charismatic leader, Tony Belcher. The first time she crossed paths with Belcher, Lexi lost her leg—and her partner.

Now she's determined to make him pay.

Vowing to end his reign of terror, the team hunts down members of Belcher's organization. But underestimating him is their first mistake. And by the time they discover the ruthless intellect beneath his fanatical persona, it's too late.

When Lexi becomes the target of Belcher's rage, she's forced to make an impossible choice: Prevent a bomb from killing thousands of innocents—or save the love of her life.

In a terror plot destined to be the worst in the nation's history, Lexi must once again put her own life on the line to do what she does best...and the stakes have never been higher.

Get your copy today at
severnriverbooks.com/series/lexi-mills

ABOUT BRIAN SHEA

Brian Shea has spent most of his adult life in service to his country and local community. He honorably served as an officer in the U.S. Navy. In his civilian life, he reached the rank of Detective and accrued over eleven years of law enforcement experience between Texas and Connecticut. Somewhere in the mix he spent five years as a fifth-grade school teacher. Brian's myriad of life experience is woven into the tapestry of each character's design. He resides in New England and is blessed with an amazing wife and three beautiful daughters.

Sign up for the reader list at
severnriverbooks.com/series/lexi-mills

ABOUT STACY LYNN MILLER

A late bloomer, Stacy Lynn Miller took up writing after retiring from the Air Force. Her twenty years of toting a gun and police badge, tinkering with computers, and sleuthing for clues as an investigator form the foundation of her Lexi Mills thriller series, as well as her Manhattan Sloane novels. She is visually impaired, a proud stroke survivor, mother of two, tech nerd, chocolate lover, and terrible golfer with a hole-in-one. When you can't find her writing, she'll be golfing or drinking wine (sometimes both) with friends and family in Northern California.

Sign up for the reader list at
severnriverbooks.com/series/lexi-mills

Printed in the United States
by Baker & Taylor Publisher Services